C000179259

IF THEY CALL

Project: Bakelite

J. Swann

Copyright © 2021 James Swann

All rights reserved

The characters and events portrayed in this book are fictitious. Any similarity to real persons, living or dead, is coincidental and not intended by the author.

No part of this book may be reproduced, or stored in a retrieval system, or transmitted in any form or by any means, electronic, mechanical, photocopying, recording, or otherwise, without express written permission of the publisher.

Cover design by: J Swann

PREFACE

Mental health in society, in my humble opinion, is something
that we need to take a little more seriously.

Decisions that are made need to be thought through.

Every action provokes a reaction.

Nothing happens without good reason.

To be truly alone is difficult. No one can comprehend the feeling. No
one can understand. Lonliness isn't an   option for some.

To be happy in one's own company is a difficult situation, to be woefully
unhappy when surrounded by people is even more difficult.

When our mental health goes into crisis, when there is an episode,
there can be so many unanswered questions, because people
don't want to be honest. Even if it's the only thing you need in
order to move on. It can be a dark and scary place to be.

Take that time to hug your children. Make that time
to say "I Love You" before you leave.

Please allow me to introduce - Project Bakelite.

CONTENTS

CHAPTER ONE:
MEET LAURA

Taking a final glance over the pristine white sideboard, Laura couldn't help but feel lucky to have such a highly finished and cared for kitchen. Every utensil has its place. Every draw was perfectly balanced to provide a pleasing aesthetic to those visiting. Each soft closer was perfectly mounted to allow a hands off approach to flush fitting doors and draws.

Walking through the kitchen in her free floating pinstripe dress, Laura gently caressed her dining table looking at the mirror clean finish. She had such pride in this one room of the house, she took perfect care of it and wanted it to stay in this way for years to come. Charcoal coloured tiles offset the brilliant white cupboard doors which were matched to the floor tiles with a grey grout and white edging. Another aesthetic finishing touch that made this place a safe haven for Laura to sit and contemplate life.

Looking at the delicate watch on her dainty wrist, Laura began to panic, she had been day dreaming for the past 3 hours, it was 14:30 and not only would her children soon need to be collected from the school, but she would have to begin cooking dinner ready for when her husband came in from work, she had been late doing this once, he had not been happy with her.

Not happy at all.

Giving a final blast of perfume as she donned her coat and left the house, Laura looked like a pin up from the 1950's, a high and tight Beehive style hairdo finishing her entire outfit off in that style. A tiny tight waist had been achieved by years of under eating and the use of a punishing corset. A reasonably sized chest in her teenage years had always bought attention to her from various school boys, but that was never what she had wanted, she had always admired older men and when she married Jerry, she had met the ideal one. This was far from what her family thought, as Jerry was controlling and on occasion rough with Laura.

Laura's family had seen and realised this happened but could do nothing as Jerry's control and hold over her was so strong. It didn't matter now anyway, Laura's family were dead. They had died in a suspicious car crash. Nothing was found, but it was investigated to great lengths by the authorities. Laura would be truly alone in the world if it wasn't for Jerry and the kids.

The kids were both very quiet. They had seen at an early age how their father had reacted when he wasn't happy. The last thing they wanted to do was end up in the hospital.

Or worse.

Both children were extremely intelligent and academic. They achieved highly in both physical and classroom based activities.

When they had special achievements it was not recognised by their father, it was as if they should be being awarded, this in his opinion was what they should be striving for. Tommy who was six years old and Hannah who was seven both had come at a happier time of Jerry and Laura's marriage.

Jerry had no excuse to be the way he was. He came from a good household with loving parents, he had a good job, being a day time manager in a large supermarket chain, it may not have had prestige, but it paid well.

Jerry had an amazing mind, he could engineer a solution within moments to any issue that could arise. He was also completely chiselled spending much time keeping up his physical appearance and ability. He told Laura he invested all of his time looking after himself for her, which is why she should actually make an effort for him. Another reason Jerry well and truly had a hold over her.

His abuse of Laura wasn't just physical, it was mental too. She felt completely indebted to him for everything he had given her in life. Stability, healthy intelligent children who would get out of this hell hole and make something of their lives. A perfect home for her to look after through the daytime and everything she would need to look after herself and keep herself in good shape for when he decided he was attracted to her and wanted to fulfil the marital role.

Laura returned to the house with the children after a long walk back from the school through the rain. She shook off her umbrella before collapsing it and walking into the house.

Removing their shoes and wet coats the children quietly retired to their bedroom to complete their homework before their father returned home. Laura tidied everything and turned the heating on to ensure that the house was warming and everything was drying. She also made up the open fire in order to have a roaring blaze going next to Jerry's newspaper reading chair.

After she had done this, which she did with a routine efficiency, she moved to the kitchen to begin cooking Jerry's dinner. As she did every Friday evening, she was cooking a fillet steak for Jerry, triple cooked chips with some fried eggs to compliment the dish, whilst Laura and the kids were left with some cheaper cuts of beef, they still had a similar meal to their father, so that he didn't feel guilty about eating better than they did. Imagine living in a household where it was frowned upon to talk.

Imagine not being allowed to have a different opinion for fear of being "taught" a lesson. Imagine not being allowed to ask a question, without the man who says he loves you flying into a rage and hitting you repeatedly but being clever about it and never hitting you where it could be seen, or torturing you incessantly about either your appearance or about the fact that you might not be being loyal to him. Imagine being in a household where there's a constant grey cloud in the room, where there's a negatively electric atmosphere and who knows what is going to ignite the next storm.

This was the fear that Laura and her kids lived with every day. She wanted to escape desperately, she wanted immediately for it to stop. But she loved him, she cared for him and she always made an excuse for him, she told herself previously it was like she had Stockholm syndrome, being madly in love with the person who is physically and mentally holding you captive. If only she could break free of the hold he had on her.

Laura hated that the kids were stuck in this position too. She could leave at any time, although she was worried that Jerry would track her down and beat her to death, but the kids had no choice. If they spoke out, it would destroy the family, it would destroy Laura, It would completely destroy Jerry, that is, if it didn't land him in prison. Laura pleaded with them to stay quiet about what they had seen their father do to her. Or indeed what he had done to them.

She began preparing the meat, as she got it out and prepared her tools, the telephone rang. She walked to the hallway, where her vintage style telephone was kept, she answered and was prepared to take a message for her husband, who the calls were usually for. When she answered, a deep monotonous voice enticed her to keep listening.

Laura didn't really understand or know at first what she was listening to. The phone call had temporarily completely disorientated her, the anxiety and stress she was feeling was making her physically warm up and small beads of sweat formed on her top lip. She could feel her heart pounding in her chest, seemingly getting faster and faster. She looked down and thought she could see the thudding of the heavily beating organ in her chest. A slight dizziness came over her, it was as if she could see pins and needles in her eyes. Taking shorter and shallower breaths, this was a completely new sensation.

All of a sudden, she snapped back into the room. It was as if someone had just bought her out of a trance, she had no recollection of the phone call. The voice on the other end of the phone was seemingly a cheery person at the end of a sales script, trying to close Laura on a change of long distance phone call provider. Obviously unaware that Laura was not the decision maker in this household and with a complete lack of requirement for this kind of service, Laura swiftly hung up the telephone.

She was in a daze, how can this have happened to her? What did happen to her? How can she have had a blank in her thoughts and emotions? What was the phone call about? Who was the phone call from? She had so many questions about the experience she had just been through, however, she knew if she didn't get on with the dinner, it would never be ready for when Jerry came in.

Laura reached for the meat rubs, to put some flavorings onto the meat so it could rest properly. All of a sudden she began to go dizzy, she was working on auto pilot, and she had no control over herself. What was happening to her? The palpitations began again, the shortness of breath, the beading of sweat on her top lip. What seemed like an eternity later, she again snapped back into the room, there were various tubs on the side around the meat.

Now worried about running out of time to cook, Laura put everything back into on cupboard with earnest without paying attention as to what was going where.

She began to cook the other parts of the meal, cutting up the potatoes to make chips prior to shallow frying them, having the eggs on the side ready to fry up at the final moment, ensuring the yolk was going to be runny enough to be dippable but cooked enough to ensure no one would get ill.

As she sealed the meat before placing it under the grill, Laura couldn't help but notice the slightly odd smell that was coming from it. She disregarded it, thinking that it would be more diffi-cult to explain to Jerry that he didn't have his routine meal than it would be to explain that the meat was a little past its best.

Bringing Laura back to the thought of what she was doing, the front door all of a sudden slammed. A booming voice demanded Laura's attention in the hallway, she was there in a flash. Help-ing her husband strip off his coat and briefcase, also dropping to her knees to untie his brogues to ensure he wouldn't get the floor wet. Even if he got the floor wet, it would remain to be her fault.

She ran back into the kitchen, to carry on preparing the dinner, Jerry without initially saying a word to Laura walked up to the bathroom to go and wash down from his working day. He made the fleeting comment "Typical Friday, you never manage your time on a Friday, you're useless"

Despite the fact Laura was working her hardest to get everything plated up and ready to put on the table, it still wasn't good enough for him. What could she do that would be?

A few moments later, Laura rang a small triangle to alert every-one in the house that dinner was being served.

She began placing cutlery and plates on the table, ensuring condiments and place settings were exactly to those routine ex-pectations Jerry had told her she had to meet. Whilst Laura was dishing the food up, the whole family silently approached the table, sat down and placed their napkins on their laps in prepar-ation.

Jerry held his hands out and bowed his head, waiting for Laura, Hannah and Tommy to link hands together so that he could say grace. "For what we are about to receive, may the lord make us truly thankful, Amen" as they all sat waiting for Jerry to pick up his cutlery, the anticipation got a little too much for Tommy. He grabbed for the ketchup. This had happened once before and it didn't have a happy ending. Fortunately, it was the end of the working week and Jerry hadn't had any alcohol yet, so, on this occasion, he let this "offence" slide, with only a dark look issued by Jerry as a warning.

He picked up his cutlery and began to cut his steak. As they were normally, mealtimes were devoid of any talking or communication or even any emotions, they were about simply getting a task achieved. Placing it in his mouth, he looked at Laura saying "meat isn't ever so fresh is it, maybe try being more efficient when you buy things, don't buy them and wait for them to get old, or are you trying to poison me?"

She had no response, all she was able to do was cut a piece of meat, put it in her mouth with a defiant look about her and chew it. This showed there was no tainting of the meat. Jerry resumed eating, scowling at her whilst eating away at his meal.

Laura felt the dizziness begin to come on again, she was not worried, she did not feel like she was going to fall down, it wasn't that kind of dizziness.

The pins and needles in her eyes came back, the shortness of breath, the palpitations, and this one seemed to last forever, although she had more clarity in this moment, she could see clearly in front of her, it was as if she was just paralysed in position.

All of a sudden, Jerry began to go very red in the face, pulling at his jumper around his neck, beginning to slightly shake. He began to shout "WHAT HAVE YOU DONE TO ME" what was a shake was now a more severe tremor.

A slight white bubbling began to become apparent at the edges of his mouth, this quickly developed into thick frothy foam and the shaking became more and more violent, Jerry dropped to the floor. He was having a seizure, convulsing violently, all Laura could do was sit and watch paralysed, a smile came to her face, her dimples appeared and what was a smile, developed into a giggle.

Tommy and Hannah watched on in shock and horror as their

mother sat still laughing, whilst their father albeit the monster that he was, had collapsed down onto the floor violently shaking and frothing from the mouth.

His convulsing continued. Laura was able to move, although it was almost a stiff and robotic type of movement. She walked back over toward the sink where the washed preparation materials were sitting on the sideboard. Although she didn't know why and she couldn't stop herself.

She reached for the tenderiser and took a firm hold of it. She wasn't really aware of what was happening, even though she was fully aware of what was happening.

Laura was still giggling in a strange entranced manner.

She turned and knelt down next to Jerry, pausing and holding her breath, listening for any sign of life from him. She could hear and see nothing.

A moment passed but a sudden gasp of air came out of Jerry's mouth, as it did, Laura repeatedly bought down the heavy hammer on his skull, with each blow small bits of air escaping, small pieces of flesh and chunks of hair, as well as pumping blood began coating the kitchen and its pristine surfaces, as she bought the tenderiser down one last time, she must of hit an artery as his head seemed to explode with a large spurt of blood covering Laura head to toe in iron rich smelling claret.

Suddenly she stopped, the laughing stopped, the dimples disappeared and as if she had awoken. Laura looked confused, why did she have the tenderiser in her hands, why was there blood everywhere? Were the kids terrified? She began to tremble and panic, what had she done? Had she just murdered her husband? Yes he was the biggest monster there was, however, she still desperately loved him. She can't have killed him.

And what would the children think? What would they say? Would they defend her, or would they tell the police that clearly she had done it on purpose?

She turned and looked as there was no noise from them. A sinking feeling came to Laura's stomach. What had she done, both children were violently convulsing on the floor. Although the convulsions were slowing, they were becoming peaceful, they were slowly looking at rest. They could finally be happy, or, they could at least finally just not live in fear.

Laura had also poisoned her children. How could she live with herself? How could she have done this?

What was next for Laura? Did she phone the police and tell them what had happened, or did she cover it all up?

How would she even begin to clear up from this, how could she begin to move on from this?

How would she dispose of the bodies?

Lost in her own questions, Laura sat cradling her children, tears forming in her eyes. She was drenched in the blood of her husband, this was when the dizziness returned, the palpitations. A smile appeared back on her face and a bout of uncontrolled laughing ensued.

CHAPTER TWO: MEET ROGER

Sitting in a smoke filled room, eyes rolling into the back of his head, a drunk and dazed Roger had been sat the entire evening recalling his time spent on service to his country. Despite the horrors he saw both in the day time and vividly in his sleep, there was also the good times, which always bought a smile to his face.

The sense of brotherhood that he had found nowhere else, the sense of belonging and purpose and reason that had helped him through some of the tough times he had been through.

A mangy cat was sprawled out on a messy ash covered floor, the tattered furniture wasn't coordinated or in any kind of condition that would entice any normal person to use it.

Rogers head rolled back as he was on the edge of passing out, a half smoked cigarette hanging out of his mouth. The near overflowing ash tray sitting next to him reminding him that he was on his last packet and needed to go to town to get some more.

He couldn't survive the pain of not having a lit cigarette constantly hanging out of his mouth.

Slowly Roger rose to his feet. He stretched and what felt like every joint in his body seemed to crack or ache, he looked at his calendar and at his watch, he had been sat in his chair for the past 2 days, not eating, not sleeping, just drinking.

He had needed to relieve himself during this time, however, he was able to do this into one of the empty bottles of whiskey he had sitting on the floor, there were plenty to choose from.

He double checked what he was picking up when the bottle of whisky in his hand was empty, before drinking it, did it look like pee? Smell like pee? The final test, did it taste like pee?

Roger was a scarred gentleman. He had wounds and burn marks all over his face. His hair grew on his head and face in patches where there wasn't any disfiguration, although this wasn't in many places.

He wore dark Raybans, even in the house, every former soldier had a pair of 'bans in their pocket, if they hadn't bought them for the service, they'd either come from a fallen soldier or been taken from the enemy, when defeating them in battle.

He had a large imposing character. He cast a broad and tall shadow, domineering in stature, yet gentle in nature.

He had always been the kind of gentleman that would help an elderly neighbour, or teach the children in his street how to wire a plug. He was a wise man even before he went to war.

He returned a haunted man who although still showed traits of his former self, seemed to have a darkness hanging over him that couldn't be removed no matter how he tried to drown it out.

Roger turned to walk when he took a heavy step and heard a crunch. Thinking he had just stumbled onto an empty bottle or some other kind of rubbish, he thought nothing of it, moving some of the dirty clothes that were strewn all over the floor.

There lay the still twitching body of his mangy cat Horatio.

Horatio hadn't been treated to a visit to the vets in years, but he was loyal to Roger and always stuck by him, he was the one thing Roger had never forgotten, the way that man loved his cat was like nothing else in this world. The cat had been the only thing he could ever have relied on in life. The cat would always comfort him through his darkest moments. Now, the cat, was dead. Without meaning to Roger had put Horatio out of his misery. If only he had the guts to do the same to himself.

Roger had become unnervingly comfortable with death. Blood, guts, gore, they didn't mean much to him. People were just once living things that were no longer living, black or white, rich or poor.

In war, both sides, both groups of people had a purpose to achieve, for a cause that was most likely unjust, it was just one was successful, the other not. Life was life, Death was death.

People were born to die. Roger loved the theory of evolution and loved correcting people when they sparked up conversation with him about it. "One of the greatest misquotes of all time - It is not that evolution is survival of the fittest, but that evolution is the survival of the most adaptable" He had a bleak view on life, that we were only born to procreate and die, so it didn't matter what you did in this life, because once you'd done your job and made a baby, what more did you need to do?

Bringing himself back into the room, Roger gently scooped up the now stiffening cat in his large hands and carefully began to wrap it in a blanket. He stumbled toward the door, picking up a shovel on the way out of his lean-to. Heading toward the back of his garden, he softly placed the blanket on the ground and began to dig a hole for it to rest in.

Within a short space of time the hole was deep enough to ensure that no predator would come along to eat the decaying body of his poor cat. He gathered up the blanket and placed it down in the bottom of the hole, he started to back fill the hole with dirt which he gently pressed into place with his boot.

Scouring the garden, he found a large piece of quartz edged flint. Roger placed this on top of the grave of Horatio as a reminder.

Regrettably there were 8 other pieces of flint within this run of the garden. It would seem that this was not the first time Roger had to bury something within the grounds of his house and he couldn't be certain that it would be a final time either.

Roger recited the words "life is life, death is death, it was an honour knowing you for the time we had together. My trusted friend Horatio" with that, he stumbled back toward his house throwing down his spade.

Wading through the piles of waste and general disorder, Roger remembered he needed to go and get more cigarettes. It was at this point that a wave of self-pity hit him and he felt, what was the point?

He headed up the stairs ducking, as not to bump his head on the low ceiling. He got to his bed and fell forwards onto it. His large frame bouncing off the filthy, stained, ancient mattress.

A creaking was apparent from the bed frame, shortly after a cracking noise began when suddenly, the cheap Swedish frame collapsed on one corner. Roger couldn't be bothered to try to fix it, permanently or temporarily, he just passed out on the bed hoping maybe that tomorrow may never come.

Unfortunately for Roger tomorrow did come and it came with a massive hangover. Although when he woke, it wasn't to the cold light of day, it was to the still of the following evening.

There was no movement in the chilly mountain air, but a mist descending and coating every surface it came into contact with.

Still stuck with his sense of not belonging, he lay back down and couldn't be bothered to get up again.

Eventually his brain managed to switch off and he was able to sleep again. This was the most he had slept since he had returned from the front lines.

Roger had been plagued with horrendous memories since he returned. They called it shell shock then, they called it PTSD now. No amount of therapy, no amount of talking about the situations could ever make him right again. The situations could never cure him. They could never make him better because they couldn't unsee those atrocities, he couldn't unsee the horror or the pain of seeing his friends die right next to him, or gathering up parts of their bodies, so their families had something to bury at home.

Drinking helped ease the pain as it meant that he didn't have to dream. When he drank he didn't dream at all. It stopped the dreams but when he drank heavily, it would often result in Roger having blackout moments. Whole hours of the day or night that he could not recall. Still this felt better than reliving any of those events he had been through.

He knew one day he would have to stop the drinking and get real with getting over this, but with no responsibilities to anyone else and an open benefits system that supported him, he was quite happy with what he was doing at present. His actions had no consequence to anyone, other than rather obviously the poor cat and those companions that had come before him.

Roger was coming down the stairs when he heard the phone ringing. It was an older phone, it had a very shrill tone, very sharp and precise.

He had bought it from the charity shop solely for this reason. He started to dig through the house trying to find it as it continued to ring.

Eventually, he found it. It was in his under stair toilet, which Roger had sealed off some time ago. It smelt like a bat cave, the stench of bitter ammonia overwhelmed him as he opened the door to it.

Stains of where he had been drunk and fallen off the seat whilst defecating were still present. He picked up the phone and closed the door, it would be a while until he went back in there again.

He answered the phone in his gravelly, unused voice "yeah what" for a moment, there was absolutely nothing there. Just a crackling line, Roger repeated himself again and again getting more and more agitated by this waste of time.

He slammed down the phone shouting and screaming at it. Momentarily he paused and didn't know what to do, for once in his life he was unsure.

The phone rang again, time seemed to slow as he could feel the rage building inside of himself. He answered but said nothing. Breathing heavily through gritted teeth he just listened. The crackling and ticking continued, as if a tape was playing and he was listening.

It was at this point that the repeated talking started "Find the girl, find the girl, find the girl" this looped time and time again. Who was the girl and what was the significance of her to him, and why the hell should he waste time going to find her.

"What a load of old crap" he mumbled to himself slamming down the receiver onto the base. Walking out of the house, he still had the phone in his hand. The door slammed, which cut the wire to the phone, the slight tug back on his arm reminded him he was holding it.

He placed it down carefully on the floor, his only communication to a seemingly distant outside world. He realised that he had lost his temper over something very small, what if that was one of the boys from his unit? What if that was a friend needing his help? What the hell should he do, he couldn't call back! Sitting on the front deck of his house, he couldn't help but spiral into guilt.

His mind immediately took him to needing more whisky, he really needed more cigarettes. But what he needed most of all was to forget.

Riding in his rusty and neglected van, Roger couldn't help but wonder when he was going to be pulled over for driving a vehicle with no MOT, no license and no insurance, that or the fact that he was most likely always over the drink drive limit.

It must have been a magnet for attention from the law. It had moss growing on every window seal and edge that it could find to grow on, green algae on the surface from being sat underneath the tree for so long.

Roger spent a large amount of time being anxious about the outside world, this limited his travel and adventures to a trip to the convenience store 3 miles from his secluded house. There and back like clockwork 3 times a week, to stock up on Whiskey, cigarettes and occasionally cat food, well, there was no longer a need for that.

Cats Dead.

Having reached his destination and now aimlessly walking around the convenience store, which wasn't the largest space, Roger wondered if he should be buying food, or maybe he should quit the drinking and get back in shape. Maybe a clean start was needed to get back on the right path.

He laughed out loud to himself, his husky tar ridden vocal chords booming through the shop. This had drawn the attention of others in proximity, who stood looking. Roger turned and looked at the shopkeeper and other customers at the counter. He was confused why they were looking at him, when it suddenly clicked. "I thought about buying vegetables" the words fell out of his mouth and without intending to, he had made both ladies smile, the familiar older lady behind the counter smiled warmly with an understanding sadness for Roger and said "5 bottles, 10 packs" Rogers face dropped to a sullen dullness, he nodded. Cutting in he quickly paid his money and slunk out of the shop back toward his van.

Arriving back at his house, sometime later, Roger sat in his van. The sun was beginning to set, he rested his arms on the steering wheel and placed his head into the point at which his arms crossed. Still having a good muscle mass despite the years of abuse he had put his body through, this wasn't the comfiest position for him to rest in, so he sat back, put his chair back, opened a bottle and began to drink.

He opened his cigarettes, placed one in his mouth and lit it flicking the petrol lighter with one hand and took a long, deep, slow drag on it, remembering how good it felt just to smoke. To have that moment of release, to have that moment of connection...to something.

As the sun began to set, a tear began to slip down his cheek, the sky was painted in a beautiful array of red's pink's and yellow's, a golden hue surrounded the hills around Rogers house.

He thought over all of the pain he had felt over the years, all of the hurt, he remembered when he had heard the bombs falling over head, he was one of the lucky ones, he survived.

He remembered the screams, remembered the pain, remembered the suffering his friends, his brothers, and his colleagues had gone through. It was then that Roger realised, he was not one of the lucky ones. They were the lucky ones. They didn't have to live with the memories, didn't have to live with the pain, didn't have to remember.

Roger poured a small amount whisky out of the van window from the bottle as the sun disappeared past the horizon "I will never forget"

CHAPTER THREE: MEET ADRIANA

Pulling around the final corner she knew she had this one won by at least 10 strides. Having pushed herself to the point her legs felt like they were about to snap. She dug deep for every last ounce of energy she pushed and pushed, she didn't even see the finish, she kept running as the world around her began to dim, the light began to fade, her legs began to fall from beneath her as she tripped over her own foot and in slow motion, she began to collapse. She could see herself from above falling face first without any energy to put her arms out to protect herself. She hit the ground, hard, a loud crunch echoed through the stadium, followed by her lifeless corpse rag dolling up the track, the world stopped for her as the gravel of the track scraped away the flesh on Adriana's face.

An angry man screamed in Slovak at the fallen body, clearly frustrated by this. He took the opportunity to kick the lifeless body and vent at her.

After what felt like forever spent in purgatory, she awoke in a bright white room. The smell of stale cigarette smoke was heavy in the air. She was paralysed and couldn't move. As her consciousness began to come back to her, Adriana felt a tremendous pain shoot through her abdomen, her face felt stiff, as she writhed in agony it felt like it was cracking.

Her legs felt like they had shards of glass in them and every time she moved them on the bed the glass was being brushed back and forth, digging it deeper into her flesh.

She tried to scream, tried to shout, but her mouth was held closed by something. Her head was being held in place by it too.

She was scared, what the hell had happened to her, she was struggling to remember how she got here. She was struggling to grasp the sheer agony she was in. Every thought that went through her head was like a piercing nail being pushed slowly through her eyeball up into her forehead. All she could do was try to scream. All she could do was try to call out. But no-one came.

She had gone from Purgatory to Hell.

An agonising wait later, the matron came into the room and she filled up the water bowl to clean Adriana down. Stifling a whimper, the matron became aware of her being conscious, she fled from the room and bought back a wave of doctors and nurses. They surrounded the gurney and this made Adriana panic more.

She began breathing heavily. Why was she getting so much attention, what had happened to her. Why were all of these people in her room?

No one would tell her what had happened. No one would speak to her. They were speaking in a language she didn't quite understand. All she had ever known was Slovak, all she had ever heard was Slovak, this language although sounding vaguely similar to any outsider, wasn't anything she had heard before or could even comprehend.

It was then that an older man hobbled into the room. He seemed frail and washed up but he also commanded a sense of authority. The kind of man that stopped people and bought them to attention when he entered a room. He gave the impression that at one time he had been a very powerful man. But now, just walked around with half smoked cigar tentatively dangling out of his mouth and smelling of home brewed alcohol, sweet, like peaches, toxic like poison.

He stared emptily at Adriana with a look of hatred and disappointment, it was all she had known from him since she was younger. Nothing was ever good enough, no achievement was enough for him to be satisfied with how she had performed.

She didn't even know what this man was to her, she knew she had always been commanded to listen to him, to obey him and to never question his instruction. But she couldn't remember why. At this point she did nothing but feel fear and undeniable agony. Every fibre of her being was hurting. She was so confused, so broken and couldn't understand why.

He wandered around the bed as all of the doctors and nurses stood up straight seemingly awaiting his instructions as he paced around the room. Eventually he broke the silence with a stifled grunt followed in Slovak with "If I'd have known you were going to be this disappointing I wouldn't have saved you, I wouldn't have pushed you, I wouldn't have WASTED MY TIME"

Adriana was scared, she barely knew who she was or what she was doing there never mind the fact that she was being made to feel worthless for being in that position. An anger grew inside of her. The flame had been lit, no matter how much pain she was in, no matter what she did, no one was allowed to make her feel like this.

She got increasingly frustrated as the old man shouted away and the doctors and nurses began to plead with him to let them tend to her. She began to shake, she began to go bright red on the parts of her face that there was no scabbing or open wounds. Her head was still held in place, but she desperately needed to move it. She needed to lash out at this abomination that was supposedly a man, but she couldn't.

In that instant, everything went black. Her body went limp and lifeless. She could hear the activity happening around her, but she couldn't do anything, it was if she had been partially sedated.

Her mind was still active but her body was asleep. She heard the crass voice of the elderly gentleman speaking a language she couldn't understand, whatever he had said, the doctors and nurses immediately began caring for the girl who urgently needed it. She had again slipped from consciousness as the staff managed her lifeless body, cleaning it and administering medication.

It was days later when Adriana awoke with a jump, it was exactly like the first time she had woken up. Agony, sheer agony and paralysis, all over her body this time, not just her head, her arms and legs wouldn't move either, not that she should have any urge to move, the pain it had caused her previously.

She lay there in wait, for someone to come into the room. It was then that the matron returned, who had come before and immediately looked over her. She could see in Adriana's eyes that she was scared. She could see that she didn't know what was happening.

Fortunately the Matron spoke Slovak and explained that there had been an incident whilst Adriana was training, she had fallen down hard and possibly broken her neck. So they had to immobilize her so that her body had time to heal the injury, she was 2 weeks into her recovery. Only another 6 to go.

Adriana had learnt that she had also had to have skin grafts on her face where she had been moving at such a pace, when she had fallen her body had slid along the gravel removing layers of skin. If she stood any chance of retaining her youthful beauty, this was something that needed to happen.

This explained the pain on her legs where they had taken the grafts from. This explained the pain in her face. Knowing that this wouldn't be the last time she would have to go through this agony to get her looks was something that terrified her.

Growing up, Adriana had been the envy of her class mates at the sports academy. Not only was she at the top of her ability class, she was also extremely attractive, she had a slender youthful face surrounded by long flowing blonde hair, she had piercing blue eyes that if you looked into them, could keep you lost within them.

But Adriana was also extremely modest about her appearance and abilities, despite being so capable she could never really fulfil her true potential as she lacked the full arrogance needed to excel at what she did. She lacked the sharp edge. Little did she know she may learn that she would need to have one sooner, than later.

Time marched forward as Adriana went through recovery. It was difficult, it was harder than anything she had ever had to try for in her life. She had to push herself to learn to move normally again. She had to push herself to be confident enough with her "new" face to show it anywhere outside of her recovery room. Even when she did emerge - it was momentary. It was a fleeting movement in the shadows. Watching others who were in recovery, waiting in the shadows and confines of her room for time to pass.

The days rolled into weeks, the weeks, they rolled into months, Adriana felt trapped and what little confidence she had in her appearance and her abilities was further dented by this incident.

What for some would be a momentary blip, a speedbump on the road to greatness, a learning point for development of themselves, for her was something that was affecting her entire life. Every decision she would make, would be made with caution, she couldn't even begin to think about competing again. It had been so long since the man had last visited, she didn't know if she was ever going back there. But Adriana also wasn't sure whether or not that was a good thing.

Whilst she lay in her room, hoping that something would happen, that anything would happen, Adriana was bought out of her daze by the sharp ring of the telephone. For all of the months she had been in the facility, not once had that telephone rang especially when there was no one else in proximity to answer it. She was in a bind, what should she do? Did she answer it and see who it was? Or did she leave it because the call most likely wasn't intended for her anyway? Why was she so torn over answering a telephone? It was just a telephone, there was nothing special about it and what did she have to lose? Why was this simple decision so difficult?

She grabbed swiftly for the receiver. It was at this point that she realised maybe her recovery was going to take longer than could have been anticipated. What felt like a hot needle had gone through her core, it dropped her to the floor, took her breath away and made it difficult for her to focus on who she was or what she was doing.

After a moment of recuperation, Adriana put the receiver to her ear, which unexpectedly hurt immensely with sharp pains arching across to her other ear. She pushed through the pain and listened to the line. It sounded like the noise you could hear on a grammar phone before the record started, like the dead air before and after a recording. The continual click of the needle skipping onto the final part of the record.

Then she heard a faint voice - this time in English and somehow, strangely she was able to interpret it. Never before had she been outside of Slovakia, never before had she spoken anything other than Slovak, but for some reason this voice made sense.

Going through this realisation, the fact she could understand meant that Adriana hadn't been listening to the content of the phone call. When she zoned into the voice, when she focused she could hear it in detail. "Let the man come, don't ask why, just do as he says"

She got scared and slammed the receiver down. What the hell did that mean? She replayed the whole message through her head. Who was the man? Was this the man who bought her here? Was this the man who had trained her? Been in charge of her and developed her abilities? Was this the man the voice or recording was telling her about? Or was it another man, someone she was yet to discover, it could be any man, literally any man in the whole world and more to the point why shouldn't she ask why? A point that felt prominent, why should she just do as he says?

By her upbringing, Adriana was subversive to the males around her, by her training she knew she had to listen to the men who commanded her to work harder, or to be more of a "real woman" so she couldn't understand why this voice on the other end of the phone had stirred something inside of her. It had lit a fire of defiance that she didn't want to extinguish.

She couldn't understand why she felt a sudden sense of resistance, but she felt admiration for herself, for feeling this way. Was this a new Adriana? Was this a confident feisty woman who wouldn't be commanded or pushed around?

Deep down, she felt a sense of excitement, but she was still curious, would she know what the call meant when something happened? Was she always going to be anticipating a man to command her? Was she always going to be submissive thinking this was the man? Then she stopped and questioned herself. What if this phone call wasn't even for her, what if this was intended as a message for someone else?

Her eyes opened. She began to question if it was all a dream. Bringing herself back into conscious reality, she was looking around. The air was dense with the scent of stale cigarette smoke. The once bright white walls had a distinct tinge of nicotine staining. She could feel the cold stainless steel gurney frame underneath her. She was well and truly grounded. But was all of that just a dream. Or was it real.

Looking over at where the telephone was, she remembered she slammed it down, or at least she thought she did do. Getting up from her bed, she tentatively walked over to the phone without taking her eyes off it. It all looked like it could be feasible, it could have rung, she could have answered it and there could well have been a message for her. But did it really happen?

Either way, she knew she was going to be pondering this for a long time to come, until maybe it either came to fruition or that it came to nothing and she returned to her normal life, that was, if she could return to her "normal" life, she sarcastically laughed to herself, life was anything but normal.

CHAPTER FOUR:
MEET SAM

Hearing a scream in the distance, Sam's ears pricked and his attention was suddenly drawn, from the moment he was in.

The late afternoon sunlight complimented his golden complexion. The shadows cast over his taught cheek bones and his strong jawline seemed to intensify as his focus was looking around for the direction of the cry for attention.

Like a sniper drawing breath, with time almost standing still, he spotted a woman struggling with a man, 200 yards up the street. He turned and began to sprint toward them. He had dropped his sport jacket, which had been previously slung over his shoulder so that his hands were free.

His shoulder heavy, muscular frame was lean and toned. He cut a line through the air as his speed built, moving both commandingly and swiftly Sam's intimidating physique was honing in on what he could now see was a man trying to take the woman's handbag.

He focused as he drew close, dropped his shoulder as he speared the attempted attacker against a wall.

A loud thud resounded through the man's body as both he and Sam slammed into the wall resulting in them both collapsing in a heap on the ground, there was no sudden urge for either man to stand up.

The would-be attacker lay broken in a heap occasionally taking a shallow breath of gargled air, his body lay disfigured from the heavy impact he had just encountered.

Sam had to take a moment to catch his breath, but soon was back up on his feet again and helping the lady to her feet with her handbag, which was passed back to her with the most sincere apology from Sam on behalf of both his gender and on behalf of society.

He looked the woman directly in the eyes, he had sharp blue eyes that sparkled when the light bounced off them. Wavy blonde hair also complimented his skin tone.

He supported the woman as they began to walk off up the street linking arms, to comfort and reassure her. Despite the incident, she had quickly become smitten with Sam. Not only was he the most gorgeous man she had ever seen, but he was also her very own hero. Not saying a word, they wandered aimlessly lost in each other and the moment for a short while.

Walking down the street Sam knew there was a pub close by that was open, comfy and secure, he took her there, sat her down in the snug and went to the bar to get a drink. Returning with 2 small whisky's the woman was confused, she hadn't asked for this, maybe Sam wasn't all he thought he could be. Whilst he made himself comfortable she waited to speak, slightly confused and now beginning to feel a little uncomfortable. He looked up with that reassuring smile, looking her deep in the eye and said simply "It will help with the shock"

Slightly blushing, the woman looked back at him and struggled to squeeze the words "oh, thank you" There came the realisation of what had just nearly happened to her, followed by an admiration of what this person had done to help.

She began to start breathing a little shallower, she got very warm, very quickly. She realised this man was watching her with an intensity, looking back at him, directly in the eye their gaze was fixed deep on each other, deep within each other.

Being lost in that moment, both of them slightly jumped when Sam opened his mouth "It's ok, I'm here for you, I'm Sam, and you've had a terrible experience. The barman will bring you over any drink you would like in a moment, but the whiskey will honestly help with the shock, we don't have to speak. I am here for you if you want to speak to me, the one thing I am most curious about, is to be able to put a name to the face of the most gorgeous woman I have had the liberty of being able to save from a would-be attacker"

Her cheeks raised slightly, her lips still pursed yet a small smile seemed to appear as she almost became a little bashful and looked down toward her feet. "I'm, well, I'm Elisabeth, thank you for everything you have done for me, I just want to sit here, right in this moment" from the way she spoke, Sam could tell she was a smoker, her slightly deeper voice had a very sexy undertone.

She had gorgeous wavy black hair. Beautiful brown eyes and an olive complexion that was the envy of her friends. She was someone that Sam was extremely attracted to, when he met someone like this, it was uncommon for him to go home alone.

They spent hours sitting and drinking in the snug taking themselves miles away from the moment and imagining scenarios that may not even have been or may never be.

When Sam suggested he walk her home, a sudden look of panic came across her face. She looked down at her hand. She remembered, she was married, she had already met the man of her dreams, and she was already married to him.

Clumsily attempting to explain and apologise for thinking she had led him on. Sam being Sam, stopped her "no apology is necessary, I didn't save you because you were attractive, I saved you because it was the right thing to do, come on let's get you home to your husband, I'm sure he's worried"

This was the type of man Sam was. Not only was he a highly attractive and attentive every day hero, Sam was also thoughtful and considerate of others. Each day he got to wake up and make a difference in someone else's life was a good day to be alive.

After dropping Elisabeth off at her house, Sam felt indebted to her husband to explain that he hadn't known she was married and that she had been in a state of shock and he primarily just wanted to ensure she was okay. Sam should have asked, on reflection, if she had a partner he could call for her.

Although this had made Ian a little uneasy knowing his wife had been drinking following a traumatic experience, he understood and appreciated the effort Sam had gone to, both to reassure him that there was nothing sinister behind it, but also that he had ensured Elisabeth was safe and comforted.

"Thank you, I will be forever indebted to you for what you have done for us, I would invite you in for a drink, but I think we need to be together on our own" Sam understood completely, he strode off doing a half effort salute and a slight nod of his head.

Returning to his spacious and luxurious bachelor pad, Sam emptied his pockets. Placing the items down in an orderly fashion at a distance from his front door, each item had its place and he ensured each was left in its place, perfectly orientated.

He began to undress, placing each item of clothing in the appropriate washing container. Walking completely undressed through the room, Sam never considered if anyone looked in through the window. He didn't have anything to be shy about, Sam was a well-endowed gentleman and even when fully clothed his abundance of manhood was clear to anyone who took more than a momentary glance. But that still didn't prevent from feeling conscious about his appearance or indeed his appendage.

When he made it to the bathroom, Sam turned on the shower and allowed it to come up to temperature, he had placed his towel in the best spot for when he got out, so that a minimal amount of water dripped on the floor.

He stepped in, and began to let the water wash away the stresses of the day. He put a small amount of shower gel onto his hand and began to lather it over his toned abdomen. He was always amazed at how this sensual experience made him feel and how relaxing the water pouring down on his head was.

As Sam moved back through the jet of water, it encompassed him and cleared all of the lathered from his body. Revealing his tight and toned physique. Watching the final bubbles disappear down the drain, Sam turned the water off and stepped out of the shower reaching for the towel and wrapped it around himself.

He walked out to his bedroom and removed the towel with his back to the window. He began to dry himself starting with his hair and working his way down.

Whenever he was doing this he couldn't help but feel he was being watched, but he secretly enjoyed this feeling. He didn't know who it was, he didn't know what they were watching, however, it helped him to have a little boost with his self-esteem, that maybe they were watching because they thought he was attractive.

Sam walked out of the bedroom toward his gym wearing only his underwear.

He sat down at his weight bench and prepared to do a small workout. He picked up the dumbbell which was heavily loaded with weights and began to count, breathing in time with his lifts. One, Two, Three, Four, Five. Sam swapped arms. One, Two, Three, Four, Five. He sat and paused for a moment before repeating this same routine and further 20 times. He thought maybe for this evening a little light arm workout would be enough.

No point in stressing over doing too much, rather unsurprisingly he ached a little after spearing the attacker earlier in the day, maybe it would be best to leave the workout for now.

Sam retired to his bedroom and got himself under the sheet, feeling the silk against his smooth skin was like a little touch of heaven. He turned on the sound system which had Holst's - The

Planets playing subtly as a background to his rest, with a sideways smile he lay his head down on the pillow and relaxed into slumber as the music took him away into a dream world.

Waking up feeling fresh, Sam got up, prepared himself for the day and got dressed. What new adventures would he be facing today? With no need to do any form of work, he was a free agent.

A few years ago, Sam had the great fortune of winning a substantial sum on the lottery. This was not uncommon for him to be lucky when he faced something that had minimal odds of being successful.

Whilst being humble with it, he had enough money to last him 2 lifetimes if he used it sparingly and only when necessary.

Sam would always give his time at no charge to anyone who needed it. Having been a former lawyer, he was never short of money anyway.

These days, he mostly spent time helping charities for those who were less fortunate or those who couldn't afford due to whatever circumstances to feed their families, unfortunately this was a common occurrence in modern society.

This was not something that could simply be solved by Sam dipping his hand in his pocket to give the charities money, although he had no problem doing this when the charities needed it, but more a case of giving his time just to be there.

To offer his professional skills or simply to do the tasks either no one else would want to do, or could do. It didn't matter what it was, Sam was able to give it a go and would usually be able to achieve a result to a reasonable standard.

Sam decided that he would head down to the homeless shelter and see if they needed any help. Throwing on a casual outfit, he was always cautious not to be too overdressed or showy when he helped out at the shelter because it didn't seem right. He approached it as a humble experience just one normal human helping another normal human.

Walking in, it felt nice to be addressed and recognised not only by the ever temporary residents but also the staff who also seemed genuinely pleased to see him. Sam walked through to the office of the centre and asked if there was anything he could do to help out. "Nothing special today Sam, maybe if you could help the kitchen staff set out for dinner, that would be more than I could ask for, of course if you wouldn't mind?" of course this was no problem for him, he smiled and nodded in silent recognition.

Being jovial with the staff at the centre was a main stay. He enjoyed speaking with them and playing about, it was somewhere he could drop his guard and just be himself. Sam grabbed the plates and cutlery and began to set them out around the food hall. They would cater for around 90 people that evening in two sittings. One table down, 8 to go.

The pay phone rang on the wall behind him. It rang, repeatedly and did do for quite some time. Not being able to ignore it, Sam wondered over. "Hello, Crane street shelter Sam speaking" there was nothing for a moment just an empty clicking, then suddenly a fearful, shrill scream came out of the receiver. This made him jump, he really wasn't expecting that, he carried on listening but he didn't know why. The clicks had returned, Sam half expected a scream to come out of the phone, but then a monotonous and dreary voice slowly began to become apparent. "You will fail, you will fail, you will fail" Sam laughed to himself, what the hell was this, Sam never failed, clearly this wasn't a phone call for him.

The voice had been repeating itself, in the continual Monotone, but it stopped, then it began again, distant at first then becoming louder and it sounded different to before "Sam, you will fail. Sam, you will fail. Sam, you will fail" again this was continually repeated. Starting to freak out a little, Sam slammed the handset down. Walked away and began to compose himself, this was beginning to become a mind worm for him, never mind, there was plenty more he needed to get on with to help those less fortunate than him.

After a long and challenging service, Sam was helping wash down the dishes. Clearing up all the mess, and of course trying to bring a smile to everyone's faces. In the back of his head, he couldn't forget this phone call, was it really intended for him. Was it real, was it just a day dream. Sam was prone to the odd day dream or two. It wasn't out of the realms of possibility.

He turned to one of the staff who worked there, he asked if the phone had been ringing earlier on, "No Sam, we saw you looking at it, head over to it and answer it, you were stood there for around 5 minutes, you were being a bit funny, we thought you were just joking about, the phone never rang" shocked, Sam stopped momentarily but then he smiled and said "Yeah of course, I was joking about, you know what I'm like"

This worried him, was this call all in his head? Did he imagine it, was he going crazy? There were no stress factors in his life, why would he be going crazy? Why the hell did the voice specify that it was aimed at him? Why the hell did the voice say he was going to fail, Sam never failed, he was a natural winner, he was naturally lucky, what could possibly change?

Thinking little of it, Sam packed up for the night and headed out of the shelter for the short walk back to his flat.

Once home, Sam followed the same routine as he had done the night before. Shower, exercise, rest. He couldn't help but lay there and wonder as he heard the crescendos of "O Fortuna" come from the audio system, how did this get on here, this wasn't Sam's usual easy listening classical music. This was turning out to be a very weird day.

No point over thinking it, Sam turned his audio system off and lay there trying to get some sleep with the silence. After what felt like forever sitting in the dark with no noise, he eventually came to rest and slept.

CHAPTER FIVE:
PERSON ONE

Imagine a white room, brilliant white, the kind of white that is dazzling given the correct lighting. There are no windows. There are no doors. In the centre of the room is a brilliant white pedestal, there is no shadow cast by this pedestal, on it, sits an off white Bakelite telephone.

On the floor is sat a young male, cross legged and appearing to be at peace. A person of average ability, average mental state and average build. There is absolutely nothing exceptional about this individual. This individual has a scruffy appearance, unshaven, straggly unwashed hair, clothes that didn't appear to have been clean for a long time. Sitting there he looked drastically out of place against the white of the room.

There is nothing but abject silence. Only the sound of the person breathing, slightly rattly, a slight whistle from the nostril. Other than this, there was nothing. Complete silence other than the sound of a being living. Nothing other when in deep thought than the sound of the person's heartbeat.

This may be the perfect place to begin to meditate. To reflect, to be in the here and now. To be just about the person, being at one with themselves listening to their body. The sounds that you make just to be alive.

The person is sat in a semi-conscious state, almost suspended in time, their eyes are open but they seem like they could be a million miles away. Their eyes look empty and soulless, but they are ever twitching.

The room is the perfect temperature, not hot, not cold. The floor although hard is comfortable. The walls, if you could find them seemed expansive. The room appeared to be maybe larger than it was. There was no real way to gauge the surroundings.

There were scratch marks on one wall, signs that someone had searched for an entrance or an exit, there was still nothing than absolute white, and the only traces were from the shadows that could be seen from the gouges that had been worked over time. That and faint traces of blood where the nails had scratched so hard they had caused damage. The blood was had the look of being smeared, as if someone had tried to clean it off.

The room other than this seemed peaceful, tranquil and a place one could be at rest. But these marks, they screamed of terror and fear.

The moment drew back in again, as a small droplet of sweat seemed to form on the persons head. It began to gather with other droplets, and form a faster moving drip running down the face, over the brow and along the length of the nose. Pausing, it hung on tip of the person's nose. Why had this happened, there was no change in the room temperature, they looked to be under no stress, there was no reason for them to sweat. They closed their eyes tightly shut.

The person began to tremble. Their heart rate began to raise, breathing began to shallow. The sound of the heart beat echoed in their ears, slowly increasing, his breathing becoming less relaxed, shallower and at a more rapid pace. This person seemed to be now conscious, of their being, of their surrounding and of themselves.

It was then that the phone rang. All of a sudden their eyes tore open. Going from the previous position of lost in a world only they would know to being terrified of what that sound would bring. The first ring always seemed to go on and on and on. It stopped, with the person holding their breath. It was only a momentary pause, then again the phone rang.

In a room of absolute silence, where there was no noise for what could have been an eternity, when the phone rang it cut through the dead air like fingernails scraping down a blackboard. A screeching awkwardness that resounded and seemed to surround everything in the vacuum of senses, but also slightly echoing itself.

The person covered their ears. They covered their eyes. Nothing could make it stop and they knew it wouldn't stop and the peace would not return until the handset was lifted.

The person desperately crawled toward the pedestal with terror in their eyes, wiping the sweat from their brow and top lip with one hand and reaching out for the handset with the other, the phone stopped its ringing momentarily just as his hand was reaching the receiver.

He stopped reaching, stopped their grasp and the hand slightly withdrew. A glimour of hope appeared on his face, all of the build-up, all of the fear and tension seemed to fade away.

This was stripped away a second later when they were thrown straight back into the moment as the phone rang one more time. Immediately the handset was lifted then slowly and cautiously raised to his ear.

There was a clicking, nothing but a clicking, like an audio tape that had no recording, this was followed by a heavy clunk. Was someone using this old technology, a tape player to cause issues with this person? Was someone trying to instil fear into this person? What could be worse than the sound of no noise in a room where there was no noise. The sound of no noise with almost the promise of noise from the telephone then to hear no noise on the other end?

Person one slammed down the telephone and turned. What was he expecting? Could he see another pedestal that had appeared, tentatively he slowly began to walk the 10 paces he had gauged it was from where he was now.

Counting, it was a way of keeping a bearing.

One.

Two.

Three.

Four.

Five.

Six.

Seven..

Eight...

The steps became slower and more cautious the further away from the first pedestal he was, it had become an anchor point for him to cling to. A safety net for him to be near.

He looked back, the pedestal seemed so far away, and he looked at it from the floor slowly raising his vision toward the telephone. It was gone.

Other than the vague outline of the pedestal the reassurance of that anchor point seemed like it had been thrown away. He was unsure now what was happening, the same fears and anxieties had come back that he had first felt when he had originally woken up there.

Cautiously, he began to turn, he knew there was only what he thought was 2 paces left until he reached the other pedestal. What was he hoping would be there? What was he hoping he would find? He took a single pace confidently and counted Nin.. as he did his head and body hit the wall with force and knocked him off his feet.

Momentarily stunned, dazed and a little confused he began to bring himself back together, slowly but dejectedly pick himself up off the floor. What did he have to lose by walking back to the pedestal he had previously known as his safe place? His gaze was fixed to the floor. With his shoulders slunk low and knees slightly bent, he felt at his absolute lowest ebb.

He began to walk the eight and half paces back to where he had been, having to force his body to lift his legs to move along the room, again he began to count in his head, the counting felt like a sense of resistance to whatever this was. Like it was a piece of sanity that could be clung onto.

One..

The paces were more labored now than ever before, they were slower and more cautious, despite his determination to push on, and every fiber of his being telling him to stop. Every breath he took, he thought may be his last.

Two..

He heard something, what was it, the abject silence was broken by something. It was a slight ring, like an old fashioned telephone being put back on the hook. This stopped his less confident stepping, it made him question whether the phone was still present.

Three..

He desperately wanted to lift his sight back up to the horizon, but he was terrified of what he would see. Why was he terrified, there was a telephone there before, but it had disappeared. What if it were back again? Had it really disappeared? Why could he just not look up?

Four..

He should be halfway back to the pedestal by now.

Five..

He began to look back up, beginning to gain a little more confidence.

Six...

The sweat began to form again, he could feel his forehead beading up, he could feel it begin to start tickling his face as the small droplets began to come together, his breathing began to shallow

Seven....

He lifted his head slightly, like when a child is scolded for their behaviour and they become hesitant to re-engage. His nervousness enveloped his entire being, he began to tremble, he was in the midst of fighting every urge not to look up, but he felt he knew he needed to.

Eight.....

As he placed his foot down on the floor, the slight click and ring came back, but this time, as his vision focused from the floor up to the top of the pedestal, he saw the phone. His breathing stopped, his eyes became fixed on the telephone. His mind became completely devoured by the disbelief that it was actually there. He was sure it wasn't there when he looked.

Slowly bringing his foot to meet the one fore stepped, he was in complete disbelief, he was lost in that moment. Lost in the essence of who was doing this to him and what he was doing there. It was then that the telephone rang again.

Immediately he felt a rush and he picked it up and quickly drew the handset to his ear. The same dead noise was on the other end of the line. A rage began to build inside of him, an anger he had been containing. He went bright red in the face "WHAT DO YOU WANT" he screamed down the receiver. The noise of this echoing around the room. The echo felt like it prolonged, like someone had put it on a loop, repeating it back to him.

Over and over, he felt like this went on for an extended period before he heard the familiar clunk that he was used to. He began to move the phone away from his ear when he heard a noise from the receiver.

Hurriedly he put it back to his ear. The noise stopped. He held the phone to his ear pressing the handset so hard against the side of his head that it was starting to hurt. He held his breath, to see if stopping breathing meant that he could hear what was going on. It wasn't a competition for being able to hear but the desire was so strong to hear something, to hear anything.

Eventually, he heard a noise as if someone was drawing breath, a computerised or digitised voice was on the line clicking in and out as if he could hear someone breathing. "Person One" this one phrase shook the man's core being. It made him realise, he didn't know who he was, and he didn't know his name or anything about himself. All he knew, was what was in that moment. That he was in a place he could not come back from.

He collapsed to the floor, a tear slowly trickled down his cheek. He was absolutely still. This had killed his final fight instinct. This had broken him. Realising that he didn't know who, what or where he was meant more to him than he realised. Not knowing how long he had been there, or what he was meant to do to leave, left him broken.

Clutching at his throat, he began to gargle on his own sputum. He found he couldn't breathe. Did he care? He began to gasp, like a fish out of water, but he couldn't bring himself to fight it, he couldn't force himself try and clear his throat. Tears began to stream from his eyes, his face reddening. Slowly he began to fade as his vision drew inwards, a rattle of breath was one of the remaining moments this man would exist. His passing thought, if he didn't know who he was, or where he was from, or what he was doing there. Did it even matter if he did exist?

As he strained through his final breath, grasping out with an involuntary reach of his hand, his fingers outstretched, his vision blurred and becoming dim. His body let go. He slumped in position on the floor. He was finally able to leave this place.

Rest in peace, Person One.

CHAPTER SIX: THE BOYS

"Come on Hermy it's time to make tracks" Terry grabbed his cigarettes, mobile phone and wallet off the counter, loading up his pockets with the essentials no-one leaves the house without.

"Stop attending to yourself and get down here, we have to go!" A portly Herman bowled down the stairs, of the house, looking like the weight of the world was on his shoulders, Terry looked at him and shook his head, "What's your drama, it's the first thing in the morning and you've got a face like a slapped backside" both men exchanged glances for a moment as they began to make their way to the front door of the house.

"I don't know why, you have to be so abusive first thing, I haven't had coffee yet and you're already starting to wind me up" Terry smiled one of those cheeky half smiles he often did when he knew he was pushing his luck, what was within the confines of friendship but also stoked the fire a little to slightly rile Herman up.

"Come on big man, you know I don't mean any harm" terry quipped as they got into the car. A tired old Ford Mondeo, which had seen many miles and clearly had seen better days. Terry prepared to turn the key, hoping and praying the car would start. As he did, he held his breath, counting down in his head, three, two and one. His will for the car to start was real, the hope that it wouldn't be another start to the day where the guys were both late for work.

"Are you starting the car or polishing your gear stick, get on with it" snapped a grumpy Herman whilst Terry was going through his daily ritual prior to starting the car. He eventually turned the key, with a little coaxing and pushing up and down of the accelerator, he managed to get the car going "I knew she'd do it, good for another 100k this old girl" he exclaimed as he tapped the dashboard with a big smile on his face.

Sounding like a World War 2 tank coming down the road, the old Mondeo showed the signs of a used, abused and poorly maintained shanty truck. The blow from the exhaust let everyone know that they were on their way miles before they turned up. They couldn't have been undercover surveillance operatives, that's for sure.

Pulling up to the station, Herman seemed to roll out of the passenger seat and get to his feet bowling up the ramp into the station, whilst Terry jumped out, apparently eager to face the day bounding like an excited puppy.

They were greeted at the door by the inspector, "Boys, glad you could join us today, we are in the business of upholding the law, which includes driving vehicles that are roadworthy. Get your sorry excuse for transport sorted and if you might be able to make the undemanding 08:00 start to the day from now on that would be just about doing the minimum you need to make it by" Both men looked the inspector in the eye like naughty school boys, saying in tandem with an apologetic and embarrassed "yes sir"

Feeling deflated following this interaction first thing, the boys headed into the kitchenette to get their coffee, after all, what other way is there to start a day, than a strong coffee and a read of the morning papers. Plodding over to their desks, with their coffee's and papers, prepared for a day of nothing exciting happening, Terry and Herman had no real drive to push themselves to do anything special, they were just shirt fillers as opposed to actual real detectives.

Sitting in front of their computers hours later, Terry looked up at Herman, wondering how he could plod along doing the same thing day in and day out, wondering how he himself could be doing the same thing day in, day out.

All they did was file paperwork and declare cases closed because investigating them would be more of a waste of resources than it would beneficial to the public. This was the kind of police station that had a larger lost and found room, than it did an evidence locker.

Terry finally piped up singly stating "lunch?" This was the first time that a smile had appeared on Herman's face all day, with an all too keen and quick response he said "you had me at lunch" they both sniggered as they grabbed their coats and made their way out of the station.

Leisurely making their way to the front door, again they were interjected by the inspector. "Boys, something has come in for you, this is a real job, it's a bit of a strange one but should it should keep you busy for a while" confused as how they were meant to take that comment, they both seemed grateful to actually be on a job. They hadn't had any real detective work since the great cat burglary of 2007, which turned out to be a cat finding its way into a jewelry store, triggering the alarm 5 nights in a row! "Just off for some lunch boss, we'll be back in 10 minutes to get ourselves familiar with the case" said Terry still feeling a little defiant toward any form of authority.

Shaking his head the inspector walked away after handing the boys the casefile. Neither of them were terribly inspired to instantly look over it, they were too interested in their lunch "come on tubs, let's go grab lunch, see if this is worth even bothering with when we get back"

Terry seemed to have an unending amount of insulting nicknames for Herman, very reluctantly did he call him by his actual name.

Off they went to grab the greasiest spoon they could find, before heading back to the station to look into this new case.

Plodding back into the station, Herman was inquisitive to know what was in the case file. He hadn't even looked at the front pages as Terry had quickly grabbed it before and thrown it on his desk. He didn't normally rush his lunch in order to get back to work, but today was an exception, he felt an excitement he hadn't had in a long time, he was eager, would he actually get to use his brain or be a detective as he was actually paid to be.

He grabbed it and sat down to begin looking through the pages, a smile came to the corner of his mouth, he'd heard about this woman in the newspapers, but why had this only been handed to him and Terry.

They were nothing special, they certainly weren't top draw detectives and they definitely weren't often handed good cases especially ones of this magnitude.

"Terry, Terry, you have to read the file, it's that mental woman, the one that got the call then poisoned her family" Terry had to take a moment to take in what Herman had just said, did he hear him right, they had been handed the case file for a definitive mental patient that wouldn't get prosecuted due to her insanity? "I bet it's just a fob off to justify us being here Hermy, but let me look"

Looking over the file Terry couldn't believe Herman was right, it wasn't just a fob off, they were going to be the lead investigators in this case and this for them was a huge deal. This case had made national headlines, not only had this woman poisoned her whole family, but she had also beaten her husband to death with a meat tenderiser. Terry's giblets began to tingle. He was excited, but keeping it cool.

"I think we will have to do something we have never done before Herm, we will be working voluntarily late tonight" they both smiled at each other, knowing this was the kind of case that might get them a job in a better place, actually using the skills that had lay redundant over the years.

They cleared their desks of anything unnecessary and cleared down the whiteboard of the "graffiti" that had been on there for so long. They began to sort through the grisly crime scene photograph that were in the case file picking out bits that could be important, reading over the initial interviews and commentaries made by the arresting officers.

This was certainly an interesting case by timeline, she had performed her normal routine and nothing had changed, had she just snapped? Had she finally had enough? Herman's head lifted and he looked deep in thought "So Terry, I've read this interview script over so many times, and I still can't make sense of it, I can't understand, she took the kids to school, cleaned the house, had a wine whilst looking over her nice kitchen, picked the kids up, answered the phone whilst preparing the dinner, claims to have lost track of time and what she was doing and then cooked the dinner, served it, poisoning the family, apparently without knowing, then beat the chap to death with the steak hammer"

This was the entire period of incidence summarised into one small statement. "Let's get our brains going, what was different to normal?" said Terry "How can she have poisoned them without knowing, was she really a bit mental, or did she plan it, let's look at the old Modus Operandi and the possible motive behind it"

Herman looked at his watch and let out a roaring belly laugh. Clearly confused, Terry also looked at the clock on the wall, on the other side of the room. He also began to laugh, neither of them had been so happy or so engaged in something for so long.

They hadn't realised the time, it was 01:15 they had been at work for nearly 17 hours, they had been solidly going over the case focusing on everything that could have happened, focusing on everything but finishing on time.

"Come on mucka, time to head home for a few hours' sleep" the boys grabbed their coats and belongings, walking out of the station with a heightened sense of self being, a sense of pride. They were actually doing real work and it felt amazing!

The boys got into their car, neither of them wanted to hear the noise from the blowing exhaust, neither of them wanted to be seen dead in this car, what had changed, how can they go from having the sense of familiarity and love for the clapped out car, to being embarrassed to drive it down the road or even start the engine.

With a turn of the key, the engine started and tentatively Terry drove the car away from the station and toward their house. Both men's brains were working in overdrive, neither of them would sleep, but better to keep routine, neither of them spoke, which definitely wasn't normal.

The journey felt like it took forever, driving carefully as not to make too much noise, but they had eventually made it back to their house. Pulling up, the boys closed the car doors gently as not to wake the neighbours, entered their house quietly and closed the door quietly. They silently headed to their rooms, silently got themselves prepared for bed and went to sleep.

The next morning, neither of them looked like they'd had the smallest amount of sleep but both of them appeared eager to be at work. Both men were at the foot of the stairs for 7am, which was highly unusual for them. Both of them were ready to leave the house at 07:05, neither of them wanted to wait. So they didn't.

As quietly as possible they left the house, they got into the car, put their seatbelts on and started the car. They made the same slow and steady journey back to the station they had made only a few hours previously. Both men walked through the door of the station, the desk sergeant looked at his watch and couldn't believe they had come in at this time, "morning boys, early start?" Terry looked at him and said "just showing some willing, you know, we're not just shirt fillers"

They headed over to their desk, where they were greeted by the inspector who for once, had a smile on his face "morning boys, looks like you've actually managed to get some decent work done, looks like you've had no sleep, but nicely done, don't burn yourselves out, I need you on the ball for this" Smiling with a sense of self pride, Herman said "we've got this sir" the inspector smiled back at them, an uneasy smile, but a smile at the thought that he had stimulated these once dragged along detectives.

He had put some sense of positivity back into their lives and back into their careers.

"Right Hermy, I guess our next step is to secure an interview with this woman, I'm a bit scared of her in honesty, but as long as she doesn't cook for us, we should be ok" they both gave a little smile to each other knowing they needed to do this to try and understand the case and the chances of memory distortion at this stage of events would be quite high, it being weeks after the event. However, they had to secure this meeting in order to progress the case.

"She's in the secure hospital, we will have to go in there with the assistants so no heavy tactics with her, we need to tread lightly, I wonder if they have done any evaluations on her, we should definitely get those, see if they have any insights into her state of mind, or anything they have that she has told them about the events of that day" Herman couldn't believe the words that had just come out of his mouth, could he really just have reeled off that piece of credible information that they both knew? Did he really sound that professional? Something had awoken inside the boys and they were excited to be able to be working on this case.

The boys had been pressing on with examining the case file when the inspector showed up again. The guys had their heads down in the paperwork, completely focused on the task, neither of them acknowledging that he had entered their office.

After a moment of standing there, he became impatient and started to clear his throat "ahhemmm" looking up the boys were a little confused as to his presence. "Morning again sir, chirped Terry, how can we help" the inspector smiled at the pair, who looked like a pair of school boys finally able to do the work they'd always dreamed of deeply engrossed in mounds of paperwork generated with their potential lines of enquiry.

"Boys, firstly, a coffee and a couple of bacon sandwiches for you! Secondly, the request you put in for the visit to your suspect" there seemed like an awkward pause, the type that's made when bad news is being broken "well, I have authorised it, however, the hospital have informed me that this woman is not only fragile, but highly delusional, she has made claims that she has no knowledge of the incident, that everything went downhill following the phone call. I just wanted you to be aware prior to your visit, you will need to be a little bit objective and speculative when you speak with her, watch each other's backs and just be careful"

Terry and Herman both cast each other a glance, "Of course sir, tread lightly, watch each other, question everything and thanks for the sarnies, I'm famished" Herman had come back with possibly the only response the inspector could have hoped for. "Good luck boys" With that he had left the room.

Herman and Terry both knew this case could be big, they knew that they had been named in the national press as the investigating officers. They were so invested after only such a short amount of time that it was like an instantaneous switch had been turned on.

Walking through the details and planning the visit and how they would "play" the interview, seemed to take the boy's hours. They knew the pressure was on them, their tiny little police station rarely saw so much as an event of cow tipping, let alone a nationally recognised murder case.

"So, I think it's best if you lead the way with the questions big man, I think it would be best if you take a nice soft approach with her, be her friend, coax the information from her, show that you believe every word she is saying" Herman was taken back, not only by the lack of insults coming from Terry, but also that he would offer for him to take the lead role when speaking to the woman.

"Thanks Terry, I guess that would be good, play to my strengths" Herman was a completely non-threatening character, the type of guy that would have many female friends, but never a lover. A big cuddly teddy bear, with a calming presence. He was perfect for the task in hand.

It was lunch time and the boys thought they had deserved a treat, they had been planning and preparing all morning. "Pub lunch?" questioned Terry, without saying anything Herman hopped up to his feet, grabbed both of their coats and started walking to the door.

"Come on then, I'll let you pay" Herman had a cheeky excited smile on his face. It wasn't often that the pair had a pub lunch and it definitely wasn't often that Terry would pay, but on this occasion he smiled and nodded.

The pair walked with what felt like pride out of the door of the station. They carried themselves confidently and professionally, this felt a little strange for both of them, not once in their entire career had they been so fired up about something.

Sitting down to lunch, the pair sat momentarily in silence, it seemed there was an awkwardness that both of them wanted to speak about, to unleash all of the thoughts going through their head.

There was almost the same awkwardness that is present when being on a first date and wondering whether the other person is going to reciprocate when leaning in for a kiss. The boys both stared at each other for a moment, having already picked their food and grabbed their drinks from the bar. They both were preparing in their heads where they wanted to start talking, about what they felt they could talk about in a place, where clearly they could be heard. Herman opened his mouth to speak, just as a rather unkempt gentleman sat down at their table, uninvited.

"Wotcha" he said as he put his drink down on the table spilling a reasonable amount of it over the edge of the glass. "Can we help? We're on a business lunch buddy, got things to discuss" the rough looking man looked Terry directly in the eyes, looking him up and down as if to show dominance, as if to show he could squash this little walking gob with one finger, to be an imposition on their lunch break.

"Actually yes, you're the coppers looking into that woman that killed her family ain't ya?" This was never a circumstance the boys had come across before, so they weren't really sure how to approach it. They usually were able to go about their business day to day not being bothered by anyone, not being questioned by members of the public, not really having to answer questions they actually didn't know how to answer, or even if they were allowed to answer. Terry quickly retorted "yes, but we can't discuss anything with anyone as it's an ongoing investigation, sorry"

The well-built man smiled as he took a large gulp of his drink, he wiped his mouth after putting his drink down, with the sleeve of his top, "Ah, no worries, I don't want to know anything really, just wanted to say that I read in the paper about the woman killing her family, obviously not a good situation to be in. I also read, she had a phone call, you see, I've had a couple of weird phone calls too, I don't want to be the next Loony Laura" the boys both smirked.

They had seen this headline in the national press. It had to be now that their food had turned up, without wanting to dismiss the man and knowing it may just, judging by his appearance, have been either telemarketers or alcoholic delusion, Terry had to think on his feet "If you have any concerns about telephone calls you've been receiving, you can pop down to the station and leave your details, with any information you have, any information you can give the guys down there might be of help to us"

Feeling a sense of pride in himself, Terry picked up his knife and fork and began to get stuck into his lunch. Herman on the other hand was using his bread to mop up any left overs on his plate having devoured his meal in record time. He quickly chimed in "Thank you for coming to us, we appreciate it" not being one to be normally dismissive, Herman was closing the conversation down so both parties would feel they had achieved a positive outcome from the interaction, without of course it having cause to disturb either of their days.

"Yeah, I'll do just that said the man" finishing up his pint, "have a good day chaps" Standing up from the table he made his way toward the bar, signalling the bar person to fill up his glass again. Both of the boys had welcomed the distraction and the need for them almost to not communicate with each other over lunch.

Having taken a gentle walk back to the station, Herman and Terry both had a relaxed and confident look about them. They came back, seemingly like coiled springs full of potential energy ready to release as soon as their backsides hit their chairs.

Unusually, Herman broke the silence first "what if it's linked?" he questioned, "what, the drunk guy in the pub getting a phone call, come on tubs, let's not over think things, let's finish our visit plan, make it happen, then maybe we can look over any details he leaves IF he does come down here, I doubt he will do!"

Chuckling, terry took his notebook out of his pocket and began writing questions he would like them to ask, although he wasn't going to be the lead interrogator, he wanted to have questions answered about the case, "let's put our questions together Hermy, we need to make sure we're on the same page"

The boys spent the remainder of that afternoon painfully slowly documenting the questions they had, slowly typing them out on the computer one finger poke to the keyboard at a time, until they had something that resembled a briefing document.

"Seems like a good place to call it day to me chaps" said the inspector leaning around the doorway to their office. "See you in the morning" taking that as it was, the boys tidied up for the day, grabbed their belongings and began to head out of the station.

As they got to the front desk, the sergeant manning it stopped them. "Boys, I know it's been a long couple of days for you but some old drunk dropped by, said he spoke to you in the pub, left his details, rambled on about some phone calls"

The pair looked at each other and smiled knowingly, "Cheers Sarge, can you keep hold of them until the morning, we're knack-ered, heading home for an early one" The sergeant agreed and the boys headed out of the station for the evening. They were just approaching the car when Herman looked at Terry and said, "Forgot something back in a mo."

Herman poked his head back around the door of the station, catching the desk sergeants attention, he enquired "out of inter-est, what was that chaps name" shrugging his shoulders the sergeant was of very little help other than stating "files on your desk"

Wobbling back into the office with a hurried pace, Herman walked quickly back to his desk. He whipped open the file and looked over the front document.

Reading only the basic details and unsure why the man's name was important to him, he was almost excited and relieved to see they were able to catch the man's name, not a full name, only given name was shown. "Roger"

CHAPTER SEVEN: NOT AGAIN!

It felt like for the past year, Adriana had spent most of her time in a hospital gown, yet another day not being allowed to put any clothes on. It was a good thing really, she couldn't take the thought of tight fitting jeans, or synthetic tracksuits rubbing against the scarring on her legs where they had removed skin for the grafts on her face.

She looked at herself in the mirror, for a long time, she had been unable to do this. She thought she looked like a monster, bits of crispy drying out flesh that hadn't been attached quite correctly during the procedure had left her with plenty of scars, but of course, it could have been worse, they could have decided to leave her as she was.

What would she have looked like then? Could she have looked in the mirror and faced herself if that was the case?

Her hand slowly drifted down her face as she stared at the reflection she didn't recognise looking back at her. A tear slowly broke free from the corner of her eye, tickling her face as it slowly made its way over the now uneven surface toward her chin hanging momentarily before dropping down onto her gown, quickly being soaked up by the unassuming fabric. She was left thinking about how she took for granted, how she had once looked and it made her appreciate how much worse it could have been.

Adriana decided, she simply did not care how she looked, that's why God had let women have long hair, so they could cover their faces, when things happened. This was something that was repeated by many of the women she knew, but what did they mean? What kind of things "happen" to women for them to need to cover their faces.

This was something that stirred the fire inside of her again, it made her angry and frustrated and she had no idea why she felt this way. Why would she feel this way? And why had this begun to start to stir the fire, this had never happened until she had received that phone call.

Looking around her room, she wondered what she would waste time doing today, she wondered how long she would be stuck in this place. She wondered why her room was locked, was she being held captive? Or was it for her own safety? But why would it be for her own safety? What had she done to herself? Nothing as far as she knew. She was just a normal person who had an injury that was now trapped in this clinical setting, when it started she had been disowned by the person who was meant to care for her the most, she had ended up there as a result of trying to be the best at what she did. Trying to push hard to please this person.

As she stood still staring lost in her reflection in the mirror, lost in her own thoughts, she heard the clank of the lock on the door, whilst it stirred her away from her thoughts, it didn't take her attention. She didn't look away from the mirror she was still absorbed within her own head and was wondering why she was there.

A person who looked like a doctor, walked into the room, she had a stethoscope around her neck and a protective white coat draped over her shoulders and carried a sense of authority when she entered the room. She sat down on the bed behind Adriana and waited for her to turn, but Adriana didn't.

She didn't want to acknowledge where she was or who this person was. She didn't want to know what they wanted or why they were there. But this was important, so it was down to the lady that had come into the room to open the dialogue between them.

"I am Doctor Yun, I've been asked to come and speak with you. You've been here for a while Adriana, It's time for you to start getting ready to leave, your sponsors don't want to support your stay here anymore, the state will not fund it, once you leave here I will organise a room at a boarding house for you, this is the most I can do" Adriana struck by the comments, turned and looked at the woman with an open mouth. Had the sponsors given up on her, why had this decision been made? Does this mean she now would never go back to the life she dreamed of, all she had ever known?

Without replying Adriana nodded and lowered her head silently, the tear that was coming down one cheek previously now increased to become a stream of tears on both sides of her face. She would now have to figure out who she was and what she was doing there? Why she had been there for so long? Why had they been locking her in the room?

Adriana finally spoke "Doctor, why have I been locked in my room? I remember having an injury, I remember my coach being here after it happened. Then for a long time I remember nothing, the first thing I do remember is my legs hurting where they took the skin. Then my memory is very little, the longer time has gone on, the less things that seem to be in my room I don't understand why I'm locked in, what have I done"

Taking a long slow breath, Doctor Yun looked uncertainly at Adriana. She sat for a moment trying to work out what to say, how would she tell her about everything? How she would explain her condition? "Well Adriana" Doctor Yun started, clearing her throat looking uneasy about what she was about to say "you have been suffering with episodes of complete psychosis, manic outbreaks, violent incidents. Your coach, you attacked him, you cut his throat. This is actually not just a medical institution, it is also a place that you are in for your own protection, you made many people unhappy when that happened and we fear they may have put a price on your head"

Struck back by this news, not only could she not believe she was capable of this, but she couldn't believe that it could actually happen or that she couldn't remember it. Seeing she was processing this information, Doctor Yun began to explain "you see Adriana, we have had this conversation many times, but, when we go through times of severe psychosis, our brain can blank out those times as a protection to how we act, it protects us from the thoughts memories and behaviours" still visibly shaken by this news, Adriana began to tremble, beads of sweat began to form on her brow, she could feel that fire ignite inside of her, the rebellion she felt against whatever she was rebelling against was rising, time seemed to slow down and every breath became accounted for.

Having seen this behaviour before from her, the doctor hit the button in the room for assistance, within what seemed like an instant two heavily built men ran into the room and restrained Adriana, pinning her head, arms and torso against the bed. The doctor had come prepared and grabbed an injectable sedative out of her pocket and quickly jabbed it into her leg, she had to let Adriana know what had happened, she had to prepare her for her release into the outside world, but she also had to prevent her from spiralling into her state of psychosis, hopefully what she had done had worked, it hadn't previously, but this time, this time there had been acknowledgement of the situation.

As the sedative took effect, Adriana's now limp body began twitching she was reacting and relaxing to it. It coursed through her veins and began to ensure that she was no risk to either the orderlies or the doctor, or to herself, they placed her rather roughly onto the bed and hastily made their exit from the room, being sure to secure the door behind them.

Doctor Yun made her way up the corridor, the hurried clicking of her heels making an echo as she went into the relative safety of her office. Being sure again to lock the door behind her, she took off her stethoscope, she took off her white coat and sat down behind her desk.

She began to talk over the situation repeating everything stated word for word to best of her memory, not only what was said, but also the visible responses to them, documenting everything each time had helped her refine how she had broken the news to Adriana, helped her to recognise the signs of her spiral, recognise when to enact her exit strategy, when to sedate Adriana.

Hopeful this time that she would hold the memory of what she had been told, Doctor Yun decided it was time to make a phone call. She needed to move the protective custody back over to the police. Whilst Adriana's condition would still need to be continually monitored, little bits of information would need to be revealed to her each day, or each time she would hit a reset. This way, easing her back into herself, removing her extremely gradually from her medication.

Somehow, when Adriana did spiral, it outstripped the power of the anti-psychotic medication even when it should have been at its most effective. Whatever had a hold in her brain, was so powerful, it completely consumed her and took over. Doctor Yun had never seen this before, she had never seen someone's Psychosis be stronger than the strongest level of medication she could legally and safely give.

Still, Doctor Yun had an obligation to report her findings to the courts, so she began to compile her paperwork. She began to document all of the information she had gathered, how to manage her symptoms, triggers for her psychosis, a plan for how to slowly bring her back to "normality"

Sadly, in Doctor Yun's mind, this wouldn't be something that would happen either in her lifetime, or Adriana's. She thought to herself, maybe it would be better if whoever put a price on Adriana would be successful in their mission, maybe this would be the only way she would ever have relief from the life she was now doomed to have to live.

With a heavy heart, the documents were placed in an envelope and put in the outbound mail. There was no turning back.

Waking up in the morning following having been stuck with a sedative was again like a glorious dawn, some people describe it as a sense of being hungover, but not Adriana. It was like waking up from taking a nap in the sunshine on a glorious summer's day, everything had a golden aura around it, everything was a little hazy, but calm, everything was soft and gentle.

She slowly began to come to, thinking over what had happened and she remembered the conversation she had previously had with Doctor Yun.

She remembered being told she had taken the life of her coach. She was still a little under the effect of the sedative, so this allowed her to think things through without starting to spiral. She was able to make sense of what she was told.

Despite her being sedated yesterday, she had now seen where the panic button was and decided maybe if she pressed it, she could get the doctors attention again to get more information to find out more of what had happened or what she had done without being fully aware.

She reached out to press it, then thought for a moment, retracting her hand slightly and pausing her position. Stood absolutely statue still whilst she thought through her options. If she pressed it, would she get to know more, if she pressed it, would she end up being sedated again? She decided that the worst thing that could happen would be that she would be sedated, so she bravely stretched her hand out and quickly tapped it.

After a second, of staring intently at the button, nothing seemed to happen, no alarm went off, no lights flashed, the button didn't even light up. Should it have done? Had she done something wrong? Should she press the button again? She decided to, what's the worst that could happen. She began rapidly pressing it, maybe she hadn't pressed it correctly, maybe she hadn't pressed hard enough, or in the correct sequence.

Moments later, still nothing had happened. She stood staring at the button and the door, she was unsure of what action to take next. She knew from her conversation she was obviously a high risk person, so they needed to keep her locked up.

It was then that, a voice came from behind her. "Adriana, please stop pressing the button, I can see you want some attention, I will be in shortly if you promise me you will be calm" Adriana looked around trying to identify where the voice was coming from. She did recognise the voice, she thought it was Doctor Yun, she trusted this doctor, she believed that she could tell her the truth. Slightly over emphasising her movement, Adriana nodded, she made her way over to her bed and sat with her hands on her lap.

The door to the room opened and Doctor Yun walked in. She had a calming smile on her face, Adriana could see the doctor had a golden glow around her, maybe this was the sedative or maybe this was her beginning to drop her guard. But she felt at ease, she felt she could listen. Adriana looked up "Doctor, thank you, I understand I may be a risk and also at risk, I understand I am to be locked in my room, I understand if I get carried away or begin to spiral, you know my signs. But I want to know more, I need to know what happened. If you can't tell me, can someone else please tell me?"

The doctor looked her directly in the eyes. She knowingly smiled and nodded. "Adriana, there will be times I will need to sedate you, there will be times I will need to give you more information than you can handle and there will be times we will need to go over everything from the very beginning. The trauma you have been through, is severe and was over a prolonged period, so we need to unpackage it slowly, but if you are aware this is the case, then we will begin to do that in the coming days" Adriana smiled and nodded.

Not only was this the most Adriana had remembered, in over a year, it was also the most interaction she could recall having. Encouraged, by this Doctor Yun slowly moved her hand to her pocket "Adriana, I am going to talk with you, but I would like to give you a little sedation to help control your spirals, are you happy for me to do this?" Adriana agreed and held her arm out, swiftly preparing the sedative, the doctor cautiously moved toward her. Gently placing the needle into her arm she quickly administered a small dose of the drug.

It didn't take long for Adriana to feel at peace. The golden glow had amplified around everything. Doctor Yun began to explain "Adriana, you have been an elite athlete for many years, you have been told continually that you are not good enough and you have to be better. You were told you didn't look good enough or you had been eating too much, these things can all take their toll" Doctor Yun took another breath. "You also told me in another instance, that you had been sexually submissive to your coach, your trainer and some other men. You said that all they wanted from you was your body and your silence" the doctor stopped. She didn't want to overload her, as it would have been when she was open to taking in the most information possible.

Adriana was quite heavily sedated, so she was now laying on the bed with a smile on her face, waving her hands around, like they had no weight to them. Like moving them could have been the one action she had control over. Adriana was in perfect tranquillity, she was beginning to get an idea of what she had been through. Things for her began to slowly drop into place, as if her mind was working overtime in the background whilst her body wasn't bound by her history.

It was at that moment, a spiral happened in very quick succession. Adriana had snapped back into the moment, like all of the sedative had been stripped away. She was back in the room, she sat bolt upright, only to find the room was pitch black.

There was no one else in there with her, the doctor had gone.

Had the doctor even been there? Had she really been given all of that information? She said out loud "what about the phone call, the phone call makes me angry, since I received that, I have had a fire inside of me" but no one heard her. No one was there to listen. But it had finally come out. A huge burden had unloaded, her body was relaxed. Her mind was relaxed, she slipped away into silent relief, drifting for the remainder of the night in and out of sleep.

The next morning, she awoke, there was no sensation from the sedative and there was no golden aura. Maybe the effects had worn off in the night. Who knows, there was no point wondering why she didn't feel it.

Waking knowing she didn't feel it was empowering. She felt the fire inside of her, she didn't know why but somehow it had a slightly different feeling to it. It had a positive, light feeling to it, it had a self-affirming quality, it reassured her, it comforted her, it made her feel like she was in control.

She gradually got up from her bed, walked over to her sink and filled it with water, she bathed herself. She hadn't done this in a long time. She had been unknowingly having sponge baths under sedation. But today, today she was in control. She was in control of herself, she was in control of the situation. She was in control of her mind. She began to remove her gown, walking back over toward the sink, she was at peace.

This was all thrown away in an instant, as the door to her room flung open. Three men she didn't recognise burst in, quickly followed by Doctor Yun and two orderlies.

Doctor Yun was physically and vocally protesting them being in her room. They quickly jabbed her now unclothed body with what she assumed was a sedative, she quickly fell into a state of unconscious being, she could hear everything happening around her, she could hear the sound of the doctor saying she wasn't ready and had just turned a real corner.

The men spoke in Russian and there was little communication

between them and the hospital staff. There was little that anyone could do, this was the last thing that Adriana could remember happening she had now completely lost all consciousness. Her body was limp and lifeless, however, they still handcuffed her and restrained her legs, a very undignified thing to happen to any person.

One of the men spoke up "Under the powers available to me, I am taking this criminal and witness into my protection for the greater good of the state" the orderlies and doctor all stood back, there was nothing they could now do.

Adriana's custody had been taken back by the state. The doctor did wonder why, why was this girl so important? What could she know? What could have happened that either needed to be kept secret or that she would need to be kept safe from.

This all happened since she had reported hearing her talking about the phone call at night. Could this be why?

The men pushed Adriana hurriedly down the corridors, demanding that all of the doors be opened for them before they even got to them.

They swiftly moved her out through the front door opening the rear doors of a dated van, barely stopping the rapid movement in order to throw the girl in the back of it in her wheel chair.

Two of them jumped in the back with her, the other ran to the front of the van jumping into the driving seat and seamlessly starting the engine. As quickly as these men had come into the hospital, they had also removed themselves and Adriana from it.

Why was this girl of such special interest?

CHAPTER EIGHT:
LOVE BUNNY

A rugged and rusty old Landover pulled up into the neglected driveway of Roger's house. The clanking diesel engine knocked as the ignition was turned off. A lean, muscular figure was silhouetted against the sunrise and morning haze.

Standing six and a half feet tall, Max cast a long shadow over the dilapidated porch leading to Roger's house. He was looking around confused as to whether he was in the right place. This was the address he had on file, but surely with the pride Roger had in his gorgeous hillside property, this couldn't be the place he had bragged about so many times over the years.

Empty beer cans and whiskey bottles lay abandoned throughout the walk way toward the house thrown and left in whatever position they landed in. A heavy smell of rotting food and urine hit max as he got closer to the house, "dear lord" he whispered to himself covering his face to try and ward off some of the stench.

He approached what he assumed should be the front door, although it could have been the rubbish chute at any commercial premises judging by the smell.

He gave it a knock, still trying to take in his surroundings. Looking down toward his feet, he saw a vintage styled telephone seemingly carefully placed on the ground near to his feet outside again what he assumed was the front door. Looking a little closer, he could see the wire was cut. No wonder he hadn't been able to get through to him. No wonder the line had just rung out over and over without an answer.

Max decided he'd give the door a try, it was still early in the morning and maybe the old boy was still asleep. He took the handle firmly in his hand and gently twisted it.

Roger had always had a penchant toward personal protection, so he half expected to run into some booby traps. Despite living in the middle of nowhere, he knew Roger had always been a little extravagant, even in his sanest of days. He gave it a gentle push - he felt a little resistance when doing so, so quickly side stepped the door and stumbled over one of the stacks of beer cans.

As Max struggled to his feet, he heard the familiar clank of a trigger being cocked behind him. He slowly and cautiously raised his hands as he felt the cold machine steel press into the base of his skull, feeling both barrels, he knew whoever was there wasn't messing around. "I have no weapon with me my hands are raised, I am now standing, may I turn around?"

For a second Roger hesitated, it was only when Max followed up with "Come on Love Bunny, you know me" the familiar name he had back in his army days paired with the voice twigged his memory.

His hands were shaking holding the gun, he hadn't held a firearm for this long with serious intent. The weapon be it small comparative to his size, felt like a ton of lead in his hands.

"Turn, move slowly, don't drop your hands and don't reach in your pockets" Being compliant, Max slowly began to turn his head slightly ahead of the rest of his body, willing himself to follow the simple instructions given despite Roger's previous junior rank to him.

With sudden recognition, Roger dropped the shotgun to the ground, the idea of who this was had dawned on him.

Regrettably he had forgotten to make the gun safe again and upon hitting the floor it discharged, setting off both barrels and leaving both men covering their heads and ears curled up on the floor.

Quickly getting back to their feet, both men held a stance for a moment, before breaking out in large full belly laughter which seemed to go on for some time.

An awkward silence dawned as the laughter dwindled away, "Max, you old devil" Roger said smiling the first genuine smile he had on his face in a long time. "Roger, I've been trying to reach you all week, had to pop up here to make sure you hadn't topped yourself" The men hugged in a strong embrace, a closeness Roger felt in many years, one Max was all too familiar with when recruiting former colleagues.

"Why the hell are you here" enquired Roger. "This is the back of beyond, I'm not really setup for visitors Cap." Max looked around and stifled a chuckle, "I can see, like I said I've been trying to call you, but I guess you fell out with the phone" both men looked down at the phone sitting carefully placed on the ground next to the door. The wire cleanly snipped through by the door frame. "Bah, I had some weird phone call and got in a bit of a strop, forgot the phone was in my hand as I closed the door" again both men let out an open and honest laugh.

"Fancy a drink?" said Roger, "I can't promise it won't have proof, but I should be able to find you something" "Roger, is it safe to go in there, am I going to catch a disease I'll never recover from?" Roger smirked, embarrassed by the state of his house, remembering how he used to talk to the boys in his unit about how it was his pride and joy, now looking more like the back end of a refuse station. "You'll be alright Cap. I promise, just a few empty bottles of whiskey, don't drink the floor whiskey though - It ain't whiskey" both men smiled at each other.

A warm feeling was washing over Roger, he could feel exactly how he had done, when he was walking side by side with this man through active war zones, through war torn villages. Or the times he was carrying his fellow soldier's bodies down the aisle of a chapel of rest or loading them into the plane to be repatriated and put to rest in their home towns. Even having been side by side when they had to white phos one of their fallen friends.

They hadn't lost that sense of brotherhood or closeness. Despite the lost years, it felt like only yesterday Max had reprimanded Roger for being drunk on duty.

After trawling through what was the wreckage of the inside of Roger's house, they got to the drawing room, which overlooked stunning views of rolling hillsides, where you could see a panorama from sunrise to sunset if you sat long enough. This was the only room in the house that Roger hadn't frequented, so it was clean, well, clean in regard to the rest of the property.

"Have a seat" pointed roger to the plastic covered rattan furniture "erm, no, I think I'll stand and I'll get to the point. Roger, I need someone a little unhinged for a special assignment, it'll either be a success or a suicide mission, I couldn't think of a better man for the job"

Taken aback a little by Max's forthrightness and the sheer lack of decorum shown, he could tell Max was in a bind, knowing what he owed this man, he asked no further questions. "Ok, I always promised I would be there when you needed me, clearly, whoever your standing for now didn't want to trawl the psych wards, so yes I'm your man" Not interested in the pay, not interested in the what, the how or the why, Roger had to get out of this routine hell hole. This seemed like as good of an excuse as any. "Kit up, transport is 06:00 tomorrow, wrap up warm, you're off to the mother land"

A little dazed and confused, Roger decided he had better pull himself together, he decided he had better clean up not only his house, but also himself and his clothes. Just on the off chance, he wouldn't make it back again.

"I will leave the file on your commode" shouted Max as he made his way back toward the door of the house. Roger chuckled to himself as he grabbed some containers from his kitchen, he began picking up abandoned half drank bottles of whiskey, or at least what he thought was whiskey, clinking bottle after bottle into the container, he quickly began to unwind years of neglect.

This kept him busy for hours, slowly he built up quite a collection of recycling outside the front of his house, it appeared to be neat and organised into containers which would be easily removed upon his return. He reached a point where he realised for the past 5 hours, he hadn't had a sip of whiskey or a smoke, so it definitely was time for a break.

Making his way into the normal living room he used, he sat down in his drinking chair. He remembered the task file was there, so he thought it would be better to have a read over it to prepare.

Whatever shadowy organisation was hiring Max was looking for a girl they wanted to extract information from, on another organisation. The target was known to bouts of excessive violence. The team must use sedative for her once they had her in their possession. They must extract her quickly and cleanly. No shots fired, no lives lost. Return fire only permitted upon the threat of the targets life. "So I really will be cannon fodder" he said to himself.

Well this place isn't going to clean itself up, thought Roger. He felt once more like he had a sense of purpose. He felt he knew this was what he needed.

It was approaching lunch time, so as a last hoorah, Roger thought he would treat himself to a pint or two in the village pub. Maybe even a meal. He needed to bulk up, no food from wheels up.

Firing up his rusty old van, Roger did feel embarrassed at the state he had let his life get into. But it had been far easier for many years to hide away and drink his feelings away than it was to acknowledge them and deal with them. Probably in the long run cheaper than therapy too, he smirked to himself with that thought.

Making his way into the village pub car park he carelessly abandoned his van across multiple parking spaces. Ambling into the pub, he found a comfy corner to perch in. Looking around the room for the nearest copy of the village newspaper, which was usually hanging around in one of the dingey corners, where the old boys sat.

Doing his familiar plod around the room, fitting in with the aesthetic like a piece of the furniture, Roger hunted for the paper whilst the barman was pouring his pint, it was just a soft one today, he had to stay focused, so a shandy, which the barman did snigger about when requested by Roger.

This had slightly riled him up and made him scowl which quickly wiped the clever smirk from the barman's face. "Where's the damn paper" Roger demanded. All the barman could do was point toward the racking behind him.

He grabbed his shandy and picked up the newspaper on the way past. Sitting down, he opened up the paper and read it thoroughly to find out how much of the world he had missed.

There wasn't much, everyone was at war with everyone, everyone loved to have an issue with some part of the royal family and in the football, some people won games and some lost. Pretty standard.

One story had caught his eye though, only because it highlighted two local detectives investigating a woman in an Asylum for the brutal murder of her husband the poisoning of her kids.

He read the story in great detail, the paper gave information not only on who the detectives were, but also had pictures of them, showing the pride of the town for having their detectives picked to handle a case of such national importance.

Roger looked up from the corner he was in, he saw the two detectives sitting across the room in awkward silence and he thought he recognised them, this was a small town and it was no surprise that he would bump into them. The whole journalistic

piece was entitled "Loony Laura" which did bring a slight smile to Roger's face, we've all known a "Loony Laura" he thought to himself.

Against his better judgement, he approached the detectives and pulled up a seat at their table. No introduction just a brief "wotcha" given as a greeting to the detectives. Roger quickly proceeded to enquire about them being the ones who were investigating the case. They did confirm this, although he did also feel like they had been a little dismissive of him.

He had read in the article, that Laura had alleged that a mystery phone call had made her kill her family. He did want to know if this was true, but realistically, this wasn't at the forefront of his mind. He was more bothered by the fact that he had also recently had a weird phone call. It wasn't out of character for him to have killed people previously, but never in his home surroundings and definitely never because someone phoned him.

Roger decided to take a stroll down to the police station, maybe the new him actually wanted to leave his details so that he could be wanted or needed for something other than just existing. Maybe he could be useful or feel a sense of fulfilment.

Filling out an information form, he gave only the bare minimum he needed to in order for them to be able to find him. He did explain to the desk sergeant that he was going away on "business" for a few days, wasn't sure if he would be back, but if he was maybe he would be able to help them with anything should the need arise.

Again being dismissive of Roger from a visual judgement, the desk sergeant just wanted the encounter over so he could return to the game on his mobile phone. Roger made a hasty retreat toward his van, he had to get himself ready for this extraction, he was in no shape to do a full op, being as his maximum daily exercise was walking to the bathroom, to excrete what he assumed was mostly neat whiskey. That was when he could actually bring himself to make it to the bathroom.

He did occasionally smile to himself at the thought that there may be a sewer rat nearby with the same alcohol dependence as he had due to what he flushed.

Pulling up, he saw everything piled up and laughed to himself - he seemed to have laughed both out loud and to himself more today than he had done in a very long time. For a few days at least, he will get to escape this reality. He will get to escape what was happening, in the here and the now. It took him away from his reality and took him back into the fantasy world he had once loved. It took him back to the days where he was the hero, where he was wanted and needed.

I can't wait for wheels up, he said to himself as he headed back into his house. He knew he had a mammoth task to undertake to prepare himself for leaving.

The first thing to do was flush all of that alcohol out of his system. He had ten, one litre bottles lined up. He challenged himself. I have to drink all of this before midnight. I need to clean myself up, it isn't going to happen overnight, but this could be a damn good start.

Roger repeated to himself, as if trying to talk himself into wanting to drink it, into wanting to make this change. Trying to reassure himself that actually everything was going to be ok, he could not only do this mission, but he could also do this mission, come back alive, get some cash, make a fresh start.

The will to reassure himself was strong - now he just had to follow through. He had spent so much time, blaming himself for the losses he had faced, feeling guilty, because he was still alive and others weren't, so much time feeling hurt by losing friends and being betrayed by them, these were the perils of having lived that life.

This is why he couldn't go back to being a mercenary previously, how could he learn to work with a team he didn't know or that could betray him at any moment. He would have been just waiting for them to make the next mistake and then not tell him about it then it might be him going home in a box, did he really want to open himself up to that kind of risk again.

All Roger had ever wanted was to be an elite soldier, it meant everything to him having that bond, having that family, those friends. He couldn't remember a time when it wasn't what he wanted. He now wondered, if it was the only thing that had kept him going all this time, that knowing one day, one of the boys would get hold of him and he would be needed, or one of them would at least drop by to check he was still alive.

Roger was a fighter, he always had been, and he always would be. He needed to prove that to himself, he needed to show himself that he could fight his way back to where he needed to be, to be happy and involved in this life again. This mission, although it didn't seem like it was of vital importance to the world, seemed like it was of vital importance to Roger. This was his turning point. This was his time.

CHAPTER NINE:
WITH THE BOYS

Another day dawned over the sleepy town, the boys had been at it since before dawn. It was the big day today, they would get to go and visit Laura and hear her story first hand. Terry was sat at their kitchen table, on his third coffee of the day, he was clearly nervous. This was vastly important not only to the current case, but also for the future of both of their careers.

Herman came back down the stairs, his second cup of the day had triggered movements that usually only his breakfast snack did. He lightly placed himself down opposite Terry and with a vague smile on his face reassured Terry, everything was going to be ok, they would be able to get loads of information, not just from what was said, but in the way in which it was said and the body language Laura may be using.

"It could be worse, we could be back in the pub with the drunks listening to their rubbish" Herman smiled at Terry, he knew he tried to think of the worst case scenario's when he became anxious about upcoming events, it was one of his many flaws. But it was also one of the reasons why they felt close with each other. They knew each other in complete depth, they knew about their worries, their fears, their strengths and the many weaknesses. It's what made them the best companions and colleagues, an unlikely pairing, but a pairing that worked well.

Herman retorted "Don't discount the small details, that's where God is" with neither of them being particularly religious, this puzzled Terry for a moment, then he thought about the phrase "God is in the detail" which he assumed was what Herman had been leading to. Maybe he was right, maybe he shouldn't have fobbed off the old army drunk. Maybe they should also follow up on that once they were back from the visit today.

"Are we sure we have everything? The last thing I want is to drive there, then have to come back because we've forgotten something simple" both men checked, "Keys, Wallet, Phone, Notepad and Pen. Two pens in fact, you know, just in case one doesn't work" said Herman. "Check & Check" Terry responded. They geared up ready for the not too distant journey and left the house.

In the car both men sat silently, it was strange not having to slightly cover their faces when driving down the street, there was no need to. They had recently decided to buy a new car, not new, but new to them. It was a cheap former executive car, highly spec'd, high mileage, but so much of an improvement on what they had previously. It was comfortable, it was nearly silent in comparison and it worked. They couldn't have asked for anything more.

It wasn't the cleanest of cars, either in look, or condition, but it certainly gave a different impression when they pulled up.

A short time later, the boys turned up at the Asylum. They had no idea the magnitude of this building, it stretched as far as the eye could see. How could they not have known previously that this place was so big? Or that it was literally on their doorstep?

An intimidating Victorian age building that had, over the years been adapted and modified to be fit for purpose. Looking more fortress like, than like the grand building it had once been, raised the anxiety levels for the boys. They pulled up to the guard's gate and presented the warrant for interview. After a brief interface and the guard teasing them that this was the wrong place, they were allowed through the barrier.

They cautiously parked the car up in a position which they

thought was close enough to not drag out the walk to the building but far enough away that it wouldn't seem like they were too lazy. They approached the front desk of the building and presented themselves to the clerk. Showing their ID and their warrant for visit, they had to fill in some documentation, detailing the length of the visit and what they wanted to do whilst there. This was so that Laura's doctor could look over the information to ensure that it wouldn't present any unnecessary risk to her.

Knowing the boys were there to dredge up the full situation they knew they may need to have the doctor in there with them whilst they did so. It seemed to take a long time once they had handed the form in for them to get the all clear to be able to go through from the front waiting area.

They hadn't prepared for the fact that they would need to talk through everything with the doctor prior to actually getting to speak to Laura. This again increased their anxiety levels. "What if we can't get to speak to her, we need to cross this off the list today" said Terry looking panicked. He could feel sweat on his palms, his breathing was shallow and he had loads of "What-if's" going through his head. Raising loads of reasons that he may not be able to carry out what he had gone there to achieve. He may not effect a positive outcome from this visit.

Herman looked him directly in the eyes "Terry, no matter what happens, if we can't do it today, we will do it tomorrow, we can deal with anything if we do it together" feeling a sense of reassurance, the noise in Terry's head seemed to silence a little, the feelings of anxiety began to calm. He knew as long as his partner had his back, he would be able to face any challenges that he may come across.

The boys wondered around the lobby area, waiting for what felt like hours and having had 2 cups of coffee, Herman started to feel the need to facilitate. With no obvious places to go, he was forced to again attend the front desk and enquire. "Unfortunately sir, facilities are all through in the secure area, you will have to wait, I will chase the doctor up for you now" This did not help the building anxiety at all. Herman began to shuffle awkwardly, pacing backwards and forwards as he did everything he could do in order to take his mind off the increasingly awkward need to relieve himself.

A short time later, a senior figure came through one of the secure doors. Ignoring the boys, the man approached the front desk directly and spoke to the clerk. He quickly turned and greeted the detectives. "Good morning gentlemen, please come through with me, you will need these" the doctor handed both of them passes "these will allow you through the doors behind me. We do have to move through one at a time, some of our long stay guests are quite challenging individuals" this again began to build the tension a little further, however, the reassuring and unassuming smile offered by the doctor was enough to put their minds at rest "and detective, momentarily we will be walking past some facilities, you may relieve yourself there"

The wave of calmness washed over Herman hearing this. He knew that as soon as he had chance to relieve himself he could get his mind back on the task, he knew that this was also not creating the best first impression he could give, but he couldn't hide it.

Walking through door one, it seemed to take a long time for each of them to pass into the secure compartment and then through door two, which also took its time.

Although Herman knew this was a requirement, he was losing his grip on being able to control himself. He hoped it wouldn't take too much longer. All three men were through into the first secure area eventually. "Gentlemen, we must leave all of our personal items here. You will find lockers behind you, once you have put everything into the lockers, we can proceed through to the next area, where we will go and sit and have a talk in my office. Detective, the facilities you require are just over behind you"

With a slightly awkward smile and with a speed to his usually sedate step, Herman made his way into the bathroom. Coming back out without wanting to waste any time, Herman quickly put his personal possessions in the locker.

Unsure on whether he would be able to take a pen or notepad in with him, he loaded them up into the locker, he did say everything must be left there, so there was no reason for him to take them through.

Meeting back up with Terry and the doctor, Herman had left all but his clothes, in the locker. "I assumed we couldn't take anything through, so I left nothing to chance" stated Herman, he hadn't realised, in his haste to make it out of the bathroom and leave all of his possessions behind, he had forgotten to do up the zip on his trousers. This of course was spotted by the doctor "If only you had taken such precaution when leaving the bathroom detective" Confused, Herman shot Terry a look, Terry looked quite embarrassed on his behalf. Raising his eyebrows and did a slight sideways nod down towards his crotch.

It didn't take more than a moment for Herman to realise what both the doctor and Terry had been hinting at. He swiftly reached down and amended the issue, awkwardly trying to explain away the malfunction. This had not created a very good first impression as to the competencies of the boys.

They followed the doctor, toward door number three and four. Having had to wait momentarily, for the more heavily fortified doors to open whilst each moved through to the security area and then on through the fourth door. This was a minor inconvenience which seemed to again increase the amount of time the boys were not taking steps forward in solving the case.

"Please detectives, take a seat in my office, I would offer you a drink but our canteen facilities are through in security area four, we are only in area two. We can head through there after we have spoken" the boys took a seat, they felt nervous. It was that same kind of feeling as when being in school and being called into the headmaster's office without truly knowing what you are there for.

"So detectives, we do have Laura here, we have undertaken many sessions with her to try and unravel what happened, we are drawing a blank, what will you be asking her? Did anyone make you aware that temporarily she had been catatonic?"

Terry shuffled in his seat, clearly, usually the more confident out of the two men, on this occasion he was struggling to find the words to come out. Herman cleared his throat and quietly began to explain "We..well, we need to find out what happened, I am sure you have maybe much more experience than us in these situations, however, we have our basic questions to ask, we want to know about the phone call"

The doctor taken a little aback by this statement, slightly changed his stance. He seemed like he didn't know how to proceed with the conversation, could this vastly unprepared, unprofessional and uneducated pair really have been sent as the prime of the police service in order to investigate this heinous crime.

Terry had eventually found his words "Look doc, I know we're not suave, smooth, senior detectives who already have all of the answers. What we want to do is find the answers as to what happened to Laura and her family. We don't know what the phone call aspect of the initial report was about, we don't have any preconceived ideas about what actually went down, but we want to be damn sure that we manage to get some answers to some of the questions we have to ask"

Smiling, in a reassured manner, the doctor looked down at his desk, saying nothing for a moment, he looked around a little, pondering his next move. "Chaps, I'll be honest, if you can get something out of Laura, I would certainly appreciate any assistance, can I make a suggestion, we send him in" The doctor pointed at Herman. "We can watch from behind the inspection panel"

Filled with the thoughts as to why he was the one the doctor had picked, Herman felt inquisitive and uneasy now at the thought of being locked inside of a room with a known killer.

The toughest person he had ever had to face, was himself in the bathroom mirror each day, judging himself for his appearance, his size and his looks. Despite the fact that the profile on this lady showed that she was only five feet tall and despite the fact that the good doctor had said that she was at least temporarily catatonic, he couldn't help but worry but, he also knew this was something he had to do.

He knew, he, was the one somehow intrinsically linked to Laura and that he could be the one that could lead her not only toward a confession, but to get the truth about this phone call.

Ever since he read it, the idea of a phone call leading to someone acting in such a way intrigued him. Maybe it was because it seemed like something based in science fiction. It seemed too unrealistic to be true. But he was approaching this with a completely open mind. After all, only new realisations are made when minds are open.

"Ok gentlemen" the doctor began to stand "I suggest we go and grab a coffee have a bit further chat, then organise Laura to meet us in the room?" Not wanting to seem too discourteous, the boys had no reason to say no. "We have to pass through area three, which is our low risk patients, then our canteen area is in security level four. I must ask that we leave any further personal belongings here, including pens and notepads, we shouldn't interface any high risk campers, but on the off chance, we don't want any accidents to happen"

The boys both stood up to join the doctor in heading out of the room, being sure to leave any remaining notepads and pens behind. They walked up and approached the door to head into the lower security area, no problem here, they passed through door five and door 6 without any issues.

It was quite surreal experience. Most of the patients seemed to be so out of their heads on whatever cocktail of drugs was keeping them passive, that it was like walking through a museum of wax works. There were many people who were still. They seemed to be breathing, however, each looked posed and poised. Each looked like they had the potential at any moment, to go off like a powder keg.

The doctor lead the way to area 4, the protocol seemed to be a little different to go through these doors. Biometric scanners were now in use, this wasn't something that the boys had noticed until the doctor had bent down to come to an eye level with the scanner. This seemed like quite a futuristic feature, although it was obviously something that worked well.

Heading through doors seven and eight, the boys now realised, this canteen was like any other. It had that same typical smell to it, cheap fried food and luke warm drinks. The odd whiff of a dodgy microwaveable curry occasionally drifted through the air as the boys were sat there waiting for their coffee's.

The doctor did return a moment later with coffee for all three of them. It looked and smelled like freshly brewed coffee, maybe even filter coffee. This was the last thing that the boys were expecting. "You have to go to the back to get the good stuff" the doctor said smiling at Herman and Terry. Handing them a cup each the boys could sense he was telling the truth, the mugs seemed well used, although well cleaned. The coffee seemed piping hot, it smelled fantastic.

Sitting savouring the taste of what was clearly an expensive cup of coffee, the boys and the doctor did not find a word to say to each other. There almost seemed to be no need to, they were just three men sitting there enjoying a coffee.

Herman caught the doctors eye "Erm, doctor, I hate to ask again, but, is there anywhere to you know, facilitate" The doctor smiled at Herman, not knowing whether this was a genuine desire for the bathroom or whether this was his nerves beginning to show.

"You have to go through what we call a half door to facilitate in here I'm afraid, this also doesn't give a very private experience, but it won't stop you from using the facilities" Herman looked a little unsure, however, he was being guided by his bladder and that told him that it was definitely time to go to the bathroom.

"I do need to go, I can't sit through an interview needing to go" Herman awkwardly stated "Where are they doc?" he questioned, the doctor gestured to a half doored room behind Terry, "head just through that half door, if you stand at a tad of an angle, no one will see anything"

Slightly relieved, although still needing to go, Herman jumped up from the table and moved swiftly toward the half door. He began almost preparing his motions to ensure he didn't begin to relieve himself too early. He got to the door and entered, not having a great deal of depth to the room, Herman barely managed to squeeze his girth in.

He had just got himself into position and began to relieve himself, he was at a moment that he couldn't stop.

The doctor looked down at his pager, for a moment, it had been uncontrollably buzzing. He pulled it up toward his face and seemed to read and re-read his message. "Oh dear, please prepare Terry, HERMAN YOU MUST RETURN TO THIS TABLE PLEASE" he shouted toward Herman who was now backing out of the half door, shuffling from side to side trying to protect his modesty. He was just removing the final parts of him from the half door, when an alarm began to sound and a light began to flash.

Herman hurried back to the table and sat down. "I will be back with you shortly gentlemen and we will then go to the interview with Laura, but for this moment, I need to sort an issue. Please remain seated with your hands out flat on the table" The doctor was quite insistent in his statement as he left the boys at the table. "Will we ever get to speak to this girl? Not only have I had to take a step to the background as the good old doctor loves you Hermy, but I'm also getting a little frustrated with what seems to be timewasting"

Herman eyed Terry up and down, not quite knowing what to

make of his statement, was this jealousy? Was he saying this because the doctor had picked him to speak with Laura? Or was he saying it because he genuinely thought that they were having their time wasted? "Terry, you're not jealous of me are you, you know that the doctor picked me to speak with her and not you" Terry knew his partner would be sincerely affected in his abilities if he were to tell him that inside he had died a little when he found out that he would not be interviewing Laura. That Herman really had never taken on the lead investigation role in any interview they had ever done, that he had never passed through any of the advanced interview technique classes that Terry had attended. That he didn't have anywhere near the level of interview intelligence that Terry did. "No buddy, it makes more sense for me to watch, the doctor obviously picked you for a reason" Terry struggled to sound like he had integrity in what he was saying. He didn't have any because he couldn't believe those words had truly just come out of his mouth.

Behind him, there was a ringing that had begun to crescendo since the alarm first started, the ringing was building to a point where Herman couldn't ignore it any longer, he knew he was meant to keep his hands on the table and his eyes forward, however, he had to look around to see where it was coming from. He spied an old phone just behind him.

This was odd, because he hadn't seen this previously when they had been walking past. What kind of place, allows a Bakelite telephone with a chord in an eating area, when they weren't even allowed to have proper toilets or a notepad and pen? It just didn't make sense.

The ringing continued, maybe it was an emergency phone that the doctor had put out, in case he might need them for something thought Herman, in this case, it would be justified to get up and answer the phone. "Terry, I don't care what you say, the ringing from that phone is getting louder and louder, I can't take it anymore, maybe someone needs our help, I'm getting up to answer it" Terry looked around, not having heard anything other than the alarm, he nodded in agreement, Herman did have his quirks, maybe this was just one of them.

Standing up, still with his hands out in front of him as if he were doing some form of core workout. He then turned, keeping his body stiff, presenting quite the sight. He moved toward where the telephone was, where the old fashioned ringing seemed to be coming from.

He spied the phone, but the closer he got over to the phone, the further away the ringing sounded. He continued to move toward the phone, still the ringing continued to distance itself, but so did the noise of the siren and the brightness of the light from the alarm. The focus became solely on this phone, which seemed to be withdrawing him from the reality around him. Herman noticed he had begun to sweat, beads had begun to form on his forehead.

Although it was not uncommon for him to sweat, this seemed like a profuse amount for saying he had recently urinated and the room was not overly hot, the beads began linking up and the sweat began forming drops that ran down the side of his face.

He could feel his heart begin to pound in his chest, what was this - what was happening to him? He was focused solely on the phone and walked toward it, still with his upper body rigid and his arm outstretched.

Reaching toward the phone, it was like he was being pulled in and there was nothing he could do to stop himself, he kept telling himself to stop, but he felt completely powerless. Each time the phone rang he felt compelled to answer it, he sensed himself being drawn in.

Reaching the phone Herman had to break from his rigid stance, the siren still blared out, the lights were still flashing but all of this had faded into the background. The phone ringing became the only sound he could hear, continuing to bore into his head the more times it rang.

He reached down and grabbed the hand set. Slowly then picking it up to his ear. His eyes transfixed on the base, he put the handset to his ear. He heard a long series of clicks and dead noise, like a needle skirting across the surface of a vinyl record. There was nothing but this noise.

Herman's eyes tried looking along the wire of the phone, it was at this point, and this point only that he realised two things. The primary point being that the telephone had no wire to the socket. The secondary being that there was no wire from the base to the handset. This was a very strange sensation, how could he be hearing these noises when there was no connection to even the base set, let alone the telephone line.

Herman slammed the phone back down, he snapped out of the daze he was in. The siren stopped, the flashing light stopped, Herman withdrew back to the seating opposite Terry. "Hermy are you ok?" still trying to come back to his senses, Herman was not only trying to figure out what had just happened to him, but also who he was and what he was doing there.

This experience had completely discombobulated him. It took another moment of controlled breathing to bring Herman back around.

"I have just had the strangest experience of my life, I can't believe it" Terry was confused didn't retort, but waited for what he had to say next.

He sat there pondering how to explain what he had just been through, how could he really explain it without Terry having had that same experience. The unbelievable desire to be driven toward doing something. The unstoppable urge, the palpitations that pulsated throughout his soul. The sweat on his brow that came from nowhere. How could he even begin to quantify how that felt to him? How could he explain to one of the people who mattered most to him, he had just had this entirely unbelievable experience?

"I don't know what it was, it was weird. The alarm went, the light flashed, I felt drawn to answer the phone, I don't know why, my heart pounded, I began to sweat" Terry stifled a laugh, which quickly turned into a full blown howl. "Buddy, I think you've been a bit freaked out by being in this place and you've also let the old drunk get to you, what's next a banner saying I believe in little green men? Or a tinfoil hat?" Herman was a little disheartened and hurt by this, not only the dismissive nature Terry had, but also the associations he was making.

"Where's that doctor then, hopefully he isn't long we have to get this girl interviewed today, besides at least now you can tell her you've had a phone call too" laughing through his words Terry didn't realise how he was affecting Herman. The sheer nature that he had found the experience his partner just had was a big joke. That he could dismiss his experiences without even thinking about them properly or listening to what he had to say.

Herman was beginning to get really angry with Terry, he was playing through the situation time and time again, thinking about the little things that had been said, that he wasn't being taken seriously.

He began to analyse everything, he began to think over how Terry was making him feel. The fact that his partner didn't believe the experience he had been through was the worst thing he could imagine. Terry was the one person he was meant to be side by side with, through thick and thin. Who was meant to believe everything that he said to him, but somehow all he felt was ashamed of his experience and feelings.

A moment later, the good doctor came back into the room. "My apologies gentlemen, there seems to be a bit of a transgression in the Asylum. You must understand sometimes, these things can happen, this is the nature of my business, especially when the moon is full or due to be" This felt like an odd turn of phrase to use. However, the boys could understand that this was an Asylum, it was a place for those with particular needs, so sometimes things were likely not to go smoothly or as planned.

"Shall we go and meet with her" Herman quickly spoke up, he seemed quite anxious now to get the interview under way. To begin to really get to grips with what had happened to Laura. The tension began to build and the doctor could sense this.

"Gentlemen, we will get there, but if you could sit back at the table for me, just for a moment I would like to confess to something" All three men returned to the table and seated themselves. "Gentlemen, I believe Laura had experienced a type of Neuro Linguistic Programming, maybe she was subjected to this on one occasion, or over many occasions. Herman, I suspect you sir, are particularly susceptible to NLP and as such, I subjected you to a little. I wanted to show you what can be achieved in a very short space of time. I can't prove it for sure, but I hope you understand that the brain is a very powerful tool and someone for some reason, maybe wanted this deed done, using Laura as an innocent party with which to do it through"

Both Terry and Herman sat there with their mouths open, not fully understanding the situation. "Terry, I trust you saw everything that Herman did yet you didn't interrupt him, but you watched and analysed, then you began to make him throw doubt on his own experiences. You, of course were gas lighting."

"Despite seeing this man you know inside and out undertake these actions, you did nothing to stop him. Herman, you will have had no control over your actions, you will have had severe palpitations and you will have had profuse sweating. These are all the symptoms I have been subconsciously dropping guides to you about over the previous days since I learned you were coming to visit, Terry I programmed you using your cynical nature which was available through your personnel file, which of course your inspector let me have. Herman, I played on your sense of wanting and lack of control or your desire to be controlled"

This again dropped the jaws of both of the boys, they couldn't believe this was happening. They couldn't believe someone could get to them or that this could happen without them being aware of it.

"So, we've just been some big science experiment to prove a point? An experiment to show it's easy or that we're idiots?" Terry's voice began to raise as he was clearly quite agitated at the thought that some old doctor had got one over on him.

The doctor smiled discretely. "No, I just wanted to demonstrate this point, that it could very easily be done. That someone could be affected in this way. I wanted you to see this isn't science fiction, If I can get the lead investigators to follow my plan, then maybe I can let them understand the potential of Laura's state of mind and maybe, just maybe, use them to help me to get her to open up"

The doctor paused as if he wanted to continue, then looked at both of them with a slightly disheartened look "Gentlemen, NLP is a pseudoscience, if this is raised as a legal defence for Laura in court, it may be very difficult to prove" Everything now began to click into place.

As Herman had an experience in what he thought was now an induced state, he could stand witness to the power of this "pseudoscience" He could also have it in the back of his head and have a sense of empathy with Laura whilst interviewing her.

He could share his experience of being drawn to the phone, he could share his knowledge of it physically making him feel like he was out of control of his own functions. It gave him good ground to be able to talk with Laura on a level playing field, so that he could have integrity when he spoke with her and hopefully got to listen to her talk about her experiences too.

CHAPTER TEN:
THE INTERVIEW

The boys followed the good doctor, although, now they had the opinion that maybe he wasn't quite as good as they primarily had done. They walked back through door eight past security and through to door seven. They were now back into the third area.

The boys were in a position where they were unsure if they could ever trust either the good doctor or the Asylum they were visiting. However, they desperately needed to undertake this interview in order to attempt to progress their investigation.

The three men arrived at a room with two doors side by side. The doctor gestured toward Herman and the left hand door, then toward Terry and the right hand door. Both men followed the visual guides given by the doctor. Herman gently pushed the door for the left hand room, the latch clicked open, there were no handles and the electronic lock was released by someone watching on the cameras. He cautiously walked into the room.

Looking ahead of him, there was a white room, with a white table and chairs in the middle of it, a mirrored glass window was to the right of the room, there was soft padding on the walls which could be seen from the entrance. Herman was sure to close the door behind him. A heavy clunk resonated off the walls of the room when the lock dropped back into place.

Herman felt like this was an extremely clinical environment, there was a good airflow moving throughout the room. The temperature wasn't too hot and it wasn't too cold. It was just right.

Seated at the table, was a woman in white overalls, it bore the name of the institution on the rear, across the shoulders. She had long brown platted hair. She sat still with her palms flat on the table and with a still, emotionless look on her face. This woman, was Laura. This was the woman who had brutally murdered her husband and poisoned her children.

Herman approached with caution and took a seat at the table in front of him. The seat didn't face directly opposite to Laura, so Herman noisily shuffled the chair over and drew level with her. She had adjusted her gaze to stare directly at him, although the look was haunting as it appeared she was staring directly into his soul.

She had piercing blue eyes, such a vivid blue that Herman was unsure this was the real colour of them. Could they be colour enhancing contact lenses? No - of course not he thought. Why would she be allowed those in here?

Herman struggled to know how to begin. "Erm, good afternoon Laura, I am Herman, I have been asked to look into what has been occurring recently and to see if you would like to discuss anything with me?" Laura hadn't changed her gaze, it stayed fixed on him. Her breathing was calm and controlled. Her demeanor was still and tranquil. This unnerved Herman. Someone who had no reaction to interview was a difficult person to talk to.

"Laura, do you mind if we speak together, or you could tell me the surroundings of the day the incident happened with your family and then I can tell you about my recent situation, how does that sound?" Laura's face began to twitch just below her right eye, her body was still, her reactions were fixed, but it desperately felt like she was trying to talk. There was no response from her other than the twitch, either physically or vocally.

"Ok Laura, maybe I should talk you through what we know about the day from the initial report, then we might be able to figure something out"

There was still absolutely no response from Laura. No acknowledgement, no nod of the head, nothing.

"So Laura, the day began as normal, you dropped the kids off at school came home, tidied the house, then sat drinking a glass of wine at your kitchen table. It was at this point, you realised the time and that you had to get ready and go and pick the children up from school. You came back in a dried off as it was raining. You got the children to go and do their homework whilst you began preparing dinner. The telephone rang, you answered it and you had a strange experience whilst you were on the telephone, then you returned to cooking dinner. Your husband came in from his working day, you helped him with his things, then returned to cook dinner, where you had a bit of an experience. In this experience you lost track of time, you lost track of what you were doing. The next thing you remember doing was putting everything back on the side but all of the seasonings had been put on the meat. You began to cook everything, at this point you noticed a slightly funny smell coming from the meat, but thought little of it, just that the meat may have been a little past its best. You called everyone down to the table, where your boy didn't wait for his father to say grace which angered his father. Your husband noticed a funny smell on the meat but continued to eat it. He blamed you for buying it too early in the week. Then he began to have convulsions, you went over to him. You grabbed the tenderiser from the sideboard and began to hit him, a total of 16 times in the head. Then the children collapsed and started convulsing. The emergency services were called when a neighbour reported hearing a woman screaming repeatedly. You were found covered head to toe in blood cradling your children in your arms. Both of whom unfortunately have since had to have care withdrawn due to severe brain damage and sadly"

Herman paused and took a long breath, now it came to reading this report out loud, he seemed to be taking it on more of an emotional stance, he was beginning to well up, he had to clear his throat "and sadly, both have since passed away" Herman's head slunk a little lower.

He eventually took a moment to lift his head back up from the case file to look Laura in the eyes, she stared back with a cold, blank stare, but something was different. The twitch in Laura's cheek had developed. It was now an intermittent, seemingly involuntary movement. A tear was slowly falling down one side of her face, quickly followed by more tears down the other side. They were streaming down both cheeks. However, her face remained completely fixed in place other than the twitch.

Herman was completely lost in the emotion of the moment and a tear also began to fall down his cheek.

"Laura, I would like to make a confession, I don't know if you heard the alarm that sounded a moment ago. I was in the cafeteria when that went off. There was a telephone, it rang and rang, despite everything I could do, and I couldn't help myself but answer it. When I did, there was dead noise and the worst part of it, the phone wasn't even connected. I'd like to ask you what happened when you received your phone call, do you remember what happened or what was said?" Laura turned her head, her lips slightly parted. It seemed as if she wanted to speak. It seemed as if she wanted to break down, but something was stopping her. She sat there and her tears seemed as if they just absorbed into her face. The ones that had fallen down her cheeks dripped off her chin onto her overall, they were quickly absorbed by the colourless material.

The good doctor was sat behind the glass watching with great intent. He was excited at the prospect of Laura finally talking. Making an attempt to speak out, he could see she was making an effort but something was stopping her. Turning to Terry, the doctor inquisitively asked "Is Herman always so open and honest? His honesty has been the key, he built quick trust, he showed emotion, he was completely different than most men had been in her life previously" there was a momentary awkward pause "I can also see why you care about him so much, this man although clumsy and disorientated and you being so aloof, this is why you make the perfect pairing, hopefully between the three of us, we can come up with some answers"

Back in the room, the expected silence continued, Laura seemed to be trying to speak and move more, at the same time she showed and gave away nothing. Deep in thought and reflective silence, Herman couldn't help but question whether this was the same situation that he had been through moments previously.

He was unable to fathom whether what he had gone through and what she had been through could be the same thing. How could she end up like this and he be back to normal? Ok, he didn't murder anyone. Ok, he hadn't suffered years of physical abuse, although he did get daily abuse, albeit of caring nature from Terry, but he couldn't put this in the same ball park as the abuses Laura had faced.

"Laura, I would like to come and visit you again, I would like to speak with you and get to understand the situation that happened. I am aware, so you know, that your husband was abusive, both physically and mentally. I won't push you to talk about anything, I will just listen. I will just be here. Is there anything you would like me to avoid asking or talking about? Is there anything you would like me to bring? I am happy to go at your pace, I am happy to do what you would like to do, or talk about what you would like to talk about"

Laura stiffly turned her head her hand began to move, all of her fingers other than her index finger curled up. Her hand began to move. It was as if she was spelling something out on the table with her hand. "Laura would you like me to get you a pen and paper?" Laura's face remained completely unchanged, her eyes and her body remaining completely still. Her hand was making macro movements which were becoming greater in their size and mannerisms.

The doctor was just behind the glass, moving from foot to foot, pacing up and down the room, he turned to Terry "all of this is being recorded we will be able to see what she's doing with her hand, it looks like she writing with her finger. But showing no emotion and not moving, completely void, it's like she's trapped within herself" Terry maintained his silent resolve watching and interpreting Herman's interview technique.

Terry was completely amazed, he never knew he could build this emotional connection with a suspect, he never knew he could draw a person out of themselves, maybe the hardball techniques he had spent years learning, could take a back seat to this emotional method in certain circumstances.

Back in the room with Herman, he was unsure on what to do next, he didn't want to prevent her from making these positive steps forward, but he also didn't want to leave it where it was. "Laura, can you tell me anything about that day? What did you use on the food? You said you couldn't recall at the initial moment in your statement. You said following receiving the phone call and again I am only going back on the initial statement taken from the arresting officer, that you had periods of blackouts or unawareness, moments of time that you couldn't remember what had happened. Is this the case? Can you think about describing those sensation to me?" Laura began to amplify her hands movements.

The white table her hand was on began to take a pink hue, he hadn't noticed at first, but it appeared her nails had begun to wear down and she was now ripping open the skin on her finger. The smearing of the blood now began to increase, so much so, that whatever she may have been trying to display was now lost. The whole time, Laura's gaze remained fixed, her stance remained completely rigid and her mannerisms were completely untelling.

"LAURA STOP" Herman raised his voice to make a straight command. At that moment, her motion became completely still. It was almost as if she had been so conditioned to routine instruction, to being bullied and pushed around, that this was now the only way to get a response.

No one, to this point, had tried this technique and this was an out of character way for Herman to act or to speak. He would never act in the way toward another person, definitely not toward a suspect who was declared catatonic by the Asylum she was being kept in.

Herman was calm again. "Laura, I am now terminating this interview, I will come back. The next time I come back, I would like you to talk to me, to talk through the situation and to go through all the details that are not currently clear. I am being direct, but please don't take this as a command"

Herman couldn't help but feel he was taking on the controlling role her husband had previously had over her. He needed to get results, if this had happened to an ordinary housewife, how many other people could this also have affected. What about Roger? Was this also what had affected him?

Herman stood up, tucked his chair in and walked toward the door, he looked back at Laura and he could see the blood was now saturating the table to the extent that there were small drips falling off the edge. He waited for the click of the door to unlock. As it did, he made a quick exit from the room, two orderlies walked straight past him into the room before the door even had chance to swing back to being shut again, with a third man, who looked like a doctor who had a medical kit in his hand.

Herman couldn't look back into the room, the fact Laura had done this to herself trying to convey a message or writing out something on the table, made him feel awful. But what had she been trying to show?

The good doctor and Terry made their exit from the surveillance room. They walked up behind Herman who looked deep in thought. "Herman" the good doctor was trying to get his attention, there was no reaction from him. The doctor gently placed his hand on Herman's shoulder. Herman jumped, it was as if the doctor had woken him from a trance, or as if he had one of those dreams where you're falling. Herman's reflexes well and truly worked.

"Doctor, how did you think that went, sorry I was deep in thought, it was the strangest interview I've ever been in the room for, I think it was possibly only the first, I've lead as a solo venture" the doctor smiled reassuringly at Herman. "You stopped that interview at the correct moment, the command you gave her, despite your unease at doing so, was also a sign of how we can begin to bring her out of this state, well done sir" Terry smiled at him "Top job big man"

Herman felt an immense sense of pride, he felt he maybe had done something right. Maybe he had made the correct moves. He had never been given this position of trust previously, but now he had it, he liked it. He was sure despite his misgivings as both a detective and as a human being, he would be able to help Laura and to find out what had really happened.

The three men, seemed to have bonded over this connection that had been made, everything had now dropped into place. The doctor had deceived them, but it had helped Herman open up to the potential experience Laura had been through. Laura had made some motion, she had tried to speak, she had shown emotion, so catatonic, she was not. She had responded to targeted instruction. Terry had seen with immense pride his partner undertake something only a few days ago, he wouldn't even have imagined him doing.

"Doc, I would like to visit again in a couple of days. Do you have anyone here who would be able to tell what Laura had written on the table with her finger?" Herman enquired as the three men began the trudge back out of the building. "Herman, I think that would be a wonderful idea, I think another interview maybe with some guidance on technique once I have analysed the footage, would help? Yes we do have someone who works with body language, so maybe if they cannot help us identify what she was writing, she could point us in the direction we may need to be in to find the correct person" The three men by this time had made it back to entrance lobby of the building.

"Gentlemen, this is where I will bid you farewell for today, I must return to my many other patients. Please, next time you wish to visit, telephone me directly, no need for any warrants" Terry having felt quite abandoned throughout this experience wanted to take a little more of a lead "Please doc, as soon as you have any information on any of today's events, promise you'll let us know. Maybe no more tricks though 'ey, not sure the big fella's ticker could take it"

With a sense of relief, Terry and Herman made their way out of the building, plodding toward the car, silently contemplating the day's events. Neither man said a word for the majority of the return journey and by the time they got back it was completely dark. They had used an entire day either waiting, having games played with them and only a small portion of the day on interviewing their suspect, they would also need to go back. This may not go down well with their seniors. But if it needed to be done for the investigation it needed to be done.

The boys walked in the door of their house, neither of them managed to muster the energy to speak to one another, they both headed up the stairs and retired to their bedroom for the night.

Tomorrow was a new day, new investigations and reports to be logged. Despite the fact that they were both wiped and feeling at their lowest ebb due to making no moves forwards, it was another first for them to feel the desire to want to get back up in the morning and get back to work following what felt a little like a devastatingly wasted day.

CHAPTER ELEVEN: WHERE ARE YOU?

Sam awoke with a slight mental haze, he had a phrase running through his head that he couldn't figure out. Mostly because it was what he recognised to be Italian? He rolled over in his bed and went to jot down the phrase. Men like Sam, high functioning ideas men, by matter of routine have a book or paper by the side of their bed, so when their genius strikes, usually through the night, they have somewhere to jot things down to trigger their memory.

Sam wasn't really sure what he was writing down, but, he had to write down what he imagined it to be 'il destino è contro di me in salute e virtù' just reading it, he figured there may be something regarding destiny and virtue in there, but this was definitely a job for the online translator.

Sam picked up his laptop and quickly went to the search engine. Where he loaded up the translation tool and typed in what he thought were the words and spellings he had seen. He was shocked when he read the translation, "Fate is against me in health and virtue" he read out loud as he continued to struggle to understand what this could mean

He thought to himself, maybe making connections that weren't necessarily there, this could have been linked with that weird phone call last night, maybe, this was what the phone call was trying to tell him, he couldn't fail, even if he did nothing at all with his life other than staying indoors and ordering takeout he would have enough money to survive for the rest of his life.

He wasn't going to let this dream control him, but he had to keep it in the back of his mind. He had to be aware of what an issue could be but not fear anything that may come to face him. This was one of the things that Sam was good at.

Sam lived by one of Sun Tzu's principles when it came to winning his mental battles. "If you know the enemy and know yourself, you need not fear the result of a hundred battles. If you know yourself but not the enemy, for every victory gained you will also suffer a defeat. If you know neither the enemy nor yourself, you will succumb in every battle." He had to know in depth what this enemy was. As a smart person, Sam was beginning to break down what he was thinking.

"Ok, so the phrase what is it and where did it come from?" Sam pondered out loud, the phrase sounded familiar, but he didn't know how he was going to figure it out. Maybe a little time spent sitting in his bed looking around the internet. He loaded up the search engine and typed the words in. The first thing that came up was a Wikipedia commentary on "O Fortuna" Sam laughed out loud, how could he not have seen or recognised this.

Of course, it was obviously a phrase that had been ruminating from the previous evening when this had come on his audio system. Sometimes this happened, sometimes it didn't this was just one of those occasions where it did.

He felt so simple, so ridiculous, that because of this phone call he had, it had thrown him into a blind panic. Was he so bothered about losing everything that when the threat of that happened, it completely threw him? Was he so materialistic that it mattered to him not only about losing everything but also about failing?

Sam had never previously shown that he had been phased by anything. Win or lose, he accepted either with humility, although, he hadn't regularly lost anything so it wasn't something that he was used to doing or even that he was planning on doing moving forwards.

Sam got up, now unphased by his dream and began his morning routine.

Routine was key to managing his mental health. It was easy for him to slip into a spiral which made him at his worst in instances such as the dream that morning.

The worst part about being a high functioning individual for Sam, was that he struggled to stop his brain from working. He struggled to stop the continuous connections in his frontal cortex, making creative solutions to issues other people hadn't yet thought of.

This also though, created an issue when Sam faced turmoil. He wasn't able to stop his brain from making connections that may not necessarily be there. He had this idea that his brain was like its own little Sherlock, except it worked completely overtime and made links that were completely fabricated.

It was why he spent his life alone, how could he trust people when his brain was telling him they were all against him, or that he was over thinking every conversation that he had? Thinking there was subtext to everything, when in fact, sometimes it just was, what it was.

Dressed and ready, he decided to skip breakfast that day. Some people were fortunate enough to be able to choose this option, although this made Sam feel guilty when he truly thought about it, but he couldn't face eating that morning. He grabbed his essentials and made his way to the door. As he reached down to open it, a knock came from the other side.

He quickly opened it, to his surprise two police officers were standing in front of him. "Samuel?" Taken a little aback by hearing his full name, no one had said it for quite some time. "Erm, yes, sorry that's me" The officers looked at each other, as if silently making the decision of who was going to talk next, the more senior seeming officer of the two stepped forward "Samuel, I am arresting you on the suspicion of grievous bodily harm with intent, you do not have to say anything. But, it may harm your defence if you do not mention when questioned something which you later rely on in court. Anything you do say may be given in evidence" taken aback, Sam wasn't really sure what he should do.

His first move was to simply hold his hands out in front of him. He didn't know what else he could do. "What did I do?" Sam asked inquisitively with a wavering voice. "This is in regard to an incident which allegedly happened recently between yourself and another male, further details will be discussed with you under interview conditions" Sam was really confused by this, he was aware of an incident, but he had saved a lady from being mugged, surely this wasn't relating to that.

A short while later, handcuffed and in police custody, Sam was standing awaiting processing at the detention desk. "Samuel, I hereby authorise your detention in order to investigate the allegations made against you, mainly being that you caused grievous bodily harm upon another person with intent. Is there anything you wish to say at this time" Sam was speechless, was this what his dream was about? Was this what the phone call was about? Was everything dropping into place, or was he making those connections that didn't exist?

Sam had everything he was wearing taken from him, he had to strip down to his underwear and was given an all in one plastic feeling suit he could wear instead of his clothes. He didn't know if this was for his own protection or if this was them believing that there may be evidence on the clothes they had taken off him.

Still handcuffed, Sam was guided down to a cell, still continually thinking over the situation that had happened he couldn't see how he could have been being treated as a criminal.

All he did was save a woman from being mugged, supported her and then returned her home to her husband. How could he have caused this grievous bodily harm? Sure, he hit the person hard, but he didn't think he hit them that hard.

They arrived at his cell, Sam was guided in, they still needed to perform a full body cavity search of him, which again he could not understand, but he didn't want to appear as if he was not compliant. He wanted to make sure they had nothing further to put against him, so if he complied with all of their requests, surely it would stand him in a better light.

Sam was instructed to slightly squat, whilst an officer lubricated his gloved hand, he quickly and forcefully inserted two fingers into his back cavity.

It felt as if he was looking through a draw for the last battery, it definitely didn't feel like a prostate exam which he had previously had. After what appeared like an age of him feeling like a ventriloquist's dummy, the officer retrieved his fingers with nothing having been found.

Sam quickly pulled up his underwear and pulled on his suit, almost urgently zipping it up as if he now had a fear of his body being violated. The officer removed his gloves and had a smile on his face. Saying nothing to Sam, the team exited the cell. He could hear them walking away, "I love this part of the job, didn't really need to do that, but worth it to make rich boy feel like one of us!"

Sam was appalled by what he had heard, he couldn't believe this was to teach him a lesson. He believed, he was quite humble person and never pushed his good fortunes on others, but used his good fortunes to help those who weren't so fortunate. How could someone treat him like this?

He sat down on his bed for the night, he put his legs up to his chest and wrapped his arms around them comforting himself. He gently rocked forward and backward, thinking to himself managing his feelings about this entire incident, not only did he feel violated, he felt as if he was being unjustly held without a proper explanation.

Wracking his brains for his next move, Sam jumped up from his position, something took over him. He confidently paced back and forth, then walked over to the door of his cell and banged it, quite mildly initially, but increasing with intensity the more he felt like he wasn't being heard. Then something happened.

Sam's arm paused mid bang. His breathing started to go a little shallower, he could feel his heart begin to pound within his chest and his neck was pulsating creating quite a nauseating sensation. Beads of sweat began to form on his forehead, the room felt like it was beginning to heat up. Sam was completely frozen. He was trapped inside his own body and head.

In his head he wanted to scream and shout out, he wanted to call for his legal representative to come and have him taken out of this hell hole, but he couldn't he was completely stuck. He was physically unable to move.

The beads of sweat now joined together and formed into runs down his face, over his nose and dripping down onto his coverall. The fabric refusing to soak up the droplets as they landed instead they rolled over the unforgiving plastic surface dropping down onto the floor beneath him.

A short moment later, three officers had made their way down to his cell, they released the door locks and opened it up to see a man who moments earlier was a fully compliant and coherent individual now seemingly frozen in position, an angered but apprehensive look on his face. He looked like a sweaty, red faced, anxious statue, his appearance was quite a spectacle, looking so blank and soulless, yet at the same time, showing emotion and physical being.

Unsure of how to react to this, they attempted to move him but his body was frozen stiff. They decided in this instance that they would call for a medical assistant to come and look over him. There was very little else they thought they could actually do.

Within the next ten minutes, medical assistance was on site. A quick response doctor turned up at the door of the cell to see this man still seemingly frozen in position.

The doctor got out his stethoscope, the man was still breathing, he was still exhibiting signs of life, so physically, other than the profuse amount perspiration, there was nothing wrong with him.

During his examination, Sam's body was extremely rigid, there was little flexibility in his joints. The medical assist declared Sam as being in a catatonic state, he needed to be seen by a psychiatric consultant.

The doctor injected Sam with some sedative and muscle relaxant. They had no clue what was going on with him, so for now, they had to treat this as a temporary mental health episode in which they sedated the patient and moved them to a secure medical facility for monitoring.

Slowly, as the relaxant and sedative coursed through Sam's veins, he could feel his world becoming smaller and smaller, his light was dimming and his body loosening. In his head, he was screaming and shouting, but even now to him, that sounded like a distant echo.

CHAPTER TWELVE: THE INSTITUTION

Coming around in a bright white room, Sam's vision was hazey, he had the worst headache he had ever experienced. The light seemed to penetrate his very core and opening his eyes was agonising.

Slowly, Sam came to, still utterly lost, confused and dazed. A booming echoing voice could be heard. Sam was so hazey, he couldn't quite make out what the voice was saying. His eyes still hadn't cleared, his vision was still blurred but he could see there wasn't anyone in the room. He could see little else other than the white walls around him.

The voice continued to boom and yet Sam was still not clear on what it was saying. The voice continued, it seemed to drill down into Sam's very being. It was at this moment something changed. The pitch of the voice seemed to lift, it began to clear. Sam could make out the odd word, one phrase in particular "Keep your eyes closed"

Sam listened, knowing the pain he was in, he chose to follow the instruction. Sam still felt completely powerless to do anything, he was willing himself to get up, to move, to find out what was going on with him. He kept his eyes screwed tightly closed, there was nothing else he would be able to do. He still felt frozen in position and fearful, what if this was now the rest of his life? What if this was now what he was resigned to be? A dribbling, broken mess.

The voice continued, it was repetitive in nature, although Sam was still finding it difficult to determine what was being said. He heard it intently, although the concentration ripped pain through his body, thinking was a task at present, which he could not undertake.

The light in the room momentarily dimmed, even with his eyes closed, Sam sensed the dimming. He wasn't having to close his eyes as hard which eased the tension on the rest of his head. The dimmed lights were helping the pain to ease off, it was helping him get a little greater sense of clarity and it enabled him to hear what was being said.

"You have had a powerful cocktail of drugs, you will be experiencing an intense pain in your head. Similar to a migraine, it will last until we are able to rehydrate you fully. We have dimmed the lights, keep your eyes closed, do not try to move. We believe you have experienced an episode of catatonia. Please do not worry, please do not think this is forever."

Sam's eyes snapped open. He had a sudden sense of sanity, the pain was gone, albeit temporarily as he would find out only a moment later when it returned with vengeance.

The message continued to repeat in the altered pitch. It felt like he was being punished for opening his eyes, if he were able to move, Sam would be rolling around the floor in complete discomfort. His head felt like it was imploding.

Still feeling like he was unable to move, the thoughts went around his head in quick concession, why him? What had he done to deserve this? Why had he just frozen, like a deer in the headlights of a car? Why, after everything he had been through had he frozen up when it came to the confrontation with the authorities? When it came to him thinking about asking for his legal counsel?

A door opened to the room Sam was in, his eyes were still closed and he could sense a person had entered but being in such extreme agony the last time he opened his eyes, he had learned his lesson about opening them. There was a strong smell of perfume in the air, which really didn't help with his headache.

Sam got the idea that he was expecting to hear a woman's voice if someone were to speak, he could sense this person near him, he could feel them doing something to him, but he couldn't make out what was happening.

Seeing his agitation, a voice softly spoke next to him, it was a female's voice, although it being a slightly higher pitch still didn't clarify the words being spoken, they were echoing through his ears, ringing repeatedly, the words having a chromatic ring to them.

Each word spoken took moments to cut into his brain "I am Elizabeth, I am fitting a new drip to help flush the drugs out of your system" the name Elizabeth rang a bell with Sam.

It would be too much of a coincidence if this was the same Elizabeth he had met previously. Who he had saved from the mugger, the same Elizabeth, that allowed him believe he was doing something wrong by trying to care for her and support her when she clearly needed someone to be there. That couldn't be the case.

Sam's breathing began to increase, he began to sweat. His skin felt like it was on fire. It was the same sensation that he had felt back at the police station when he had frozen in time. Frozen in position, was this happening to him again?

He sensed the door to his room open again, not knowing why or how he had sensed this and despite how he felt, there was a complete sense of familiarity. Sam's hearing had mostly returned to him and other than the sensation like he was insatiably overwhelmed by whatever was happening, he felt as if calmness had entered the room.

An elderly gentleman walked over toward Sam, he rested his hand gently on his shoulder. "Sam, I am here for you, I guess you probably won't remember, but are collecting frequent flyer miles with us, we will patch you, we will get you back to you. Don't worry, this is all only temporary"

Still with his eyes closed, Sam sensed a feeling of closeness, a feeling of warmth. It began to calm him, his breathing began to slow, his temperature felt like it began to normalise, and the sweat began to soak away. Who was this man and what did he mean by him having frequent flyer miles?

Sam began to drift away into sleep, whoever this man was, he seemed to ease whatever was going on with him. He seemed to take way the sensations and feelings he was having. How could this be the case? Someone Sam didn't know seemed to be able to make him feel at complete ease with himself.

A few hours later, Elizabeth returned to tend to Sam. She replaced his drip she wiped his face over with a damp cloth and tucked him in for the night.

Another morning came and with it Sam awoke with a clear head. He was able to open his eyes, he was able to see without the splitting pain in his head. The door to his room opened, light streamed in through it.

It was odd. What had been so impactful to him the previous morning, now made little difference. Elizabeth walked meaningfully into the room, her heels clicked on the vinyl floor. Sam could see even under her tunic that her hips swung from side to side with each step that she took. Her perfectly formed chest seemed to fit so well within the top as if it were fitted solely for her. Sam couldn't help but begin to feel a little aroused seeing her silhouette enter the room backed by the hazy morning light.

"Don't worry Sam, that's normal" Elizabeth nodded her head down toward his crotch, which seemed to be expanding the longer he was in her presence.

Embarrassed, Sam slightly turned to the side to hide what he was ashamed of. The smell of Elizabeth's perfume in the air wasn't helping. It was like a familiar scent that got into Sam's core, it made him close his eyes and feel the warmth, care and love he so desperately craved.

"Sam I have bought you some food, you need to eat. The drugs will wear off soon and you will have a hunger like never before. It's good to see that you are able to move, this is a quicker come-back than we have seen from you previously" This struck Sam into deep thought. How many times had he been here previously? How much had he needed this care in order for him to be a "frequent flyer" Sam realised he needed the toilet, with great intensity it hit him like a freight train.

He went to get out of bed, but realised he couldn't. Seeing this Elizabeth turned to him "Sam, you are currently strapped in place for both of our protection, don't worry, if you need to use the facilities, you have a catheter fitted, you wouldn't remember but we had to fit this for you, it's been a week you've been here resting"

This news shocked Sam. He had lost a whole week of his life and hadn't known about it. How could he have been unconscious for a whole week? Either way he needed to utilise the catheter, but with Elizabeth in the room it was a very difficult task to undertake.

Elizabeth walked out of the room having sensed Sam's frustration at struggling to relieve himself. After some time, he did manage to go, although it was an extremely unnatural and uneasy process.

Sam was thinking about his experiences back a few weeks ago when he had saved the woman from the would be mugger, the time he spent with that woman was so special. Assuming this was why the police would be speaking with him. He couldn't possibly think what he had done. Maybe the person he ran into got hurt? Maybe the woman had made a complaint about him, but what had he done wrong? Sam simply didn't know and didn't understand.

The hours had whiled away whilst he had been thinking, strapped in his bed, quite at ease in his own company and thoughts. At the same time as he was tearing himself apart asking himself why he had been arrested he was also curious as to why he had the response he did, why his body went into that state. Why was he feeling so ok now?

The older doctor entered the room, "Sam, I think maybe it's time we tried getting you up to go for a walk, maybe you could accompany me" Sam nodded in agreement. The doctor began to unstrap him, being careful as his wrinkled mature hands seemed to struggle with the restraints. "Sam you are going to feel very sore when you stand, but we will take it carefully, you must trust me I am here to help you, I always have been and I always will be" Again, Sam nodded at the doctor, he slowly began to shuffle around to bring his knees up toward his chest.

The doctor supported his shoulders and slowly lifted him into a seated position "Sam, let's just pause here for a moment, usually after a moment you have a slightly dizzy spell" the doctor was spot on with his comment, Sam had a deep feeling of being tipsy, his head was spinning, he felt slightly out of control.

How could this doctor know so much about how he reacted? He must have been here many times before, but why had he been here so many times before, every little action was causing Sam to slip a little deeper into excessive thinking, then question everything he was going through and had clearly previously gone through.

"Ok Sam let's stand up" the doctor seemed frail, as if he might not be able to support Sam if he weren't to be stable or if he fell down. He knew he was on his own with this and had to put every ounce of effort into not putting the strain on the doctor. "Sam, take a deep breath and count toward ten, exhaling as you stand" He clearly hadn't been paying attention to what the doctor had been saying which caused the carer some frustration. "Sam, pay attention to me, let's work as a team, don't let your mind wonder, you will understand everything shortly, just stay here in the room with me"

Sam knew he had to focus, he had to concentrate on what he was doing and he was ready to put every ounce of will he had into standing. He took a few deep breaths and prepared, "Ok Doc, here goes" taking a deep breath of air in, he began to tremble whilst initially putting weight on his legs. "One, two" he put his arm down to help push himself up but also to steady himself "Three, four and five"

His legs were wobbling like a newly born giraffe, he knew he had to push through this barrier, "Six, seven, eight, Ni...." Sam was upright, his legs were locked in, his knees now rigid, he didn't even want to think about trying to move his feet at that moment.

"Ok Sam, you've done well, interestingly, a count of nearly nine, this is exactly the same as previously, you are following your normal pattern, which means you are doing well, let's keep it up. In a moment, we will definitely get moving but let's let your body normalise in this position for a moment"

Sam agreed, he really didn't feel stable either mentally or physically in that moment. He could feel the life blood flowing back to his limbs bringing with it strength and vitality. He felt refreshed and renewed, he felt strong yet apprehensive. "Ok doc, let's go" Sam lifted one of his feet slowly and cautiously, he found he had the strength to support his frame easily which meant that he grew in confidence and after placing the first foot down, he took a second step. It was like he was learning to walk all over again, but with the knowledge of how it already felt, this was a strange yet invigorating sensation.

Slowly putting one foot in front of the other, being guided by the caring doctor, Sam began to pick up the pace. The doctor had now stepped aside offering Sam his arm for support, Sam quipped "I should be supporting you, old man" the doctor knowingly smiled at him "If only that were the first time I'd heard that joke" Sam smiled back at the good doctor, but had the instant thought that maybe he shouldn't have made the joke.

Walking out into the grounds of wherever they were, the gardens seemed to have a golden hue to them – a slight taint at the edge of their being.

Everything seemed so beautiful and peaceful, maybe there was a reason for him to be in this place. Maybe this was a place he found comfort and calm. "Sam, this is now the eighth time you have been sent to us, it's a good job you're wealthy. You have episodes completely disabling you, Elizabeth has been your primary carer for a long time now and she has pioneered your restorative care and is mostly responsible for you being safe and well"

Sam was a little taken aback by this truth. "How doc, how do I not know that I have been here before, I mean, I don't even know where I am? I don't have a clue why I am here, I know I froze up when the police had me in custody, but I am not sure why. I know they arrested me for an incident that happened, but I don't know what incident, I saved a woman a few weeks back, maybe I hurt someone badly, I didn't mean to I just wanted the woman to be safe, she was being attacked. I know I have some issues, but don't we all? I know I need to manage my mental health, but I guess we all do."

The doctor smiled at him "Did you save the woman, or did the woman save you?" This set Sam off on a wild mind path, his day dreaming began to run free. How could he have been saved by a woman, it hadn't escaped his mind that this woman had the same name as the nurse that had caught Sam's attention in that place. But how could she have saved Sam, how would that be possible?

"Sam, the police were concerned, they had found a man collapsed in the streets, he was a vagrant, he was trying to mug a woman, in the process of saving her, you did quite seriously injure him, you did rescue her from this situation, you did return her to her house after taking her to the pub, that all happened. But my questions was, did she save you, did she allow you to play the hero, to be the nice guy you truly are" This straightened out most of the questions in Sam's head. He finally knew why he had been arrested, he no longer questioned if that situation actually happened. Now all he had to do was answer the police's questions.

The thought that Sam had previously been held in this place, wherever it was, seven times and this was his eighth resonated with him, but it had slightly drifted to the back of his head, to become a worry that he no longer had.

Sam was more concerned as to what prosecution he may face. "Sam, I know you are worrying about the police. You will simply tell them this – Under section three of the law 1967, you were protecting someone who you suspected was having unnecessary or unlawful force placed upon them. You used a pre-emptive strike to disarm the alleged assailant, you had no intention of causing any harm to the alleged assailant, however, you did mean to effect a positive outcome by assisting the alleged victim. You will also state that you regret not following up with appropriate first aid treatment for the alleged attacker, you also regret not following up with the authorities regarding the incident, it was not your intention to purposefully deceive anyone, however, you were not aware of the seriousness of the persons injuries." He paused for a moment "Do I make myself clear Sam, this must be your statement, this must be your only statement, you must not guess as to anything else you would want to tell them or let them lead you down another path of enquiry that could incriminate you. Any other questions they have should be answered with a no comment, I will have your legal representative be present and you will make the above statement written and will not actually speak with the police. You must obey, you must not fail me!"

Sam suddenly felt like a naughty school child. He felt like he had purposefully done something wrong despite, in his opinion, the fact he felt that he had acted in this persons best interests. Why was he being briefed like this?

Surely this man wasn't Sam's legal counsel but was a doctor of some sort "Sam I know where your mind is going now. I know why you acted like you did, I have spent many hours listening to you talk, I have helped you figure out who you are, so I know what you're thinking right now. You can refer to me, as the good doctor, I will give you no details other than this, as we agreed previously, I have helped you, I supported you in your low points and helped you get to your high points"

Sam felt as if this man was able to read his mind, he knew what he was thinking and when he was thinking it. "Sam your disorder is very routine, we figured it out on your fourth visit, and we are hoping by tweaking our responses, we can extend the periods where you do not need our interaction, you shouldn't need to return here for a while. The garden is particularly beautiful at this time of year, so maybe we should reflect a little whilst we are here, maybe we should sit down by the lake, you have previously enjoyed it" Sam agreed and they walked down toward the tranquil lake but he couldn't help but wonder in particular what made him "good"

As they sat watching the world around them in complete silence, this was the perfect place for Sam to be able to reflect on everything that was happening and the information he had to absorb. "Doctor, why don't I remember any of it. Why is there so much of the information I cannot recall?" The good doctor took a deep inhale of breath "Sam, it is difficult to simplify it, but, like a computer, from time to time, they need to shut down in order to clear the temporary memory, well, that function doesn't really switch off for you when you sleep, every once in a while, your body responds to this by literally pulling the power, doing of sorts a hard reset. By making you freeze up like you did do in police custody, it was a full on temporary memory and sensory overload. Nothing more nothing less"

The fog felt like it had cleared, everything felt like it was explained, Sam was at a point where he had few questions left about his condition. But he also did know, he had many questions about his personal life, his wealth, his desire to help others. He wanted desperately to know what this place was, he had assumed it was a mental health facility, but walking around the grounds, it seemed rather less functional than it did luxury.

Sam felt like he was ready to leave, but he didn't know if he was allowed to. He did have a feeling of imposition, or imprisonment, a slight uneasiness like he was trapped there. "Doc, can I leave here? I think I'm ready" the doctor looked him straight in the eyes, "Sam you will be taken from here in three days, this will be into police custody where you will assist them with the statement you will prepare with your counsel. We need to make sure you are a fully functioning unit before releasing you back into the world"

He could now understand the feeling of being trapped and why had he just referred to Sam as a fully functional unit, surely this wasn't a way to make him feel real. This made him feel like a programmed robot. This made him feel like this was more of a commercial enterprise than a facility that worried about his health and wellbeing.

"Doctor, where am I?" the doctor looked uneasy with this question, he shuffled on the seat he was sitting in, awkwardly, looking like he was trying to find the correct phrase or words to say. "Sam, I cannot give you that information, you know this already, but you maybe cannot recall it, we fixed you, when you were written off by others, we took you in when others had resigned you to medication to sedate your condition, we helped build you up and make you a functioning member of society again, do I need to explain further information or will this suffice"

This had done nothing to answer Sam's question. This had not helped him in any way at all. He was now beginning to spiral as to where he may be. Although he knew he only had to sustain an impression of not worrying for the next three days, after which he would be in the police's custody. This could be his forever escape, from what, he did not know. But something inside of him told him not to trust the doctor, told him not to trust wherever he was. If he had ever had a dark day, this was that day.

The pair decided to head back into the facility as dark clouds began to appear on the horizon, moving rapidly toward their position as if chasing them back indoors.

The afternoon had whiled away, it was getting toward the time when Sam was due to eat, he hadn't thought about it until that very moment when it was like an anchor had dropped within him. He was feeling an intense hunger like never before, he was feeling pain from his throat down to his gut which told him, if he didn't eat at that moment, he would collapse in on himself so this is the hunger Sam thought to himself.

Elizabeth had warned him. He hadn't realised what it would be like. It was one of the most intense feelings he had ever had the displeasure of experiencing.

Having returned to his room, with the good doctor parting ways, Sam couldn't wait to rip into the food he had left in there earlier on, he knew there was some juicy looking ripe apples, a few packs of crisps and some other bits and pieces he hadn't really acknowledged. He walked through the door, toward his bed, only to see the tray was no longer there. He also had to do a double take as it appeared he now had a plain white desk against one wall, with a white chair placed at it. There was a second chair next to it, why would he need 2 chairs, he didn't want to acknowledge any of the realistic functions for this equipment being in place, it was easier to fantasise about the weird and wonderful reasons it could be there for.

On the table lay two breakfast oat bars. He didn't care that the other items had been taken away, he was so hungry, and he could do nothing but tear open the packet and begin to devour the bar. "Sam, take it slowly your stomach has shrunk and within moments will be filled" the voice was over the loud speaker in his room, it didn't help with the feeling of being watched but he didn't care. He just needed to get that food inside of him, he needed that fulfilment.

Very quickly, Sam regretted his decision. Two thirds of the way through the first bar, he reached a point where he felt physically unable to continue. Throwing both back down to the table, he was defeated and feeling ashamed of how he had acted, the fact he hadn't listened to the advice he was given even though he knew that it was most likely right, proved that he was still the person he had always been.

This was a sense of reassurance for him, but it was also a point at which he realised he was completely exhausted, having been comatose for a whole week without realising, then going on the emotional and physical journey he had just been on had worn him down. Quickly he fell into a deep state of sleep, resting and restoring.

Sam had a hell of a few days ahead of him, little was he to know what he was yet to face.

CHAPTER THIRTEEN: OF A DENIABLE NATURE

With a cough and a splutter, Roger rolled over and woke himself with one big last snore of the night. His alarm began to buzz and vibrate, his eyes opened wide, it was operation day and it was the day he got to be back in his prime.

One more time for the glory days Roger thought to himself with an excited smile on his face. He rolled off his mattress onto his feet, quickly grabbing his cargo trousers, vest and socks, throwing them all on in a disorganised fashion. Still straightening his t-shirt, he grabbed his toothbrush and began to scrub his teeth furiously, I won't be doing this again for a few days, he thought to himself, as he hacked away at his neglected gums.

Throwing down his toothbrush, Roger managed to finish packing up his entire kit bag the night previously so he could be ready and waiting for the transport when it turned up.

Not wanting to take any outdated weaponry, the only item that would differentiate him from any other tourist was his Fairbairn-Sykes, hanging freely on full display for anyone to see. There was no point him hiding it, this weapon was specific to his former days, his former role, his former life. Not only did this tell any person with combat experience, he was one of the best and earned this through a tough career, but that he still has it and knowing where it comes from, would still happily use it if necessary. This was not just a killing blade, this was a statement.

Looking more like a lorry driver these days than a soldier, He had packed plenty of cigarettes, he didn't think he would smoke them all, but he also didn't know how long he would be gone. The assumption was that this would be a quick in and out job, "Home by dinner" he laughed to himself as he loaded up his bag onto his back.

Roger lit a cigarette up as he slammed shut the unstable door to his house. He looked down and saw the phone still stranded in the doorway – with all the effort he had gone to, to clean the remainder of the property, he hadn't made too much effort on the front deck. This triggered Roger to think back to it being there, why had he had that weird phone call? What were they talking about – was this some kind of phone call from Max? Or someone within the organisation he was working for? "No matter, let's do this!" He said to himself, not trying to overthink the connection between the phone call and Max's visit.

Shortly following stubbing out his cigarette, Roger reached for the packet and lit up the next one, he was clearly more anxious about going on this mission than he thought he would be. A snatch and grab was the easy part, no shots fired, maybe not so easy knowing he was off into Eastern European territories.

He didn't have much time to think this over as an unmarked white van turned up. A man jumped out of the van as Roger was making his way down the driveway to where the van had stopped. The driver opened up the rear doors of the van and motioned to Roger to get in. His aged bones took a little waking up, maybe this was the drink wearing off, but he could definitely feel the strain from his kit bag on his legs as he awkwardly climbed into the back of the van. "Floor job is it, it's been a while" Roger suggested to the driver, who nodded in acknowledgment but made no other effort to communicate.

The doors quickly slammed shut, as if he were almost being snatched and grabbed himself, the driver was back in the front in no time at all. Roger imagined the driver might not have even had the time to put his seatbelt back on again with the speed at which the engine began to wind up and the vehicle began to move. This definitely wasn't going to be a comfortable or fun ride for him in the back of a decked out van on his way to who knows where, which would take goodness only knows how long. There were so many unknowns.

It was at this point Roger began to question everything. He hadn't imagined he would ever need to question what he was doing or where he was going especially if it were a previously senior officer that asked him to undertake a task, he just knew he would do it. Now he was in this position, all kinds of anxieties had begun to arise, maybe this was just alcoholic's remorse kicking in. Maybe he was just coming to his senses, after years of passively trying to drink himself to death he was now making all of these changes as the result of someone asking him to undertake a small mission for him. Was this the wisest move to make? Who cares, *what do I have to lose!* Roger thought to himself.

Around an hour and many bruising bumpy lanes later, the van containing Roger pulled to a final halt. He was cautious as to what the doors might open to, he wasn't paranoid, but wanted to make sure he would be protected if the worst case scenario would be what greeted him.

He squatted placing his kit bag upright with his blade to hand. Posing in a caveman like fashion, coiled like a snake he was ready to strike should he need to.

Eventually after what seemed like an eternity of waiting and paused breaths, listening to the sounds being made around him, the back doors of the van flung open. Slightly tightening his pose, bright floodlights shone in from the distance and despite him being able to see Max's familiar silhouette, he could make out many others in the distance too.

"At ease bunny, everything is above board, no one is here to harm you" Roger felt reassured upon hearing his voice. He grabbed his bag and sheathed his knife, crouching as he made his way out of the van. Stepping down out of it clumsily, he came to his senses, placed his bag on his back, stood up straight and to attention at the rear of the vehicle.

No matter how far distanced the time was, when a Rupert commanded your attention, you buckled down, stood to attention and prepared for a beasting.

"At ease Roger, we are not so formal here. I want to introduce you to a few people. A lot has changed since our time, modern technology has developed, there are lots of new tricks to make this an easy job for us to undertake. but I still need one of the most experienced men I know by my side, someone I can trust to have my back if it gets messy" Roger felt a little easier hearing this, he wasn't aware that Max would be going in with him, he thought he would be flying solo or working with a team ill equipped and poorly trained for the task.

"What, where and when – I'm there, let's do it" Roger seemed a little over eager to know all of the details "You know a good soldier follows commands, not asks questions. Trust me, this one is easy, we just need to use everything at our disposal to achieve this relatively covertly, but, I need you to trust me and the team I have spent years building and training to bring them up to the standards expected in our time" Again the reassurance was an overwhelming feeling, Roger felt tingles up the back of his spine, he felt alive and invigorated. He remembered this feeling, this was a feeling he used to relish.

He had been told many times that the mission would be an easy one only to come back from it with yet another war wound, or another unbelievable story to tell to the rest of the drinkers in the local establishments, that in fact seemed so farfetched that it may just be true. Or in the worst case scenario as on some occasions, coming back with his friends in boxes.

Roger's head was alive with thoughts, emotions and feelings, he knew this was the result of the adrenaline coursing through his veins, it was the result of him spending years trying to repress those feelings by drinking the days away so he could end up in a box, but he couldn't contain them, he couldn't even hear what was being said by Max who was standing toe to toe with him.

"Bunny, come back to the room, get your head in the game, wheels up in 2 hours, briefing and intro's to follow" Roger clicked back in, almost only for the summary of what had been barked at him a moment ago.

"So you're from the old days, why does he call you Bunny, seems a bit of an odd one?" A young, intellectual looking man questioned Roger without making eye contact or even taking his eyes away from the laptop screen he was staring at. "I've never seen him bring any dinosaurs like you back" Again he quipped taking verbal shots in an arrogant and insulting manner. This began to wind Roger up, he didn't know if he would be able to stand these children around him "Am I bothering you bunny, you seem to have gone a little red in the face" By this time Roger was trying hard not to lose his cool, but he was feeling a rage build up inside of him.

This was quickly extinguished when the screen of the laptop was closed and the young person stood up, he was only the same height of Roger's chest – built like a bean pole and with glasses with the thickness of milk bottle bases, all he could do was laugh at this little boy. "Max, why have you recruited a child that looks like a skinny Ronny Corbet, no wonder you needed me" Roger roared a belly laugh as the young man shrunk away embarrassed and slightly upset, this forced him to laugh even harder "Ah, he can give it but he definitely can't take it" Max walked over to the young man and bought him back over to Roger sighing as he bought them together "Bunny, be nice, this one is Digi, he does all of the computers and comms for us. I like your description, but try to keep on his good side, this boy has saved my skin more times than I care to think of! He's just a bit of a smart arse"

They both smiled, Roger offered out one of his big paws to shake hands with Digi. The young man offered out one of his nimble hands obviously being rather dwarfed, he now felt both insecure about his appearance to Roger and his physical being.

"When you don't know someone my good man, best not to insult them." Roger raised his eyebrows as he bent down looking eye to eye whilst shaking Digi's hand with patronising effect.

Both men smiled "I thought you squaddie lot didn't get upset with little insults, lesson learnt" they shook hands meaningfully and walked away from each other. "Come on chaps briefing time" Max shouted through the hanger they were in. The noise resonated off the empty building, echoing in each of their ears, echoing in the still of the morning.

"Fall in chaps" the boys quickly lined up, with Roger and Max seemingly standing literally head and shoulders above the rest of the team. All of the men had an elite military past, so they were prepared for what was about to happen "We all have a common goal with this mission, we all have one thing to achieve, to grab the girl. If we can manage it, I'd like to also come back alive. I don't know about any of you?" The lined up squad seemingly showed no emotion, this seemed at this moment, like a standard mission brief. "We fly now in one hours and forty five minutes, the bird is being fuelled and loaded as we speak. Those who are going in, will drop in at targeted locations. You will be in teams of two, you will follow orders and you will hold your fire"

This had started to take a slightly alternative turn, Roger had never been through this much briefing which seemed so vague on detail. He tried not to overthink it, he tried to listen and be in that moment. To take in what was actually being revealed to him.

"Alpha team, you will drop in first, you will setup a boundary watch covering with long range weapons, North and East Infil and exfil from the site, Bravo team you will setup a boundary watch covering South and West Infil and exfil from the site again with long range weapons, Charlie team which is Bunny and I, we will undertake the task in hand, Delta team you will prep for sharp shots from far off, if it goes belly up, save a round for me and a round for bunny. We cannot be captured under any circumstances"

This seemed like it was shaping up to potentially be a mission that Roger may not come back from, the black dread seemed to wash over him, the thoughts that he may not make it out alive had taken many of his colleagues over the years.

That seed of doubt doesn't have to be sown too deeply in order for it to take root and begin to grow. Once it sets in, it becomes a point of main focus and as any good soldier allows you to know, nothing can be on your mind except the mission, any distraction can be an extraction in a box!

"Is this girl worth it?" Roger questioned whilst Max continued his briefing, detailing the plan for retrieving her. "Bunny, it is not my question to ask if anyone is worth being retrieved, it is my job to get on and do it, it is your job to get on and do it, let those above us worry about if anyone's life is worth it!"

Roger felt like he had maybe embarrassed Max, he felt a little guilty as to why he had asked that question. Years of being around very few people had obviously limited his social skills. It had limited his abilities to not just speak whenever something came into his head. He had to make a conscious effort not to do that again. He didn't want to be responsible for compromising the operation, or for compromising the belief that the task was worth undertaking.

"Right chaps, brief is now ended, grub up, 60 minutes to wheels up, on transport in 15" All of the men fell out from their position, they made their way to where the food was and grabbed whatever they could do to keep them going, it might be days until they had a hearty meal again so any quick snacks they could pocket may just keep them going whilst they were in the field.

The time flew by, one by one, they grabbed their kit bags and headed toward the plane. A commercial small scale airport, as the one they were at didn't really have the capacity to accommodate the Airbus A400M that was sat on the runway waiting for its payload of troops. However, the plane had managed to land there so Roger was sure there was enough room for it to get them back off the ground again. It didn't help the awkward feeling he always had prior to a mission that everything would go wrong before they had even left the ground.

The anxieties Roger was building began to overwhelm him, it had been years since he had done anything like this, what if he had forgotten his training. He knew when he was on the ground and had Max by his side, he would be in the moment and he would recall all he had learned over the years, he would rely on his reflex memory.

He wouldn't let Max down, not on this one, it seemed like it was too important. His sense of owing to Max was what was driving him now. He needed to complete this and come back to life not just for his own sake but also for that of his former captain.

The teams took their seats, Roger could see Max had taken the seat at the very back of the plane. He had done this on many occasions when they had flown out of places previously although he wasn't sure why. The rear was the worst place to sit, it was the bumpiest, it was the most prone to turbulence and was also the coldest when the doors opened, if you weren't first to jump. But still, for old times' sake he opted to sit close to him.

Maybe this was for a little reassurance for himself rather than to show solidarity, maybe this was just because he was anxious about speaking with any of the team around him.

Everyone was now buckled in place, they all had their kit bags ready and parachutes fitted. Now was when the nerves began to really build. Now was the time that caused any troop the most stress and anxiety. Now was the time that preparing one's head was of vital importance.

The engines fired up, the sun had barely properly risen as the large aircraft engines began to whirr into life. Within moments, the momentum of the plane taxiing onto the runway became apparent. This was it, this was wheels up. There was no turning back now.

CHAPTER FOURTEEN: GET IT DONE!

Four hours in and the journey in the back of one of these planes never got any easier. It was cramped, which was ironic. It was uncomfortable in extreme measure, your backside was hard pressed against an inflexible metal plate with the harness pulling your back into the rear of the seat which again was an inflexible metal plate. The idea was, that having a parachute bag on and other protective gear which should pad it out and make it a little more bearable, it didn't, it made it all the more uncomfortable with little option to move.

It was noisy, noisier than you could ever imagine, the sound of the wind constantly howling past the tail of the plane, the movement of the flaps with the continuous corrections being made throughout the flight. The sound of the jet turbines powering up and continuously pulsing throughout reverberated through the fuselage.

"Time to get ready to drop in chaps" Max shouted up the breadth of the plane. The team simultaneously pinged their seatbelts off, stood and began preparing their kit.

"All ready Bunny?" max shouted toward Roger, he nodded, but the truth was he wasn't, he didn't actually know if he was at least. It had been many years since he had dropped out the back of an aeroplane, many more since he dropped out the back of one into a none agreed territory.

The hatch dropped and the noise began to crescendo, as the

cabin began to equalise in pressure, it felt like their ears were about to explode, this was always a part of dropping that Roger had not enjoyed. The lights turned on at the rear and the teams began to pair up in the order they would go in, Digi was still seated with his computers fully functioning around him and Roger envied him. Why did he get to stay in the plane in the relative safety whilst these skilled individuals had to go down and potentially be fodder?

The answer was obvious – they were the ones who were skilled. They were the ones who had the ability to make this mission a success, they were the only ones that this mission was critical to. Roger suddenly realised, he had gone along with this, but he didn't know why, he didn't even know if he was getting paid, smiling to himself, he knew that the reason he had agreed was because he missed this life. He missed the rush, the thrill of not knowing if he was ever going to come back alive.

The first light flashed green signalling Alpha team to drop. They were flying low, so chutes would have to be opened exceptionally quickly, but they needed to be low in order to avoid any radar detection. This made the drop all the more challenging as it meant that everything had to be remembered in double quick time, only 5 seconds of stable freefall prior to opening the chute.

Alpha team jumped, this was no issue, and they went. Next up Bravo team, Rogers's leg began to shake. It was an adrenaline shake and he knew nothing he could do could stop it, he just had to ride out the storm and make sure he was ready when that light changed over. The light changed and Bravo team jumped. It was mission critical that there were no delays in the jump. It was vital that everything went to plan. Roger heard the comms come up in his ear, he had been seemingly deaf to this up to this point. "Bunny, get your head in the game, it's the cap and you up next. Listen to my command I will lead operational procedure as well as feeding you information whilst you are on the ground"

Double clicking his chest mic, Roger confirmed. Both legs were now trembling, but he didn't have time to think about how anxious he was, their light had changed over to green. It was time for them to go! Almost without hesitation, Roger ran toward the rear of the plane without stopping. He continued to run through the air for a few seconds, which although an unconventional exit, achieved the same end goal. He had forgotten how freeing this sensation was. Falling freely through the air, the wind rushing past, looking to get eyes on Max. He spotted him a small distance away, seeing only the small red flashing LED light that they were all wearing around their necks. This was the problem with dropping in the dark, everything became that little bit more difficult.

Watching his altimeter, the 5 seconds the guys had to wait seemed like forever. Then it was time, this was another part of dropping that wasn't the most fun, when the chute opened. The sudden sensation of gravity as your stomach wants to continue falling but the rest of you slows as the parachute fills with air and takes the strain.

The controlled fall was a short lived prospect, the time seemed to fade away as they were preparing to hit terra firma. Comms came over the radio "3, 2, 1, and that should be the big boys dropped off at day care"

Both Max and Roger seemed to hit the ground rather hard considering they were using parachutes to slow them. But still, seconds later they were both back to their feet, weapons drawn and at the ready with their parachutes off their backs and hidden in the undergrowth. In the distance stood the target building. It was bland and undefined, no obvious points at which would cause concern. Max gestured to Roger as they evaluated their position and synchronised their watches, little went over communication channels other than a series of clicks on the throat microphones to confirm each team were in position.

They stalked in a low orientation through the trees, working their way toward the target. This location did not seem to be of particular importance, there seemed to be no external security, there were no fences and it was just a building in the middle of nowhere. "Don't let your guard down bunny" whispered Max through the comms "it looks deserted but we need to be sure. You know the plan, we go in, we get the girl, we get out and we hit the RV point. Intel says she is in the central room, 5 guards should be inside with her, either that or no guards and she's been left alone to slowly become forgotten about, either way don't drop your guard"

"Got it cap" quickly replied Roger, he knew this was his chance and he loved it! The adrenaline was coursing through his veins, he could feel every sensation amplified, he felt alive, for the first time in years his system was pumping and ready to go. This was his day to come back to life, his chance to have a real shot at making himself new again, his chance to be someone who makes a difference, even if it is in the shadowy unknowns.

They approached the 50 yard proximity mark. "Hold, hold, hold" came over the comms, both men went to ground being as still and silent as possible. "The penetrator shows mines, not many but a few, keep your course due east, enter the door directly in front of you this should avoid any unnecessary loss to life and limb"

And like that the game changed.

It became real, there was now a real risk to life. Not just some wargames happening for fun. "Bunny, lets proceed, I'll take lead, keep a hand on my shoulder and follow my footprints, if you hear the click then move quick and make the RV forget the girl and exfil the team to safety" the amount of trust that Max was placing in Roger seemed like a large undertaking. He was trusting him if things went wrong to get everyone out safely. "Cap. If it goes belly up white phos me, I don't want to be put in a hole in the ground, I'd prefer to be the cop out" Max nodded. This was something no soldier ever expected to have to make the decision to do, however, it was an option and clearly one Roger had contemplated. But this also told Max that Roger was willing to do what was necessary for the mission. He always had and he guessed he always would do!

The adrenaline was at an all-time high as the two men reached the door of the building. They fitted breach charges around the handle and potential hinge points. They knew they had to do this part in a less discreet way, but without drawing attention from too far out. They plugged the wires in and stood to the sides. Each man checked his weapon, Roger prepared himself whilst another series of throat clicks went across the comms. "Breach in 3, 2, 1" and almighty flash of fiery smoke came from the door accompanied by a muffled thud of covered plastic explosives being set off.

Roger reached around the side of the door way and threw a stun grenade through the doorway, it seemed only milliseconds after he had thrown it than it had gone off and the two men had stormed into the building. The men entered, wearing night op goggles enabled them to see several men on the floor of the building covering their ears and heads. They ran straight in and whilst Max applied quick cuffs and gags to the men on the floor, Roger stood guard and scoped out their next move.

Having quickly dealt with the three men in the first room, they knew there was a chance of seeing 2 more at least. Leading with their silenced weapons the men began to move through the first room cautiously into the second, not wanting to move in a predictable motion, they didn't use a grenade when entering the second, seeing the guards in the first only had one handgun between them lowered the risk of injury to a bare minimum.

This should have been the central room, however it lead them into a corridor where they had several other rooms to investigate. "Let me take point Bunny, I know what this one looks like from the file, there could be others here too" Roger slowed and crouched whilst Max took the primary position. Leading the way he managed to quickly check through three of the other rooms, they were all vacant, so after a quick check they proceeded on down the corridor. It came to a final room, it seemed the building was leading them to this point.

They slowed on their approach to it, silently motioning to each other for the plan of attack. Max was trying to tell Roger not to worry, for in one of the three rooms he had checked, he had started a small fire, hopefully drawing out any remaining guards as it began to take hold. They paused, it was only for a few seconds but they paused.

Within the next moment, time seemed to slow and be moving in a slow motion. There was shouting in some sort of Eastern European language that whilst sounding familiar could not be understood by Roger. Two men seemed to be communicating and heavy footsteps came toward the door they were hiding by.

One man passed through, it didn't seem like he was hanging about for anyone, he didn't look back, another man could be heard approaching the doorway along with the sound of dragging and some muffled screams.

The second guard just walked through the doorway when the butt of a rifle was bought down on the side of his temple heavily, making a loud cracking sound as it made contact with his skull.

The man dropped to the floor like a dead weight. He dropped the weapon he was carrying. He also dropped the person he was dragging out with him. Roger looked down and laughed "it's a Twofer" he jubilantly proclaimed. Both Max and Roger bent down and picked up the person being dragged along the floor. "Name" Max demanded of this person, they said nothing but still stifled screams.

Both Roger and Max could tell this was a female from her build and from her vocalisation. "IMYA, NAZOV" Max was now screaming in various Eastern European languages at this woman, knowing the HVT couldn't speak any English. "ADRIANA, ADRIANA, ADRIANA" she retorted in the loudest and clearest voice she could bring to with a gag in her mouth.

Max came over the radio "HVT acquired, making our exit, one ran for it has anyone exited?" "Cap we have eyes on the door, negative, no eyes on the x-ray" This again changed the mood, from excited to dangerous, both Max and Roger had seen the man run off with an assault rifle.

They knew he could be waiting around any of those corners. "Let's leave this building in a noisy way Bunny, weapons are released for primary intervention, do not wait to be fired upon" Roger took point on leading the way out of the building, keeping low and checking each corner and doorway as he went toward and through them.

He could now see a raging blaze from a room down the hall. He knew the man wouldn't have run into that room. He checked the first he came to, raised his gun and looked for the heat signature in his night vision goggles. There was nothing here. He moved quickly back out of it on toward the next room, again checking thoroughly to find nothing. Roger closed over the door of the room that was on fire whilst Max was hanging back with the HVT. The handle to that door quickly became too hot to hold.

Being an outside of the box thinker was one of Rogers's special talents. So neither Max nor himself were surprised when Roger quickly whipped the door of the room back open again, causing a flashback to move out into the corridor and throughout the room as the oxygen rushed back into it. If there was someone hiding in there, they wouldn't be hiding for too long as the room was fully engulfed in flame and heavy black smoke.

Both of the men and Adriana were still crouched on the floor when the muzzle of an assault rifle appeared around the corner of the door frame from the first room. Neither of the men had seen this and before they knew it, they were in an open corridor with no cover being fired at. "Lay Low, Ležať nízko, Zalozhit'" shouted Max to Adriana as the walls seemed to absorb this disorganised array of bullets being fired. "Clips emptying" shouted Roger as the gun was hastily withdrawn from around the corner.

Pulling one stun grenade and one frag grenade from his tool belt, Roger hoped for the best when throwing them through the doorway, the best outcome being unfortunately the loss of life of the four men, three of whom were previously cuffed and gagged. This would leave the way clear for the three to exit and begin to head toward the RV.

A series of bangs, accompanied by a flash of light and the sound of many small metal components hitting metallic surfaces resounded through the corridor. The location they were in was seriously heating up at this point and no matter what they were to face in the next room, they knew they had to move sooner than later. "Bunny, let me take point. As we go through we cover front and rear just in case, let's get this one back alive and deprogrammed" Roger clicked down his throat mic to confirm he understood.

They rounded the corner moving closely with Adriana wedged between them. They saw the three men who were previously cuffed and gagged all laying slain on the floor, there was still no sign of the fourth man. He hadn't exited, he must still be there. The boys scanned all of the corners. Roger saw the faintest reflection in the light available of something in the further corner away from them.

He went over to investigate, it looked as if the grenades had done their job and he seemed also to be down, an empty magazine on one side of him, what seemed to be a full magazine the other side. Roger kicked away the weapon from his hand, he didn't want to take any chances, and he had been in this position before. The thud off silenced rounds although not a large sound, still seemed to resonate momentarily in the main room as the boys made sure all four really were despatched.

It was never a nice feeling knowing that you had taken someone's life, but if this girl was worth all of this risk, then there must be a reason she needed to return with them.

The two men quickly headed toward the door of the building

still a little hazed from both the smoke and the firefight. Sandwiched between them still was Adriana who still looked completely lost, still cuffed and gagged.

They paused for a moment to catch their breath and get their bearings. "It's Digi, head due west from your current location to miss the mines" "Will do" checked back Max, sometimes just having that voice to remind you could help clear everything up. It could quickly bring you back into a sense of reality.

"Bravo team – vehicle inbound from the south with 8 potential x-rays, are weapons still free?" "Negative – no unnecessary attention drawn or loss to life" Max turned to Roger "Double time Bunny let's get this girl out of here" neither of them had noticed her silently beginning to slip away, neither the men nor any of those watching over their progress had identified where she was walking.

It was only when they heard a click and the sound of a whizz that they both hit the ground as quickly as possible. Looking around they saw a cloud of red mist. Body parts landing from the site where someone had trodden previously. Adriana had escaped but had run across the patch of mines triggering multiple explosions. "Oh for F..." Rogers frustration was quickly intervened by Max "No time for that now bunny, let's get out of here, it's about to get noisy"

There was nothing else the men could do at this point than make their way to the collection zone. "All teams head to RV, wheels up 6 minutes" Max sounded incredibly disappointed. He didn't like failing a mission, but none of the team did. This was a woman who likely didn't even know she was being rescued. This was a woman who was excessively violent but had suffered at the hands of many through her short life. This was a woman who was now in pieces due to the rescue attempt. The silence on the return to the RV point was deafening.

The thoughts resounded with both men, they nearly completed the mission and they nearly returned the girl. They should have had eyes on her instead of being distracted by their own sense of satisfaction. Their own sense of the glory days relived. Hitting the RV was a sombre affair, no one talked. No one made eye contact. No one dared breathe too loudly. This had been a massive waste of time and resources. As well as a horrendous waste of lives, four men possibly five lost without cause, one woman lost albeit due to her own volition. But that didn't matter at this point, all the men could think of was returning. You could never dwell on the lives lost or the lives taken otherwise they would eternally haunt you.

Jumping into the helicopter, the men knew it would be another long and silent return journey, not only that, it would be even more difficult on their return. This team with a flawless record, never having lost a target or failed a mission, took a risk on a former asset, which had since lead to the loss of the HVT's life. Max would have to justify this to his boss. He would have to show that neither he, nor his team had made any mistakes. They would have to show how they could have rectified the issue, how they could have stopped it from happening.

These thoughts were resoundingly loud within the heads of everyone there. Not only did Roger have to deal with the guilt of taking those men's life, but also the girl losing her life and the worry now that he would be scape goated.

He would be the cop out despite it not necessarily being his fault that this had happened. Despite him following every order to keep weapons out of use. To keep everything grab and go, as discussed in the brief.

Nothing else to do now other than sleep the hours away until they were back. They had no control over anything, what would be, would be.

As the sun rose over the horizon, the helicopter pulled into a private airport. The men had to swap over to a smaller capacity aircraft for the remainder of their journey. It created a bit of an issue, as there was lots of kit and lots of men, but little space. It presented a tight squeeze, but they needed to do it to get back home. No one on that journey home was comfortable physically or mentally. This wasn't a group of people who were used to losing battles. This was a group of men who were used to succeeding and getting paid well for doing so.

Several cramped hours later, the plane landed at the same private airport they had left from such a short time previously. The men began to filter off the aircraft grabbing their equipment as they did. There was no way they wanted to return to the plane once they had left it. Within a few short moments the whole team were back in the hanger, awaiting the debrief. Max looked over them, it had been a difficult night, he had some tough decisions to make and lots of explaining to do.

In the corner of the shadowy complex there were a group of people lurking, the stench of cigarette smoke was heavy in the air and this made Roger have an urgent intense craving. He hadn't had a cigarette in quite a while and now he had smelt one being smoked, all that was on his mind was getting one and smoking it, taking that time to reflect on the nights events. The crowd hung in the shadows appearing eager for an explanation.

Max strolled over and was having a rather animated conversation with them. A laugh erupted from that general area, this intrigued Roger as he didn't think this would be how those from above, who he assumed Max was talking to, would have taken the news of the failed operation.

Max walked back over to his team, which included Roger now returning to it with a cigarette in one hand and petrol lighter in the other. He had his trademark smile on his face. "Well chaps, they've said it was one of the expected outcomes, not ideal, but at least the information can't be had by anyone else, so still a positive, we will still be paid, we did undertake the task, we were never here or there" despite what the team thought, for Roger the wave of relief wasn't as fulfilling as he had expected.

Just because this group of people deemed the mission to be a success, doesn't mean in his eyes that it actually was. He thought it was the exact opposite.

"Grab a beer, let's go and debrief in the lounge" Max instructed. Each of the men didn't really feel deserving of going to grab a beer, but they still did, they were told to.

They moved their way up to the lounge abandoning the kit bags they had on them previously. The comfortable seating provided in the lounge was a welcoming area especially for Roger who felt that he really needed to rest properly after going through the process of flying in and out of hostile territory in just a single day having "failed" their mission to bring the HVT back for interrogation. He felt like a failure, even though it was along the lines of one of the projected outcomes.

"Chaps, this girl we went to save, she was part of a previous trial for something, somewhere and I have limited details. She was prone to extreme violence, she had been in a mental hospital for the past year or so. Reading her file, she had also murdered, in a cold blooded fashion, her coach. No one knows why, but when she was questioned, she claimed she'd taken some strange phone calls that had driven her to do it"

Roger suddenly stopped his party of self-pity, sat up and listened. "She may well be in the best place she could be now, wherever that is" Max smiled, Roger was a little annoyed at his dismissive nature at the loss of human life.

He knew they needed to disassociate from the situation to help handle the guilt of taking lives, but he still felt they owed her something. This girl had strange phone calls that allegedly made her kill someone, which was strange, he was at the point where he needed more information on this.

He had heard of Loony Laura, he himself had a weird phone calling telling him to save a girl. How was this all linked, it had to be in some way, it had to be undeniably linked, but he just couldn't fathom why.

"Fall out chaps, return transports 2 hours off, I've ordered pizza's let's have a chill out and a few more beers. We all need It now, we all need to unwind" Max left the room, which left Roger smoking a cigarette in the corner, whilst the rest of the team were laughing and joking.

To Roger, this seemed very disrespectful and he didn't want to partake! He did however indulge in the beer and pizzas, why not, he deserved it after all he had been through that evening.

CHAPTER FIFTEEN: AN INTERVENTION

The day began like any other would do. Terry in the kitchen drinking his coffee, Herman bowling down the stairs just in time for them both to walk out the front door. Herman definitely was not a morning person.

Following his typical morning routine, Terry grabbed his keys, wallet and mobile phone placing each where it belonged for easy access, before they both headed out of the door. Getting in their nice new but used car was still something of a novelty for them.

They were pleased to be seen driving down the street in it, proud that they had lifted themselves out of the gutter or at least the day to day routine.

They were now arriving in at the office early, which was far from the achievement of previously only sometimes making it there in time. They still had the same laid back attitude, but they managed to have an invigorated nature along with it.

"Right Hermy, we've got to go back and see that Laura, you ready for another visit today? Or did you want to put it off temporarily in case the doctor plays any more tricks on you, we also have to follow up with that drunk, what do you fancy?"

Herman huffed, he knew the good doctor had got one over on him and that never felt very nice. That never felt like a positive outcome to a situation. "I think we should definitely follow up with Roger. He seems like a good guy, just a bit eccentric. Yeah, lets drive out and see him, find out what his story is" Terry acknowledged Herman's decision and agreed, surely it was worth a punt, maybe this was associated with whatever was going on, but maybe it was also nothing but an old drunk veteran.

They headed out of the station grabbing the file on Roger as they went, one of the junior civilian staff had done some background research on Roger, which included his military service, his social information and everything that had happened with him throughout his lifetime.

This file was big! "Wow, years serving his country to be dishonourably discharged" Herman gawped at it, he couldn't wait to speak with this man he seemed completely intriguing. It showed unfortunately he had faced the loss of his partner, which was under questionable circumstances, following discharge, maybe this was something that wasn't looked into, and maybe he was drinking away his guilt.

"He's just another drunk you know" Terry tried pointing out to Herman. "But, what if he's not, what if this is bigger, what if he did something wrong, what if his partner's loss wasn't questionable, but he is able to answer those questions?" Terry shrugged whilst driving, he didn't know how to answer Herman, he didn't know how to help him see the situation the way he did do.

He guessed he would have to let him just find out for himself. They pulled up to the driveway, having interviewed many drunks in their homes previously, they knew to expect the worst, they knew to expect a room filled with rubbish stinking of stale smoke, litter on every surface. A person who would just do nothing but lead them as far away from the truth as possible. Or purposefully lead them down paths of enquiry that would make them look foolish.

You can imagine the look of surprise on Terry's face when they pulled into the driveway and saw the neatly stacked piles of rubbish, ready to be taken away. The cleaned and organised exterior as if someone had sorted this place out. "Well stone me that is not what I expected. Maybe I will be wrong, maybe we will find something worthwhile here" Herman had a big smile on his face, he knew he needed to trust his instinct, he knew it was driving him to this meeting. He wished he had never ignored it in the first place. "Let's go, I can't wait for this one!" Herman chirped and seemed excited. Terry had never seen him this enthused, for anything other than a pub lunch.

They both got out of the car and walked a little way up the drive. "Doubt this has an MOT" Terry said as they walked past the dilapidated wreck of a van sitting in the driveway. Herman followed behind looking it over and agreeing, it really was a mess, he hoped this thing wasn't driven on the road.

Climbing up the stairs of veranda, they got to the door, looking for a doorbell or knocker, they found no joy, but decided to give the door a heavy knock. After waiting a few moments, there was no answer. "Maybe he's done himself in" said Terry with a slightly hopeful inflection to his voice. "Nah, squaddies like this wouldn't do that I've got a feeling this is going to be good. Would you say Terry that your concern for his welfare warrants just cause to enter without a warrant?"

Terry was not very often shocked by Herman, but this was something he would never have expected him to say...or do. "Erm, well, I guess we could, before you go getting all James Pond, try the door handle" Herman smiled at getting Terry's approval for being a little daring and for the first time in his life, he was taking a risk on something. He was risking his wellbeing, who knew what a guy like this would be capable of.

Herman slowly reached his hand down and placed it on the door handle. He cautiously began to twist it, whilst he was looking down, he couldn't help but notice out the corner of his eye, there was an old telephone with a broken wire down on the floor. This piqued his interest and slowed him down when he was holding the door handle "Look Terry, the phone, do you think it's connected?" Terry smirked at Herman "That's the problem big boy, when you're looking for a connection, you'll often find one in the smallest of instances that seem to make sense, even when it's not connected at all"

In awe of this statement, Herman couldn't help but look upon his partner with admiration and desire. This was maybe one of the wisest things Terry had ever said and despite his gut telling him this "could" be connected, maybe he needed to ignore it on this occasion. "I'll leave it, I'll remember it, but I'll leave it – remember Terry, God is in the detail"

Herman returned his attention to the door handle. He slowly and nervously began to twist it, his imagination was running wild, surely someone who had the history Roger did, would have prepared traps to stop people breaking into their house. Who knows what could await them on the other side of that door.

Having twisted the handle so slowly, a metallic clunk could be heard. It almost sounded vaguely familiar to them. Although they were not so sure why, slowly, Herman began to push the door but felt some resistance, surely if someone was there and alive, they would have heard the noise from the detectives by now. Was there any point continuing or should they go for a look around the building first? "Terry, I'm not scared, but do you think we should go for a look around the building first?" Terry smiled at this big man who usually never stepped out of his comfort zone.

He was showing his fear, he was showing his true self. This was when he was at his weakest and Terry enjoyed his company the most. When Terry could be there for him, could help guide him and give him the confidence he needed to progress and become the great man he knew he was. "Come on big man, you've done the first part if you're scared, stand to the side and give the door a little kick"

Herman did just this, which he was relieved he did a second later as a muzzle flash burst through the door and wood was scattered everywhere. The boys were down on the veranda the moment the gun went off. "Terry, Terry, are you okay, are you alive?" "Yes big man but if you could get your backside off my leg, I'd be even better" thankful for a moment, that his good friend had his back. Herman turned around and gave a big hug to his partner. "Ah mate that was close!" Terry mumbled as he was being consumed by Herman in a big bear hug kind of fashion.

The shock could only last a moment before a vehicle screeching to a halt on the road at the end of the driveway could be heard. Both of them quickly got to their feet and stood in a guarded position looking for what was to come up the driveway. They waited for a few moments but nothing happened, no one came. The vehicle could be heard speeding off, neither of them knew the next move to make, but they assumed it was to go and investigate what had just happened.

They slowly and cautiously made their way back down the drive, back past the wreck of a van, back past their car. It was only a little lower down onto the road, they could see something bundled down on the floor, and there was some camouflage material with whatever was bundled.

They apprehensively moved toward it, still not knowing what it was. For all they knew it could be a bag of kittens, but they didn't want to think that it could be anything untoward. Somehow there was a feeling though that it was.

Terry made the first move over to whatever it was. He cautiously began to investigate what the material was. He began untangling the mass of camo fabric. It felt like there was a bag in amongst whatever this was. "Hang on wait, it's a person, it's a mass of person, in a parachute"

Terry had a sense of urgency now in his voice as both him and Herman began to unpack it. Whatever it was, whoever it was, they were quite cold, quite stiff and pretty much not in a good way. The person was almost wrapped in what became obviously a parachute as if they had been packaged up, securely and respectfully for transport.

As soon as they had finished, neither man wanted to address the other, neither man wanted to ask the questions they felt they should do. Neither man felt they needed to state the obvious. "I'll call it in" Herman said as they both stood there looking down at the body which was covered in blood, of a whole range of colours. Under the blood, under the disfiguration, Herman could see who this was. "Yes, I need an ambulance assist and a doctor to call on a body I've just found, I believe it has been dumped out the back of a vehicle. I also need a cordon team and SOCO"

"Terry, that's Roger" Herman said with a shaky voice. He knew he thought it was stating the obvious when he said this, but he also thought Terry might also be in a little state of shock, maybe Herman had been right all of this time to trust his gut. That there was something not so right about this situation, that maybe there was some link with this person. That God really was in the detail.

Terry confirmed Herman's thoughts by nodding in agreement. He looked over the body, noted the time in his notepad and the stepped away from the body to light up a cigarette. He hadn't smoked in a while, it seemed to be a grounding technique he used when he was feeling a little out of control.

A short time later, there was a whole host of people present at the scene, including the inspector. He wanted to know why they were even looking into this line of enquiry, he wondered how this was linked to the case they were working on. "Well sir, you see, he had reported some strange phone call to us whilst we were having lunch in the pub and we asked him to pop down to the station to leave some details as we were planning the visit to see the suspect at the Asylum. This took priority, so we made this visit the first one of the day today."

"There was no answer and knowing the guy was a bit of a local drunk and having seen the circumstances in which he was flagged on the computer system, we decided to investigate the property with concern for his welfare. When we opened the door it seemed to explode, luckily neither of us were injured –

but I do thank you for your concern – we heard a van pull up. It was there momentarily then it sped of down the lane. We investigated what we thought was an abandoned package, only to find it was a body wrapped in a parachute, we called it in and now I'm stood here explaining myself to you"

"Well boys, that's quite expansive, will I get a break down of your daily bowel movements too? Get the reports done and if there is a link, find it. If there's nothing, write up a new case file and this becomes your secondary following on from the Loon"

Herman took the lead in their response "We will sir, thank you, it is quite interesting. If..." he was halted in his response to the inspector. "Quite honestly I don't care boys, just get it done. I'm not rushing you to wrap the cases up, but I want to see the positive light thrown on you both be worthwhile, prove me wrong, prove to me that it is worthwhile you working these cases" "Will do sir" Herman responded as if he was a scolded school child.

The boys took stock of the situation, they looked around the scene, it was a major investigation, the road had been closed off, the evening was now drawing in so the SOCO team were putting up floodlights around the tent in which they were protecting and investigating the body. "Let's go and have a look around the house to see what we can do" Terry said guiding Herman away from the body.

They wandered back toward the house, Herman got a little panicked as they approached "What if there's more traps" both of them thought about what they may find when they entered, what horrors lay awaiting them. "Let's just be cautious and slow as we walk through it. I bet it's a bit of a mess but nothing should be beyond us being able to deal with it" Terry said trying to persuade Herman that there was nothing to worry about when in fact he was just as nervous about going through the house.

They entered, bypassing the shotgun which was behind the front door, they turned the lights on as they moved through the building, looking on surfaces and in cupboards. There really was nothing of note, the house was vaguely tidy, and it looked like someone had actually made an attempt to clean it. This was a strange experience for someone who lived like Roger did, it was out of the ordinary, and it didn't seem to make sense. They continued to investigate the house finding their way through to the back garden, they continued to scout out, maybe to see what they could find out about Roger.

They came across his little animal graveyard, which although a little creepy wasn't anything that particularly concerned them. Although it did seem quite strange, why would someone have so many dead animals, assuming they were all animals, although with names like Lovey, Bunny & Max, it seemed like a reasonable conclusion to draw.

"I think we've seen everything here Hermy, let's go and get our paperwork done and call it a day, I'm starving, chippy on the way back to the station?" In agreement, Herman hadn't even thought about how hungry he was up until that point. He knew they had quite a large report to do, he knew they had quite a lot of information to portray in the right light. He knew for sure that they needed to find God in the details, because to his mind, there was more to this than they probably could even begin to imagine.

CHAPTER SIXTEEN: ASYLUM BOUND

Sam awoke on the morning of the interview, it had been two long days of thinking over everything that had lead him to this point. Everything that had made him who he was. Most of it he couldn't remember. Some of it was coming back like a kind of amnesia that had kicked in when he had been catatonic.

Sam ruminated over his entire life, how had he come to this, how had he ended up back in this place. How did he end up back potentially at stage one?

The heavy clunk from the door lock bought him back into the room, he was showing no physical effects from either the cocktail of drugs given to him or from his episode, which was good although he was still bemused at the fact he had been locked away like a caged rat.

The door opened and as with other mornings, Elizabeth walked in, Sam couldn't help but be drawn to fantasizing when he saw her walk into the room, maybe one day outside of this he would get the chance to meet her and maybe, they could go out for a drink and see where it went.

Bringing himself back to reality, he knew nothing like that would ever happen, why would she pick someone like him? Just a normal guy with no job, no ambitions and a really bad reaction to fear and threat.

Enough of those thoughts, he had a big day today. He had to face the police interview that he couldn't face previously. It was a scary time, what if it did all happen again, what if Sam froze up and ended up losing another week of his life. What if he had done something wrong how would he live with himself? At the same time, how could he live without knowing if he had done something wrong?

"Come on Sam, I have bought your suit in, this is one you have used previously when leaving here, we know it fits you, or at least we know it did do Try it on, the transport will be here to collect you in a couple of hours. We need to get you interview ready"

Sam got up off his bed, walked around and had a good long look at himself in the mirror, he admired his physique, the way his body looked so chiselled and toned, he hadn't noticed recently but he did really enjoy the way he looked, he could get lost looking at himself for hours on end. It did just then click, that what he was looking in was in fact a two way mirror.

"Who's there? Who's watching me, I'm not really this vain. Turn the light on, let me see whose watching." Nothing happened, for a moment Sam waited, maybe he would get to know who it was, maybe it was the doctor watching him, maybe and most realistically it was just an orderly told to sit and watch him around the clock.

What if it was Elizabeth, did she watch him? Did she like to look at him, whilst he was sleeping, whilst he was getting dressed?

Sam decided again, enough was enough, time to get dressed and ready. It wouldn't take him long, but he wanted to make sure he was presentable he wanted to make sure he looked at his best. Why wouldn't he, after all first impressions that are made are often the only ones that last. If he looked like a crazy man, that is how they would treat him. If he looked like a respectable member of society, then maybe he stood a chance of getting away with whatever it was that had been done.

The few hours passed quickly, they often did when Sam was lost in his own thoughts. He had barely gotten himself together.

Having put on his shirt and trousers but still looking like a scruffy mess, he had spent so long in thinking about making a good impression, that in fact he may just not make a good impression.

The heavy clunk of the door went again and Elizabeth came rushing in "Sam we need to get you dressed, the transport is here to take you for interview" rushing him to his feet, pulling at his trousers to straighten them up Elizabeth was dressing Sam as if he were a naughty school child, who hadn't got dressed when he was told to.

Quickly pulling together his tie and suit jacket Elizabeth put them on him and tied the perfect Windsor knot. Everything she did, seemed like perfection, everything she helped with she did with compassion, why did Sam feel so intrinsically linked with this woman and how come she was so kind to him?

Elizabeth began to rush him further "Sam we have to put these on you for the transport, you have to appear to be under control." Elizabeth cast forth a pair of handcuffs, Sam understandingly held out his hands, he would do anything for her, go to the ends of the earth or lay down his life, but why?

"Sam, I'm going to lead you down to the front now, can you please be compliant for me and listen to my voice, I will not hurt you but it must appear that I am in control" he nodded in agreement, carefully following where she guided him. She led him by the cuffs like a horse being led by its reigns. What had he done to deserve such treatment? Why would she be guiding him like this, there must be some reason, something he was missing, and something he was yet to be told.

"Good afternoon, Officers Brent and Prior here to collect prisoner known as Sam for transport to Queen Street station for questioning, is he ready and available for handover?" Elizabeth guided him forward "This is Sam, he is now free of his Catatonia and is ready to answer any questions you ask. Will you need an assist for interview or are we relieved of the prisoner" The officers looked at each other, with the knowledge that this could all go wrong again, but, they needed to risk that they could interview him without compromise.

"We do not require assistance at this time, if we do, then a medic will be on standby in order to see to Sam, if he does require intervention he will be taken to the state run care facility. But it's all going to be OK isn't it Sam, we're going to get this all sorted aren't we?" Sam had been acknowledged for the first time in this conversation which was a little unnerving for him, but he simply nodded in agreement. Elizabeth paused whilst signing the paperwork for the transfer, "You are aware that Sam must have a legal consultation once he has heard the charges to be bought against him so they can be explained at his own pace in a way that he will understand?" again the officers glanced at each other, they could already sense The Institution were beginning to make their lives difficult.

This had happened before with others and no matter what they did to try and just collect a transfer, it would always end up with the prisoner getting away without answering for any of the crimes they allegedly committed.

"As is his right under law, we will ensure that his legal team are briefed of the charges and he will be allowed to meet with them prior to interview." Elizabeth smiled at them "That's perfect, just for the record, we have captured that confirmation on our surveillance system" The officers again both looked at each other, they both knew that no matter what Sam was there for, he was simply going to give a prepared written statement and say nothing, as many others from here had done before him.

"Come on then Sam, lets change those cuffs over for ours, then we can get you in the car and get on the road" The officers placed their cuffs on him, he was already beginning to feel a little uneasy, with something as small and simple as taking away the comfort of the cuffs that Elizabeth had put on him, but he was strong, he could do this.

He could answer the questions the way he was told to answer them. Sam showed compliance at every step of the way and the officers, although already feeling rather frustrated, showed Sam every ounce of compassion they could muster.

"Okay Sam, you're doing really well so far, we're going to walk out to the car now and get in, we will help you sit down in the back of it then Officer Prior here will strap you in the seatbelt to ensure you arrive at the station safely" Although the tone was slightly patronising Sam thought it best to refrain from commenting on the fact he was a little bit mental, not a little bit slow. He knew they were trying to keep him at ease by informing him of the steps they were going to take and for that he was truly thankful.

Sam accompanied the officers calmly out to the car and needless to say the remainder of the journey went without any issue. Sam didn't want to say anything he shouldn't and at times he really felt driven to ask questions, he felt like he had to have an explanation for where he was coming from, what the institution he had been held at was. He felt like he needed to know why he had been there before, would they be able to tell him? He doubted it.

It wasn't too much later when Sam realised he had been ruminating again, completely lost to this world in a day dream. It was beginning to get dark, they must nearly be at the station by now. "How much longer until we arrive, I could do with using the toilet if possible please" Sam was being as kind and courteous as possible with the officers. "About 10 minutes Sam, can you hold it?"

Sam winced, but he would prefer not to go through the humiliating act of being paraded through a supermarket or convenience store handcuffed to an officer just so he could go to the toilet. "No problem, thank you" Sam had to focus, maybe if he let his mind drift he would be able to close himself off from the need to go to the bathroom.

The car soon pulled into the station, the officers, aware of Sam's desperate need to facilitate, moved quickly. "Sam, we need to get moving if you could do with using the bathroom, we will hold off on processing you, but one of us will have to stand in the bathroom with you, is that understood?" Sam nodded in agreement. He was at the point he would agree to anything in order to relieve himself. They got him out of the car and frog marched him into the station, they reported in with the custody sergeant and let him know they would be taking him to the toilet prior to processing. Sam was so relieved to feel the compassion and kindness, he didn't know why he'd felt this, or hadn't felt this before.

It seemed like Sam was taking a long time to relieve himself, maybe he had been holding it in for a while. But once it was over he felt the most awake he had in a long time. It felt good not to be relieving himself through a tube, it felt good to feel like a man.

Sam washed his hands and made sure that he dried them thoroughly. He didn't want to overdo it but he hadn't felt like he had been able to have a decent wash down in a while.

He was still remaining silent, not volunteering anything other than the occasional confirming smile. He offered the basic information required of him at the custody desk. "I understand your name is Sam, no given family name" Sam replied "Yes sir that is correct." The custody sergeant was a little taken aback by his attitude to being held "you are of the address: The Penthouse, 54 Upper Road?" again he confirmed "Yes sir, that is correct" There seemed to be a pattern emerging. "Sam, I hereby authorise your detention and transfer from The Institution to ourselves in order to investigate allegations made against you to the charge of grievous bodily harm with intent, do you understand" With one final confirmation Sam replied "Yes sir, I do" after a short pause Sam followed up "I understand my legal counsel is aware of my potential detention and should be coming to help me understand the situation and explain it to me fully, prior to us preparing a written statement for you in response to the allegations made"

This request and knowledge of process did take the custody sergeant back a little. Whilst some people knew they had a right to it, not many would request it in the manner. Sam followed up "Obviously my previous arrest didn't go too well, so I'd like to approach it with more caution than usually deemed necessary so I can help you address the allegation. I trust you will understand this and I also trust you could accommodate me during this time. Thank you" Again, almost lost for words, the custody sergeant looked at Sam trying to figure him out. "I think Sam, if you ever find yourself short of a job you could always apply to come and join us, you seem to have a good knowledge" Sam smiled at the officers surrounding him "Unfortunately officers, having previously been involved with the legal side of life, I have a little background knowledge, but don't worry, I will comply with all you ask, there will be few, no comments from me, I know they are frustrating for you"

Sam had just amazed himself and had offered a little more information than he thought maybe he should have done. He let slip about his former legal profession, he had given them a slight upper hand when it came to dealing with him, which of course was never a position that anyone with legal knowledge wanted to be in.

"Would it be possible to wait for my counsel in a soft suite please?" requested Sam. This was not an obligation that they had to comply with, but knowing they could be in for a tricky interview, the sergeant agreed to let this happen.

Only moments after Sam had been bought into the suite, the door knocked and in walked a mature gentleman who looked physically well to do. He had slicked back, white and silver hair, it looked like he had been preened thoroughly prior to him leaving the house, and his suit looked like it was pressed to fit him. He was sure he had met this gentleman before but from where, he couldn't recall.

"Sam I am Ricardo Hernandez, I am your legal counsel. I will be preparing your statement with you. I understand the doctor has briefed you prior to you leaving The Institution is this correct." Not quite sure what to make of this interaction, Sam looked at the lawyer, silently trying to assess him. "Sam, this happens each time, this has happened before, this no doubt will happen again, you have met me many times before, you are a successful former lawyer who had a win on the lottery, you now spend your days helping others less fortunate than yourself. Now we are over the introduction, shall I go and grab us a coffee whilst you process this?" He nodded at the lawyer. What more could he do? Why did he feel like he was being told everything about his life as if he had all of these connections with all of these people? When in fact, despite the familiarity, he felt like it was the first time he was meeting them in real life.

Sam's mind wandered off again, his day dreams had to become less controlled, he knew he could easily end up going down the wrong kind of path if he let them carry him away, he knew his mind was powerful, but he also knew at this point he had to take control of it. He had get back in charge of it.

He was swiftly bought back into the room when Ricardo walked back in with two vend cups of coffee for them. "Sorry, its cheap rubbish, but it's better than no coffee!" Sam took the cup from him, he hadn't had a coffee in a while, so to him, this tasted like pure delight, although the undertones of powdered milk did spoil it a little.

Ricardo grabbed out a notepad and began writing the date and time down, as well as some headings on a piece of paper. "Sam, the police allege that you caused GBH with intent 21 days ago, the victim was a vagrant who was looking through a waste disposal area from one of the restaurants on that stretch of the high street. They say you hit him so hard when you ran into him that you broke multiple ribs, the intent part of the charge shows that you meant to cause this harm to him. Well for a start, I have read what you had said at The Institution and I am aware of how you perceived that interaction. So straight away we can show that the charge will be lessened simply down to GBH at the very most, however the briefing I believe you had is very straight forward, but I will need to get the statement checked over as to my own briefing, so Sam tell me what happened"

Sam had to think for a moment, he was still wrapped up in how much he was enjoying the cheap coffee. "OK, well, I heard what I thought was a scream, I thought I saw a woman being attacked by a man, it looked like he was trying to take her bag, so I ran toward that location and I shoulder checked the man against the wall."

"Essentially I just ran into him. I then picked up the woman and her bag and took her to the pub for a whiskey, after a few hours of calming her, she made it known that she was married, so I took her home to her husband and explained to him what had happened and who I was and that I just wanted to help and was happy to bring he home to him. It was nothing more than this, however, I have been told to make my statement to the effect of, under section three of the law 1967, and I was protecting someone who I suspected was having unnecessary or unlawful force placed upon them in the perpetration of crime."

"I used a pre-emptive strike to disarm the alleged assailant, I had no intention of causing any harm to the alleged assailant, however, I did mean to effect a positive outcome, protecting the alleged victim, I regret not following up with appropriate first aid treatment for the alleged attacker, I also regret not following up with the authorities regarding the incident, it was not my intention to purposefully deceive anyone, however, I was not aware of the seriousness of the persons injuries."

Ricardo gave a big smile. "Between you and the doctor, I shall soon be out of a job! This is the statement we shall give, we will not lead the officers astray, we will not give them any further information, I don't think there will be anyone pushing for a follow up to this, I think you shall be out of this station shortly good sir" He sat patiently and neatly writing up the agreed statement. It did seem to tally with what Sam had said, it did give answers to questions. They felt it was a good statement to give.

There was a knock at the door. "All ready for interview?" it was officer Prior who has helped transport Sam from The Institution to the station and had shown kindness to him. "Our statement will be ready and signed in five minutes, we would then ask if we could pose this prior to any questioning or accusations being made" Officer prior gave a thumbs up and exited the room. "Sam I need you to read this and sign it if you agree. I have combined your recall of events with the statement the good doctor advised you on" Sam took the piece of paper from Ricardo, he read it word for word, although none seemed to sink in, he had made it sound so much more proficient than either the good doctor or himself had made it sound, he had made it sound like he was a hero. When he felt like anything but! He quickly signed it knowing his five minutes was quickly drawing to a close.

Another knock came a second later. Three police officers entered the room, tape recorder in hand. "Good evening Sam, I am officer Smith, present also are officers Prior and Brent who helped with your transport here today. I understand you have a written statement to read to us, would you like me explain the allegation against you at this time?" Sam shook his head. He knew what they were, his brief had explained it "I would just like to read my formal statement if that is okay?" Officer Smith agreed, he wanted to hear what Sam had to say about the events prior to asking any questions about it.

Sam sat and read word for word what Ricardo had written, paying intrinsic attention to how the wording had been placed in order to make him look like the hero. Not like the aggressor. Sam finalised with "This is my full and final statement and I would direct any further questioning toward my legal counsel at this time"

Officer Smith clapped his hands, "Bravo Sam, that was quite the comic book story. I understand this is your statement of events and honestly I agree with you up to the point at which you left Elisabeth with her husband. You see the allegation wasn't only from the vagrant, it was also from the husband. I will quote from the attending officers written report, I attended a scene that resembled a horror movie, there was blood covering every surface surrounding the front door of the house. There was a man lying face down who appeared to be choking on something, every time he coughed more blood spurted out the side of his neck. After I had called for immediate medical assistance I tried to look at how I could help, there was something large and sharp looking sticking out of the man's neck. There was a few holes in his neck and I didn't want to risk exacerbating the condition of the casualty" the officer took a pause as he was aware of Sam's delicate state. He was looking directly at Sam and could see it was like a ton of bricks had just been dropped on him, as if he couldn't believe he was capable of doing this. As if he was now questioning himself.

"Sam, I need you to remain calm, but I also have to explain, your charge is being raised from GBH with intent to attempted murder. Your alleged victim, survived, somehow." The world felt like it was coming crashing down around Sam. The walls had been dropped. Attempted murder was a huge thing, but he was sure none of that had ever happened how could it? That wasn't in Sam's nature. He wasn't out rightly violent, he wasn't aggressive, and how could he have done something like this?

Ricardo spoke up "I need to have a moment of confidence with my client gentlemen, may I?" the officers were happy to leave them alone together, although they weren't comfortable leaving a single person alone with Sam. "The red buzzer is for immediate attention" said Officer Smith as they were leaving the room. Ricardo gave an assuming wave disregarding the comment from the officer. Whilst this had been going on, Sam had gone into one of his signature spirals, trying to work out how this could have happened, trying to figure how he could have done this, surely he couldn't, why would he? He had nothing to gain from doing it.

"Sam I need you to remain in the room with me. I need you to prevent yourself from slipping into catatonia again" Sam hadn't even acknowledged Ricardo speaking, he was on a journey that he couldn't draw himself out of.

How could anyone draw themselves out of that spiral, if someone had done this to another person how could they not recall having done it.

Sam had become unresponsive to outside influence. He was not listening and was off on a journey that Ricardo knew there was no recovery from. He hit the red buzzer and stood well away from Sam, he didn't want to become a victim, he knew Sam in-depth but he had no idea he was capable of something like this, but genuinely thought he could be if he wasn't in the right space of mind.

The room suddenly flooded with officers, Ricardo had lost count and Sam much like before was pretty frozen in position, one arm slightly raised off the desk, one arm across his body supporting himself. They began to evaluate the situation but knew they couldn't move or communicate with him. Thinking quickly, Ricardo pulled out his mobile phone and began to call The Institution, it was quickly snatched away by one of the officers. "No calls sir, specific orders for incarceration of this one in the state Asylum if this happened again. No private fancy clinic, no secret squirrels and funny handshakes" Ricardo wasn't quite sure how to take this, however, he had to report back to the institution either way. It would have to wait until Sam had been taken away. The on call doctor had been prepared this time, following the last report from the clinic he had been at, he took it a little easier on the medication, which still managed to achieve the same result, but would maybe not have so much of an after effect on Sam.

In all of this, the same sensations had filled Sam, a feeling of deep remorse, although he did not know what the remorse was for. A feeling of spiralling out of control of himself and the situation, as if he were falling away from his own sense of self being. The sweat became profuse, the palpitations began to rock his very core, feeling like soundwaves pulsating through his entire being. His arms began to involuntarily raise in the air, when it happened it was almost of another worldly nature. A man frozen in position whose arms seemed like they were on pneumatic lifters slowly raising in the air like a heavy car boot struggling to lift its own weight.

"We need to get him over to the Asylum within the hour, he needs to be there and be strapped down in a cell until we can bring him back up again to see if we can lift the catatonia" The doctor seemed to be panicking. With little time to actually get to the Asylum the decision was made to transport him in one of the police vehicles with a cage in the back. It was maybe not the best decision, but would be quicker at this time of day than it would be to wait for an ambulance and have to top up the medication.

Sam was placed in arm and leg restraints for everyone's protection. Everyone was concerned as to what they were facing, either, he was an extremely good actor or there was something really not right with him. The journey was perilous in the police vehicle, it didn't bode well, although being so relaxed meant the damaged Sam risked suffering on route, would at least be a little limited.

Pulling into the gate of the Asylum, the police vehicle was granted immediate access, it sped through the gate toward and inbound entrance at the rear of the site. Sam's body was quickly flung onto a gurney and strapped into position.

He was then wheeled through the hospital passing various security gates, he knew all this as well as the medication hadn't quite knocked him out but had relaxed him to the point he couldn't move, even if it weren't due to the catatonia, it would be due to the medication. He was wheeled into a room, which in nature was much the same as other rooms he had been left in. Bright white, with intense lighting and a two way mirror. The smell was extremely sanitary, like a combination of bleach and other disinfectants, they only vaguely covered an odd smell, which could only be described as resembling multiple bodily functions.

He was left in the room alone, he could do nothing, he could not move due to the multiple influences inflicted upon him. His eyes closed over, as he slipped into unconsciousness, maybe this was the best place for him to be in now, maybe the only place he should actually be in.

What was to become of Sam and would he ever stand for the crimes he had allegedly committed, that he wasn't even aware he had committed? Only time would tell.

CHAPTER SEVENTEEN: A SERIES OF EVENTS

Another day, another case file lands on their desks. Terry and Herman were both getting a little fed up of having new files landing each day, before they showed any willing to work hard on cases, they just got to drift through the days without any need to really do much at all. Since they had been getting extra caseloads, they hadn't had time to disagree about much. It even looked to Terry like Herman had lost some of his bulk.

"So, Hermy, let's go and visit Laura again today, lets chuck you in a room with her again, see what happens? See if you, my big old bear, can get her to talk" Herman cast a glare at Terry, he hadn't affectionately called him a big old bear in quite a long time, he didn't want to tell him that he liked it when he did it, but he did do. Eventually Herman offered a half smile to Terry as a sign of his acceptance.

He knew he was the one that had bought her out of the catatonic state, that he was the one that got her to react. So maybe he would be the one that would get her to talk. The one who would unlock the key to the mystery. Who knows, maybe he would draw a blank. He thought it better to think that this visit would effect a positive outcome, that way with a little bit of luck he would be right.

"You know what, this other file looks a bit of a mess, this is the new one they bought down, they had the guy in for interview for that attack the other week, some posh fella that's lost his marbles and keeps turning into a possum" Terry had a cheery and sceptical tone in his voice. "Maybe you should talk to him too" laughing to himself, he knew Herman would take the humour in the right way.

Making light of the dark circumstances was what made the difficult times bearable, it made it seem like it was easier to deflect, a self-defence mechanism that prevented the horrors from getting in and becoming niggles that could easily throw a person off a normal path of thought.

Herman was deep in thought, it wasn't often he didn't have any off the cuff remarks to make, but, he was so deep inside of his own thoughts everything in the real world was faded into the background. He suddenly seemed to come too and reached down to pick up the case files of the three different cases from in front of him. He had thought of something that hadn't been obvious at first, but now, maybe more so.

"Hang on Tel, I've just noticed something, well thought of something at least. I hadn't seen it before but it is similar in all three of the files. Laura, Sam and our mate Roger. None of them, not a single one, gave a surname. I mean, Laura did, but that was her married name, showing on her marriage certificate, is just Laura, no family name. In Rogers file, no surname, in Sam's file, no surname. It's quite odd. It really is" Terry snatched the file from Herman, he didn't believe something as basic as this could be relevant, but it did seem a little too obvious to be a coincidence. "How can we have not seen this before Hermy, I agree, it is a little bit too coincidental for it to not have some kind of link. Well, well, you always say, God is in the details"

Herman smiled, it was one of those smiles someone gives to themselves. A gift only for them, from themselves. When they have an incredulous sense of self satisfaction and self-pride, when they have a feeling of winning, he didn't know what he had won, but it felt as if he had won the lottery.

He was quite quickly bought back down to earth with a thud

"Saying that, it could be for any number of reasons, but let's look into it. Maybe that should be on your list of questions to ask the good old doctor, maybe we should actually interview him under caution, you know just to see if he can shed any light"

This made Herman disappear off into his own mind again. It made him think deeply, if this is one of the quite obvious links, maybe they need to look for less ordinary motive, less mundane questions, think way outside of the box. Really search within those small details to find something that could guide them on the right path.

"Come on Hermy, grab your jacket, let's get over there he said we could come at any time, I'll call him en-route, you can drive" Herman quickly responded and got to his feet. He really wanted to make a success of this case and something told him not to discount the fact that these cases were all linked. Not to detract from the fact he had made that first link, he also had another thought to himself "Terry, I think my jacket is getting a little loose" Terry looked him in the eyes, smiled only a smile a partner could "I know, I had noticed, you're losing a bit of weight, but you'll never stop being that big cuddly teddy bear!"

Herman slightly blushed, he hadn't realised but, this was not only a form of compliment from Terry but also it was a great feeling that he had started to improve his own appearance, his own health, without even trying. Imagine what would be possible if he set his mind to it. Today was turning out to be immensely positive for Herman and he could do nothing but relish the feeling.

The boys jumped in the car, taking again nothing but notepads and pens, they had notified the desk that their phones would be left in the car for the duration of their visit, because it just made life that little bit easier. Terry jumped straight on the phone as Herman got to driving. It wasn't often that he was allowed to drive the car, but on this occasion he was going to take it in the positive stride he was taking the rest of his day. "All sorted

Hermy, booked in with the good doctor, actually, I want to know why he's called the good doctor, I want to know his real name"

The boys had a really good drive out to the Asylum, they had the windows down in the car, the music turned up. They sang along to songs and enjoyed the journey, they knew they would be in for a harrowing few hours, so wanted to make the most of the time unwinding before facing such an experience.

Finally pulling up to the gate again, the boys pulled out their ID cards a little more prepared for the guard's humour than they were on the previous occasion. "Thank you gentlemen, I must warn you to be careful, you know the inmates run this place" He smiled at them and it did take a second for it to sink in. "Ah" chirped Terry quickly getting the joke, "the inmates run the Asylum?" answering the guard with a question seemed to deflate and disarm the potentially negative thought process that could begin when they were about to be face to face with known murderers who had a lack of compulsion control. "Maybe not the best joke to make buddy, but it is always a pleasure" Herman stated with a completely straight face.

The guard who previously had a cheesy grin on his face had now lost this, in fact his face had dropped and he looked extremely humiliated about maybe not completely thinking through his joke. "Sorry chaps, I will let reception know that you are on your way"

Herman raised a hand in thanks to the guard as the barrier lifted. He pulled into the car park and took nearly the same position they had done previously. "Nicely done Hermy, although I think you made him feel a little bad, are you prepared for this, it's going to be difficult, but even if they separate us again, I will be right there with you. I will be watching and waiting until I'm back by your side, you know I've got your back" Herman was taken a little aback by Terry's feelings and words. This was compounding the positive vibes he had been feeling all day. It was enhancing his own sense of self-worth and belief. It had been many, many years since he had felt this positive about not only himself but also about his outlook on life in general.

The boys got out of the car after emptying their pockets and stashing various items throughout the many hidey holes they could find. "You know he made us wait last time, I think that was him trying to demonstrate that he was in control, that we were there with his permission, his consent to undertake the interview, not that he had a choice about it really but I picked up that kind of feeling from him. You know I bet this time he's there like a flash because it's on his terms" Herman not only was feeling good today, but he was also thinking quite deeply, maybe over thinking in some respects, but even the most well rounded individuals are guilty of this at times.

They entered the reception, showed their ID's and announced that they were on site to see the good doctor who had agreed to see them at short notice and agreed to arrange for them to interview Laura. Momentarily the good doctor was out to meet them in the reception. He was smiling and shaking hands with the boys. He seemed genuinely pleased to see them, maybe he had some news for them, and maybe they had managed to work out what Laura had been trying to write with her hand on the table.

"Doc, could we please sit down with your good self-first and have a chat about a few things? Some new cases have come to light and I bet you're the only man who is able to help us." Terry was thinking as to what Herman had said whilst they were walking into the building, it appeared that he had been correct. So maybe if they played on the sense of self-importance the doctor felt, maybe he would open up to them or help them. At the very least he hoped he wouldn't play a trick on them again. The doctor agreed and walked the boys through the security doors, today, it seemed like counting the doors would have no effect and if they did it, would it again be playing into the mind games the doctor had played on them previously?

Moving smoothly and swiftly through all of the security areas, abandoning the few belongings they had bought in with them this time at the lockers, the boys soon found themselves sitting in the doctor's office as if they were speaking with him in his professional capacity as opposed to questioning him, although this was good as it would mean this would make him feel as if he were in control of the flow of questioning and this allowed him, without necessarily knowing it, to open up to them.

"So doc, Herman is going to take some notes if possible, we want to document as much as possible of our conversations so that we don't miss anything, is that OK?" The doctor agreed, he had no reason not to, but again, Terry asking for consent gave the impression this was all still on the good doctors terms, that he was in control. "Sorry, I must apologise, I keep calling you doc, we only know you as the good doctor and it feels incredibly rude to only refer to you as this, may I enquire as to your real name?" Terry probed in the least imposing manner he could do, the doctor didn't seem best pleased about this, but he didn't feel he couldn't answer the question. "My name gentlemen, is Aridam Kek, which is of both Indian and Egyptian origin, I often don't use the name due to the connotations it invokes. You see those who named me, did so based on their beliefs, not because of any heritage or family name. I don't use my name in normal practice, because of its subtext"

The boys were a little shocked openness of the doctor. "OK, so we will look into those definitions back at the station if you would like? Save a bit of time?" The doctor agreed, it would be more time efficient for this to be the purpose and process. "Doc, if I am still ok calling you that? I would like to enquire as to whether you had made any revelations with what Laura may have been writing on the table with her hand when she last sat with Herman?" The doctor again shuffled uncomfortably in his seat. "Yes gentlemen, we did, it isn't terribly reassuring, especially given that it has been a repeated experience since, but, having medicated her a little differently, she has since stopped it, her catatonia has lifted marginally since then too, so she has made some progress, it would seem that whatever was done to her, may be starting to unravel, I was excited to hear you were coming again. I would like to put Herman in the room with her as he was, in my opinion, the key to unlocking her"

Herman couldn't get any more enthralled by his own being today. He was on cloud nine. Often this could be seen in any man as a portrayal of over confidence, but for Herman, this was one of the most positively affirming days in his life. Terry abruptly interrupted, despite the doctor and Herman smiling at each other. "So, we have a few new cases, one of the suspects to a crime I believe has ended up here in the Asylum, I would like to ask you some questions about him if possible?" the doctor insisted they proceed with the questions, he wanted their minds to be free for helping to deal with Laura to see if Herman had the magic touch in order to free her completely of whatever had been holding her within that state.

"Doc, the man we are enquiring about is simply known as Sam, do you have any knowledge of him? He has a similar kind of Catatonia to Laura, however, his was caused twice when he was questioned. He completely froze. The odd thing is, both Laura and Sam have no family name. Laura did have her married family name, but nothing given on her marriage certificate in terms of maiden family name" the doctor looked overwhelmed. "Yes, we do have Sam here. Yes he is having similar symptoms and if you have any ideas as to what triggered him then I would be intrigued to know. We had to take his sedation to a very deep level" Reading between the lines, they knew Sam wouldn't be someone that they would be able to speak to today.

"Ok, do you think we should go and see Laura now, the sooner the better?" The doctor agreed and all three men stood up. The boys waited for the doctor to lead the way, they knew they would need him to do this, as this was not a familiar place for them to be in, alongside the fact they would need to utilise his security clearance.

Again the doctor suggested himself and Terry go into the supervisory position and that Herman go into the room with Laura.

Herman followed the same process, waited for the heavy automated lock to release on the door, slowly opened it and walked into the white room. He was met again with an almost identical scenario to what he had been exposed to previously. Laura sitting handcuffed to the table in the middle of the room, wearing a coverall. He again took a seat opposite her.

"Good morning Laura, I am Herman, I am a police detective, I visited you previously, I wondered if we could talk today" Herman waited for a response but didn't expect to get any from her, he knew this was going to be difficult, but he needed somehow to try and get her to open up to him.

The other two men were sat in the observation room. Terry suddenly realised, the doctor had not divulged on what Laura had actually been writing on the table "Doc, you never told us what she had written on the table, could you please share it with me?" The doctor, realising he hadn't, apologised, "Yes, sorry, It appeared that she was writing in Latin. Mors Vincit Omnia – which roughly translates to – Death conquers all" This startled Terry a little, although it shouldn't have. He was more than aware of what Laura had been capable of, he had seen the photos of the aftermath, the trail of destroyed life that she had left.

"That is quite unnerving doctor, I'm not so sure I am comfortable with him being in a room with her now" Terry had a worried tone to his voice, the doctor had picked up on this. "You really feel quite deeply for him don't you, he means everything to you" Terry smiled and nodded like a bashful school child. "Doc, I honestly don't know what I'd do without him"

Back in the room with Herman, he had faced a few moments of abject silence when Laura turned her head to face him, staring directly into his eyes, it felt like she was not only looking at him but through him at the same time. Like she was staring into his core, it was a haunting look, the look you would expect someone to give you shortly before attacking you. This put Herman on his guard. It made him want to be more aware of how dangerous this woman could potentially be.

"Laura, I want to ask you something, it shows on my records that before you were married, you had no family name, would you mind asking me why this is?" Laura's expression changed, her face was slightly distorted as if she was trying to force words out, as if she was trying to speak but something was holding her back. There was a crackle of noise coming forward from her mouth, her lips parted then in a hushed monotonous manner she let forth "I am Laura, I have no family, and I have no family name"

Herman was astounded, she had spoken. When she did so, she sounded so calm and haunting that it really began to frighten him. He didn't want to stop there, she had spoken, and maybe he was the key. Maybe he could get her to unlock completely. Who knew where this could go now! He was excited but trying to hide displaying this to Laura.

"Laura, is there anything you would like to tell me?" She continued staring at him with vacant eyes. "I am Laura, I have no family, they're dead" whilst this was progress hearing her say a similar phrase was frustrating. Which under the circumstances was quite understandable. "Laura, would you like to say anything else?" Herman had a sense of angst in his voice which was picked up by both the doctor and Terry in the observation room. "Herman, let's have a moment outside of the room please" The doctors voice was resonating throughout the room.

Herman quickly stood and exited the room, he could feel Laura's eyes following him as he left, and it felt as if she were boring a hole into his back.

He reached for the door, which seemed to take forever to open, but quickly did. Herman exited as swiftly as he could do. He was scared not only for himself but also for Laura. There was something very wrong with this woman, but what it was, he had no clue.

The three men stood outside of the room. None of them at least in that moment could easily find the words to say, awkward smiles and half glances were exchanged intermittently. "So, she speaks" said Herman rather clumsily. He was excited that he had achieved enough to get her to speak. He was confused as to why he had this ability to get her to unlock, but at the same time couldn't help but overthink her comments. Maybe she was a realist, she had killed her family, so yes, she had no family, but the boys really needed to get the answer to the question, which was the why she had done it!

"Ok chaps, let's take a few moments here to calm ourselves, this is exciting stuff! Herman please take some deep breaths and compose yourself, we need you completely level headed no matter how this makes you feel, you can show no stimuli at all. You must remain as monotone as possible but be yourself. I feel it's your physical stature that allows Laura to speak with you, so let's use that" Herman had moved himself to being seated taking some deep breaths with his eyes closed, when the doctor had said this, it stopped him from his method of calming and had slightly upset him, he thought to himself *hang on is he saying she's only speaking with me because I'm fat?* Shrugging it off, he continued to attempt to calm himself and level his head.

"Ok, I'm ready for round two" Herman claimed as he got to his feet. The men parted ways, the doctor and Terry again to the observation room and Herman into the interview room.

As Herman entered, Laura's head was pivoted staring at the door, he body was still fixed in position and it looked like the most awkward angle to hold a head at for an extended period, how had she done that, she almost looked like an owl, nearly turning her head completely around to adjust her gaze following him across the room as he moved to take his seat again.

"Laura, let's get straight to it, a few things puzzle me from your statement, I would like to ask you a few questions is this possible?" She stared emptily through him, it was a haunting stare that he didn't think he would ever be able to forget. "Laura, you said you took a phone call and all of these things happened following the phone call, if this is correct? What was the call and who was it from? We did check your telephone records and it showed that no calls were received that afternoon"

She continued to stare through Herman, as if he weren't really there, but at the same time making him feel uncomfortable like she was trying to read his mind. Again there was a crackle from Laura's mouth "nēmini cōnfīdō, walk the path you are, what happened before is now gone, what happens next is expected" Utterly lost for words, Herman wasn't quite sure what to begin addressing next. "What do you mean what happens next is expected Laura" She had clammed up again, he mouth did not move she showed few facial expressions, she just had the remaining cold and daunting stare she had maintained throughout their time together.

In the observation room, Terry and the doctor had sparked conversation over the phrase used by Laura, it would seem that she had quite the knowledge of other languages or at least some phraseology from them. "Doc, any ideas on the foreign language?" he seemed to be deep in thought, Terry probed again "Doc...Anything?" the doctor turned and stared at Terry, "You know, sometimes, one must take a moment to mull over an answer from a patient with a severe disorder. I think she may be using Latin again, but I can't be sure, I will let our linguist have a listen to it, this is all proving rather revealing, don't you think?"

Terry looked at the good doctor blankly, he felt absolutely nothing had been answered, for him, even more questions had been raised, the only part that did intrigue him was regarding the past being gone. Maybe a look backwards before looking at the present was in order. Was there some sense of commonality between the cases from the past in which they could begin to draw some links, no matter how vague they were?

Herman was sat there, still trying to get Laura to speak with him again, maybe she had said something in the interview that would be telling, but on the surface he felt he had come away from this with nothing other than a haunting face that he assumed would forever visit him in his dreams. "Laura, thank you for your time today, I appreciate you meeting me again, and maybe you would like to meet in the future? Discuss a little more?" Herman was to get no further responses from her, maybe she felt that she had given them enough information on the situation for them to be able to move forwards.

Herman stood and tucked his chair back under the table. He walked toward the door, moving lightly listening for the familiar crackle of her voice to see if she would say anything as he left. She didn't, he was standing almost wanting her to say something or to guide him on what to do next, how he forged further interaction.

He was well and truly ready to terminate this particular moment, as he stood by the door, it again seemed to be an extended period in which he had to wait for the lock to be released. Eventually though, he was freed from the room. He was back in the corridor, the doctor and Terry joined him as well. "Ok there big man?" Terry questioned as he was reunited with his partner. All Herman could do was nod, he wasn't ready to speak at that moment, and he just wanted to play that interview over in his head, reminisce on what Laura had said. "Boys, I have other patients I need to deal with, this was a massive step forwards again today, can you come back again in a few days? Give me a few days to settle her again then we try to see how much further we can get her to go?"

Both Terry and Herman agreed, they wanted this interaction. They wanted to be the team to bring forth whatever had been happening. No matter how many visits it took to the Asylum in order to achieve it. "I think we should make our way out now doc, I better go and get big guy rested up for in a few days' time" Terry was still quite protective of his partner. He was more so driven by the desire to effect a positive outcome from this experience.

"Ok boys, please follow me back to the entrance, we shall get you signed out, then we will reconvene in few days' time." They all traipsed back through the building. The doctor stopped at the lockers whilst the boys retrieved their belongings "chaps I am being paged to an incident, I will have to leave you here, I will instruct security to let you out, the reception is just there, and please see the desk clerk who will sign you out." Terry and Herman said their goodbye's in a rather rushed fashion, but understood that when the doctor was required, there was no time for a drawn out exit.

They headed through the reception to sign out, waiting patiently at the security door. "So how do you think it went?" Herman asked as they waited. Terry had no response at that time, he had taken on board what the doctor had said. Maybe it is worth taking the time to think, maybe it is worth having some silence to develop thoughts thoroughly in his own head before opening his mouth. The silence became a little awkward. The door then opened releasing the boys to the reception, where they very quickly signed out and headed out of the building.

They made their way over to the car and in silence, got in, it was assumed that Terry would drive as this was normally the case. Still an awkward silence was consistent between them. This was maintained throughout the journey home.

They both exited the car, walking slowly toward their house. Still nothing but silence. They walked in the front door and proceeded toward the kitchen. "I'm ordering in a pizza tonight, do you want anything special?" Terry asked as Herman placed himself down at the kitchen table. "Just the normal, we don't need anything special, I'm pretty tired in honesty and I want to think over today really, it's been quite an experience" This was something that they both agreed on.

Today was a day that was an experience, it had been a development not only for Laura, but despite the limited content of her interview, there was the underlying suspicion that maybe she revealed more than they initially suspected.

"I'm really proud of you for today, it took so much courage to do that. Well done buddy" Terry had a beaming smile on his face. This instantly restored not only the good feeling that Herman had earlier in the day, but also the reassurance that he was doing things correctly, that he was developing himself and building himself up. Taking a compliment was never something that Herman found easy to do. But he managed to push out a whispered "Thank you".

The boys turned the TV on to zone out for the evening. They needed the time to process the events of the day. They needed time to document it, but that could wait, Terry had notes they could recall tomorrow, for tonight, it was time to relax.

CHAPTER EIGHTEEN: A MEETING OF OBSCURE MINDS

It had been 2 days since Sam had been admitted to the Asylum, he had been kept under deep sedation through that time. But the stage of his recovery had come to the point of him being bought back out of it, back to the land of the living. The good doctor was overseeing Sam, with keen interest.

"When he comes around, I want to be observing, the limited notes requisitioned from The Institution show that he bounces back quickly I want to guide him through his come up" The orderly sitting in the observation room agreed and said he would page the doctor when the time came. The doctor looked slightly sinister. He had gone from being a kindly older gentleman with concern for a patient, to someone who appeared to need to control the come up of this seemingly simple gentleman who had issues when he was arrested and told about a crime he had potentially committed.

This was a second nature behaviour for the Doctor, he seemed to be very good at disguising his true being to show he was no threat to anyone. Although that isn't the truth about who he was.

The morning came and with it, saw the rising of Laura, she got herself up and dressed. She sat prudently at the table in her room, waiting for the orderly to come around with her medication. She knew she had to face another day sitting there motionless following her medication. She knew it stopped her from being who she was, it was the medication that was controlling her. But if she didn't take it, they would strap her down and force her to have it by injection, she disliked that even more.

It reminded her of when she was younger and Jerry would pin her down, he would tear her clothes and pull her about. He would strip her naked and tell her how he was disgusted with how she looked. He would make her feel guilty when she didn't want to make love to him, he would completely destroy her self-confidence. But she could never have left him, she could never let it be known the horrors she had faced from having to live with him from a young age. The terror she had lived with every single day. It had calmed down the older they got, the abuse became less physical and more aimed toward her mental state, although him becoming physical with her was never off the cards.

Her mind had been whirring away for quite some time, when the door to her room opened, the corridor outside sounded alive with activity, there were a whole host of stimuli that were making her feel alive again. To her surprise, the good doctor walked into the room. "Hello Laura, how are you feeling? I wanted to have a little chat with you today is that ok?" Laura agreed, she hadn't had her medication so she would be free to talk, she would be free to feel emotion instead of sitting there with a head full of medication designed to stop her from feeling, to stop her from being whom she now could be. "Laura, you've had some very positive reaction with the detectives who have been questioning you, however, you have been on medication each time they have and you have fought it, you have managed to overcome it, you have managed to speak, although it has been in slightly cryptic circles. I am going to propose something to you; if you refuse to talk with them, if you act like you are still in the state of catatonia then I will make sure you no longer have to take the medication. If you do talk to them, unfortunately I will medicate you until you rot in your bed. Until no-one recognises you, until you don't even remember yourself"

Laura was shocked. She was being forced to withhold information, to lie to the police. To pretend she was under the influence of medication when she wasn't. Laura was an open and honest person, how could she pretend to be in a state she knew nothing about. How could she turn him down, the fact she had this freedom for the first time in weeks, the fact that she had acted out those atrocities to her own family, she had no clue why it had happened but she knew she had done it. She could admit that surely.

"Laura, you have admitted to killing your family, if you remain in the semi catatonic state, you stand a chance of having an easy life living here for whatever remains of it. If you admit responsibility to the officers and they can see you are of sound mind, then you will spend the rest of your life in prison. I am going to leave the decision down to you. I will allow you to free roam the day room today. I will allow you to interact with other patients, I trust you will come to your own conclusions"

She had been given freedom, even when she was free she had never had freedom, she was locked to her house, sometimes she had been physically locked in her house. But now, this man was showing her freedom, albeit limited freedom.

It felt good, someone was allowing her to be herself, but, who was she? This was something maybe if she spent the rest of her life doing, it would get tiresome, but she would also get to be free. Whereas prison, she would be there until she died and who knows what she would have to face. She was now in a dilemma as to what to do. Just a day being free to walk around and mingle would be good. How would she figure out who she was?

Laura accepted at the very least the day of freedom, she wasn't really given a choice about not talking to the detectives. She was given the choice of relative freedom or going to prison if she was proved sane.

The good doctor seemed to be losing a little good about him. He just seemed to be The Doctor now, it seemed his intentions were less patient centric and more conspiracy related. Laura smiled to herself, *conspiracy in the Asylum* sounded like a good title for a book. Maybe she should write and hide her woes in the subtext.

Still she had her freedom for the day at least, so decided to go out for a walk around the day room. It was a bustling, bright, sunlit room where there were so many things going on all at the same time, not all good things but everything did seem to be gilded by the sunlight. This sense of freedom and wellbeing was a little overwhelming and Laura did have to stop herself from time to time. She still retained her vintage style even in the coverall, with limited options for doing her hair and makeup.

She took in her surroundings. Is this what it was like to be as free as she could be at this time? It felt good, she felt out of control, she felt overwhelmed and her senses felt full to bursting point. She couldn't remember a time when she had ever felt like this before. Did it take a tragedy in order to free her from the prison she'd been trapped in? Would she manage to be free of despair and be filled with the fortitude to make it seem like she was still suffering.

Her eyes scanned the room for someone to talk to, she couldn't see many people who she would want to, she wasn't used to starting conversations and previously she had never been allowed to.

How would she even start a conversation? There weren't many topics she could think of as ice breakers. In that moment whilst she was thinking how to start a conversation with someone, without knowing who she would begin a conversation with, her eyes caught site of an attractive gentleman across the room. He looked as though he was struggling to move, she knew that feeling all too well, maybe this was her ice breaker moment. Maybe this was how she would make a friend, not just any friend though, an attractive male friend.

She began tingling all over, she got goose bumps up the backs of her arms, she was feeling excited at the prospect of talking to someone of her own volition.

Walking over, she slowed down, she started to become nervous. What if she couldn't speak? What if he couldn't speak? What if she looked silly trying to open up a conversation? All of the self-doubt began to flood back in and she was soon trapped back and withdrew from her approach, quickly finding a free table to sit down at where she saw a boxed jigsaw puzzle. She had never done one before, so felt it would be apt to swiftly begin to do it. Only she had no clue where to begin. She was now worrying about how she would do a jigsaw puzzle, how had she become like this!

She took a deep breath, composed herself and tipped the pieces of the puzzle out on the table. She felt a presence behind her, she continued with turning the pieces over on the table, so all of the picture was revealed. She found three of the four corners of it. She still felt the presence behind her. The goose bumps returned but not quite in the same fashion. This kind of feeling was fear, was she safe? She felt like someone could be breathing down her neck and she couldn't acknowledge it for the fear she would be drawn into a conversation she didn't want to have. This was a feeling she knew all too well.

"If you are going to sit, please do, otherwise please stop standing behind me" Laura surprised herself when this statement came out of her mouth, all she heard was a grunt from behind her which was slowly moving to the side. It was slowly being drawn away from directly behind her, moving around into her peripheral vision. It was the good looking gentleman she had seen across the room. Although he said nothing to her and moved as if he were a character in a horror film. Stiff and awkwardly, he dropped himself down at the table beside her.

She looked up and made eye contact with him. "I am Laura, may I know your name?" Slightly avoiding the eye contact, the man dipped his head, but still checked out of the corner of his eye.

He managed to raise a part smile from one side of his mouth. But as he did this, a large globule of drool fell out the corner of his mouth, down over his chin and after pausing for a moment dropped down onto his coverall. Laura was trying to force the eye contact, she could see deep within him, and this man was a man who needed a friend.

She got lost for a moment in his blue eyes which resembled a tropical lagoon. They were so blue, that they took her breath away. Perfectly offset by his olive skin tone and blonde hair. The only detraction from attraction, was the drool, that and the tear that had formed in the corner of his eye, which began to grow in the following moments and break free tumbling down his face.

The man did not talk, but that didn't seem to be an issue for Laura. She enjoyed just having someone to sit with and he seemed quite happy, yet sad at the same time to be sat down next to her.

A siren rang out, it resembled an old air craft warning siren from the war time. Laura looked around in panic, she could not see anyone rushing to move, and she could not feel any sense of urgency to react to it.

Was it an alert? Did this go off normally?

She had never heard this in the time in which she had been at The Asylum. Was it new?

What if it was a warning and none of them knew, maybe a fire alarm and they would have to sit there and burn to a crisp because nobody had told them to get out of the building. An orderly was walking through the day room and Laura looked for their attention "Excuse me sir, what is the siren? I haven't heard it before, is there an issue?"

The orderly took a seat on the other side of Laura and opposite the man. "If there was any reason to worry miss, would I be sat down next to you? You will hear those sirens from time to time, sometimes they are to alert the staff to an emergency, sometimes they are at certain times of day and each one will sound slightly differently so that we know how to respond to them without concerning our visitors too much."

Feeling incredibly reassured, although not sure why, Laura thanked the orderly who was more than happy to oblige. A moment later, several other orderlies came into the room, they were pushing stacking trollies, piled high with portion trays covered with disposable cloths.

It clicked, in her head, she had gone off to this centre of catastrophe, whereas in reality, all she needed to do was ask a question and she would find out that it was time for lunch.

Maybe this was a point at which she would start to change her patterns of thinking, to not identify in the worst case scenario when it was an unfamiliar situation, but to take the time to really observe and evaluate.

The nice orderly who had sat next to her bought over a tray "double pudding today, result!" the tray of food looked good, there was fruit and vegetables, there was tasty looking ham sandwiches on doorstep bread, crisps and two chocolate cakes on the tray, this certainly seemed like a situation she could tolerate being in for the rest of her life! This was a place she could imagine making a life in. New people coming and going all of the time, people to come into and go out of her life, it was definitely preferable to being segregated on an isolated prison wing.

She was almost deciding to side with The Doctor, maybe she would play on her catatonia, maybe she would hide the fact she was a functioning individual in order to deceive the detectives. She had never been a good liar, if she had ever lied to Jerry, even in the smallest of ways, he would always come down hard on her, both physically and mentally.

So she wasn't even sure if she could pull it off. Maybe if she spoke with The Doctor and asked him to give her some of the medication to ensure she was zoned out for when they returned it would help portray the situation. At least she would only have a vague memory of it and wouldn't quite feel so bad about it.

She decided to begin to eat her lunch, she felt like she maybe hadn't eaten properly in so long that eating it would be a real treat for her. She picked up one of the sandwiches and took a small mouthful, she closed her eyes, and it took her back to her far younger days when all she could recall was happiness. The smell and taste of the bread, freshly baked was like a memory in a mouthful. The ham, wafer thin but not reconstituted, realistic tasting meat, this was turning into a wonderful lunch that she thought she would always remember, not just for how nice it was but also for the memories in invoked.

This is definitely a place in which she wanted to remain.

The man sitting at the table with her, again attempted a smile, she regretted looking at him, as another globule of dribble fell from the corner of his mouth, clearly he was on some quite strong medication. He hadn't moved to eat his lunch, could he even do so? He was able to walk of his own accord, but were his other movements functioning?

She didn't really care, if she was being honest with herself, why would she. Why should she have to care about this other person that she didn't know? Maybe she was just a caring individual? Maybe she was just a fool, maybe she didn't know what she was and she had to spend some time figuring that out.

Laura was tired by the time she had finished her lunch, despite the chocolate cakes having lots of sugar in them, she felt she needed to go and have a nap and try to rebuild her strength.

Maybe that was enough of the puzzle for today, or enough of the day room for today at least "goodbye, maybe we will speak soon" with the quick comment to the man, she stood up and returned to her room. The tiredness had hit her like a brick wall, she needed to get into her bed before she collapsed.

She lay down and was very quickly drifting off into a deep sleep.

The doctor stuck his head around the corner of the door, with a terrifying grimace he whispered "rest well Laura"

CHAPTER NINETEEN: FINDING GOD

Another day dawned and the boys were already on their way to work, it was going to be a long day of report writing and analysing data. They arrived and strolled into the station, with a little less gusto than they had in the past few days.

Slumping down at their desks, Terry cast a glance at Herman. "So, we really got nowhere. The weird woman admitted to killing her family, the doctor answered no questions. Where does it leave us? We have no leads, other than vaguely, no one has a family name" Herman breathed a heavy sigh "I hate sounding like a broken record Terry, but we need to find God" Terry was a little confused, he didn't know if he thought he was losing it and thinking they needed divine intervention in order to succeed or if it were something else. "I don't think becoming born again in this situation will help us solve whatever crime has been committed. We know that Laura has admitted to killing her family, we know that Sam was being questioned for the murder of some random bloke, we know that Roger's dead" Herman signed "No Terry, we need to find God in the detail, we need to look for those little things, that will help us get there, like, a while ago you were sceptical that Roger could be linked to any of this, now I'm more convinced than ever. There's no such thing as coincidence" Terry's face looked like a grey cloud had passed over it, he hated being wrong about anything.

"Hermy, what did Rogers post mortem say?" Flicking through the mass of paperwork scattered across his desk, Herman looked through a case file that had been sent over by the coroner. "Well, it says that he died, believe it or not from a 'Cytokine Storm' I'll have to look that one up!" Herman tapped away on his computer "Looking on the internet, it says usually it happens in an overreaction of one's own immune system as a result of having something like the flu. I'm not being funny, but if he died of the flu, why was he in combat gear and wrapped in a parachute?"

Tapping his fingers on the desk, something didn't seem to add up when Terry heard this, he understood where his partner had been heading with his thought process. Maybe, he thought to himself, God really was in the detail.

"One thing I have noticed, the investigation on his clothing shows an excessive volume of gunpowder residue, not just that but traces of explosive too, which is odd as apart from the booby traps, there was not that much at his house in terms of weaponry." The boys were momentarily lost in thought "Don't forget Hermy my old pal, we found him wrapped in a parachute, who knows where he had been!"

Terry had the three case files in front of him, he opened them all to the same pages, to see if anything looked similar. "First thing I notice my old pal, is that none of them have family names which we knew, but we didn't look at – well apart from Laura. But that was after she was married. Before she was married, she had no family name.

Let's have a look into them earlier in their lives, what happened to them on the system? Where did they lose their family names?" Herman grabbed one of the files from his partner's desk, he sat there for a while, he was never very quick at reading and this was always something that had frustrated Terry.

He continued to browse, he would occasionally pause for a moment looking up as if he were about to reveal something, then he would take a breath and return his head back down to the file. After a considerable amount of anticipation, he spoke up "Terry, what year does your record go back to for Laura and Sam, you see Roger's only goes back to 5 years ago, no information prior to that, no birth certificate and no registration within the system. Just a hospital discharge letter to make sure that he is flagged on the system as a potential risk."

Terry, now sensing a glimour of hope, flicked through Laura's file. He moved to the very back of it "10 years for her, again flagged on the system, no record before that, no information, no family history and until the recent event nothing of special interest." Herman sat feeling a little less defeated than he was. *Maybe this is my God*, Herman thought to himself. It was as if they'd possibly put a chink in the armour of the case and could be leading down a path that would guide them toward some answers.

Terry excitedly chirped "And Sam, nothing about him, no history. 6 years ago there was a flag put on the system. Then the recent event, other than that, nothing" The boys had found it, they needed to find out where the flags had been raised on the system. At the very least they could apply for a warrant for the information to be released to them. This was the first step and it felt not only relieving, but also as if something had ignited inside of them.

There was a feeling of buzz within the room, the interest in the case had returned. The thrill of the chase had reinvigorated them. "Ok, so, next steps. Get the warrant, get the information, find the doctor who flagged them, interview them and we've got it, case solved" Herman stopped his celebratory thought process, initially only to take a breath but, he didn't want to assume this was the end game for this case. Maybe this was just the beginning.

"Terry, hang on a minute, let's not get too excited." Herman waited for a moment "Let's not think this is the case solved, we have found one thing that links them. Ok, this is one thing and it is not coincidence, there's no such thing as that, but, there's more to look at. Sam is a multi-millionaire. Roger, was an alcoholic former squaddie, Laura was an abused house wife. There are no other links" Terry stopped his celebratory dance, he stopped his thought process.

His partner had killed the moment, dead.

"So, Hermy, where does that leave us then? Ok, we know they all have one thing in common. OK, so what's next, two of them said they had received a phone call. Did Sam have anything like that? I didn't see anything from the limited statement they got that said he had a phone call. Plus if we try to investigate too far with that I assume his lawyer will twist us up so far we will end up losing him to litigation"

The boys despite this minor positive, felt drawn to a point where what they had to go on might never lead them forwards. "Let's get IT to look into the place and doctor who created these three on the system. That has to be our starting point, that's what we know." Terry for once had a positive inflection in his voice as if he were feeling the details could be the answer.

"Sam, he's an odd one, he has all these bad things happening to him and then he somehow gets lucky and wins the lottery. He had previously been a lawyer, he had no worries in life. Since winning the lottery, he stopped being lucky, but he spends most of his days, feeding the homeless down at that shelter in the town. Fancy a trip for a free meal?" Herman had a big smile on his face, Terry wasn't sure whether this was because of the potential of a free meal or whether this was because he thought this may be a place they could harvest some information for the case.

Either way, he was in "Grab your coat, let's get down there and see what we can find" The boys immediately sprung up from their desks, there was an enthusiasm about the way in which they prepared themselves.

Leaving the station, the boys decided a walk down to the shelter may stand them in good stead, maybe this would this would help bring about some fresh thinking or fresh ideas.

There were long awkward silences on the walk, neither of the men seemingly knew what should be said, there was the odd shared word about the weather, or about that poor state of repair of the pavements, both men seemed focused, but they didn't want to distract each other by sharing their thoughts.

The weather was good that day, the sun had been shining since early on in the morning. There was a slight heat haze coming from the road ahead of them, the miles and the time seemed to pass without notice.

The boys had eventually reached their destination, the homeless drop in centre seemed to be ramping up to full swing. There were a huge number of people moving into and out of the premises and it looked as though they may well struggle to get a word with anyone, this place was a scene of bedlam.

Entering the drop in, the boys felt not only overdressed but also out of place. Approaching a more mature lady that seemed to be giving commands to others who were there assisting, Terry opened the dialogue "Excuse me, I'm DC Terry Picket, I am looking to speak to someone about a man named Sam, is there someone here who can help me?" She looked at him, she also looked at Herman.

Not being one to miss a chance a sly smile appeared at the side of her mouth she boomed in a deep and broad Scottish accent "I'll be able to help you , but I have lots of people to feed here first, if you fancy pitching in, go and get your hands washed, pitch in and we can sit down and chat with a coffee after service, how long that will be depends on how much you can help" The boys feeling obliged, rolled their sleeves up and walked over to wash their hand.

A short while later, after serving a seemingly unending number of "customers" the cue began to dwindle and the room became less active. The Scottish lady walked over with 3 cups of coffee on a tray and signalled to the boys to come over and join her at one of the tables. They made their way over to go and have the promised conversation. Sitting at down at the table, the initial silence needed to be broken Herman seemed happy to oblige "I can't believe how good it feels, helping out, I know we didn't do much but these poor people don't have a thing and they were so grateful for the little bit of food we were able to serve them. Maybe we could come down more often, of course if you need the help?" he mused taking a sip of coffee.

Terry shot a glance at him, looking quite annoyed at the prospect of having to come back to do this all again, why should he spend more time helping them, they don't do anything to help themselves "I think your wee partner there doesn't look so keen on that idea. Nevertheless, you had some questions about our bairn Sam, I'm Angy, the drop in manager" The partners took out their notebooks to begin their questioning. "Sorry, yes we have quite a few questions, but mostly we would like to ask you about Sam as a person, who was he, who is he?"

The woman eyed at the pair still trying to figure them out, they seemed to approach the conversation completely unprepared or at least unprofessionally maybe showing a little of their inexperience "Our wee Sam has been with us for a while, he struck me as odd when he first came, but he is one of the kindest and most giving people I have ever met, not only has helped us financially here over the years, but he helps all of our clients with anything from housing to welfare payments. He's also one of the last to leave here whenever he comes in, he's very committed to helping, and it's one of the things we love about him. Now if you're coppers, what's the little scamp done wrong now?"

Terry and Herman silently glanced and drew breath, unsure of how to break this news to her and tarnish her perfect view of Sam. Terry spoke up "Well, how about you tell us more about Sam's behaviour a while ago, the last night maybe that he was here working at the drop in, then maybe we can go over a little of the information we have and the reasons why we want to find out a little more about him."

She smiled, "So, a fishing mission your on is it? Ok, no problem, the last time Sam was here, he was little out of sorts. He talked about receiving a telephone call toward the end of the evening and one of the other ladies had seen him pick up the payphone over there and he appeared to have some kind of interaction on it, but no one had heard it ring, but that's not uncommon with the noise that there can sometimes be going on in the room. He then left, he had a rush on that evening for some reason, not really sure why and it was odd. Come on boys, now it's your turn"

Somehow neither of them could bring themselves to tell her of the terrible actions he had taken or the downfall or spiral he had taken in the weeks since she had seen him. Neither of them could explain how he had brutally murdered a man, or how he was now trapped in an Asylum. "Well, you see" Terry paused for a moment trying to think of how he could warp the truth in order to not let her feel like there was any reason to be concerned

"Sam has become a person who may be able to assist us with some of our enquiries, but before we speak to him in detail, we want to get a picture of who Sam really is. Do you hold a personnel file for him? If so, I'd be interested in having a read of it."

Again looking them up and down Angy was making a judgement based on what she had been told, having a common association with many people of the street gave her a sixth sense for when the truth was being withheld from her, she knew the boys had a bigger story than just needing to speak with Sam. "So where is Sam, we haven't seen him for a while. Every so often he does disappear for a few weeks, we're not sure where and we're not sure what for we have noticed when it does happen he does become a little vague, maybe checked out and although the timing can change sometimes a few months, sometimes a year between the disappearances, they do happen, then a few weeks later he is back and just like his old self again."

Herman beamed from ear to ear. He couldn't hide his emotion at thinking this was the next piece toward helping solve the puzzle. But how would random disappearances at random times be another piece? This was completely unknown to them, but it was that gut feeling that maybe they were onto something.

Angy could see his outward smile "Aye, I guess that fits with something you're looking for then. We do have a personnel file for Sam, although, I haven't ever completed it properly, not many of our volunteers even offer to fully complete a file, they turn up, they complete a basic piece of paper and then they pitch in. They don't usually last too long, the going is tough and we see some right old states, it can be quite frustrating, devastating and depressing." The boys although a little unsure of the lack of vetting could completely understand where she was coming from. If someone is willing to help those who have nothing, they wouldn't just turn down the help for the sake of improperly completed paperwork.

"Angy, do you think we could have a copy of Sam's paperwork? It may help us in our investigation, it may give us some small pieces of knowledge, some minor details that we wouldn't otherwise have known, I know you may think that there's nothing there that will help us but there is a good chance it could do." She took a big swig of coffee, looked the boys up and down again and shook her head, she stood up from the table without saying a word and walked off. They were left alone at the table. The awkward silence returned, they weren't quite sure what to make of this situation.

"Terry, even if this leads nowhere, at least we may find something, or even a lack of something, that actually gives us something." Herman's voice had inflections, this was him becoming excited at the prospect of finding another lead, something that could progress their investigation and potentially improve their personal relationship. He seemed hopeful, his ever loyal but cynical partner wasn't quite in the same place of thinking. He didn't quite feel the same way his Herman did, he didn't know if he felt the enthusiasm for their personal or professional relationship. How could he when he felt lost himself?

A moment later, the manager returned. She threw a thin file with little paperwork in it down on the table. "This is it, nothing much in there. I will tell you this, but this will be my last words with you" she took a moment appearing to be choosing with how she progressed the conversation. The boys were hanging on her next sentence, quietly, Herman was counting in his head:

1.

2.

3..

4...

5...

6...

7...

8.....

Her lips pursed on the cusp of him counting to nine, this seemed like a coincidence, but then, neither of the boys believed that anything was ever a coincidence. Whether Terry had also clicked onto the count, hadn't skipped Herman's mind and he was trying to catch his eye to see if he had counted too, but Terry's gaze was completely fixed on this strong and passionate woman.

"Sam has done more for this drop in, than any benefactor, than any volunteer or than any well-wisher could ever do. He came here when he needed building up, yes he disappeared occasionally, but he always came back. He always gave all of himself to these people that had nothing, physically, financially and mentally. So if you want me to say a bad word about him, you're looking in the wrong place"

The boys knew they probably were no longer welcome, so they made their exit shortly after this. They took the file although they felt they shouldn't, but if this could provide some insight into the entire situation, maybe it could help.

Walking back the same route they came, the boys had been walking in silence. Each one of them building a picture of Sam in their heads "I tell you what Terry, next time we think it's a good idea to walk, let's think again." This single comment was enough to remind him of why he felt so strongly for his partner, a small school boy giggle could be heard from the detectives as they walked along. They had such an in-depth task to complete but they also had a care free nature returning which seemed like something they had been missing for a while.

Dusk was drawing in as they reached the station, the temperature had dipped and the sky was clear. They walked in and headed toward their office, little could be said for what they had achieved that day. The boys did feel a little deflated, like they had an artificial high point in their day getting some information. Only to return and realise that there was still a mountain to climb in order to figure this whole thing out.

Sitting at their desks, the day rounded up with a little paperwork, a little report filing and documenting the information they had attained from the drop in centre.

Flicking through the limited paperwork that was in the file that Angy had given them, Herman was a little lost. "Terry, this file is little more than a basic personal details form, everything fits with what we know. His name is documented as Sam, no ID is provided but a box is ticked to say they have seen ID, his address is his home address, I do now know that Sam likes classical music and exercising. So, there is an absence of new information, but in a way, doesn't that kind of tell us what we need to know, he maintained the same information we already know, the information that was already on the system. Maybe what this tells us, is that this is the only information he knew, maybe there was a reason there is no copy of the ID, maybe there is a reason he has only stated his given name."

"Or maybe Hermy my old pal, it's because he was hiding something or didn't show ID and a place like that wouldn't as such be willing to push someone to give information that they don't want to give. Let's be honest a generous chap shows up who can help homeless people with complex paperwork and gives large donations to help keep the place afloat, would you then push to get ID from them, or would you willingly accept it so you could continue with your mission of ensuring that these people with absolutely nothing in the world, get fed, that they get clothed or housed."

This caused both of them to sit there in silence, their desk lamps being the only things now lighting their dingy office. They both sat deep in thought but didn't want to offer up anything for the fear that each of them may have thought of a counter for the others point.

"Let' call it a day now Hermy, I can't think any more about this today. My brain is mashed, let's get back at it early doors." The boys retired for the evening wearily dragging themselves to the car, leaving their desk lamps on knowing that it wouldn't be long until they were sat back there again trying to figure out where they were going to turn next.

CHAPTER TWENTY: MAKING FRIENDS

The crisp morning sunlight entered the narrow cell windows at the Asylum. It moved as time passed like a sundial across the room. Shining strongly onto the face of Laura as she slept silently.

It seemed to pause for quite some time whilst on her face which slowly began to heat and wake her gently, she was dreaming of lying in a field at the cusp of spring, the sun feeling warm and soothing on her skin, feeling comforted and completely at peace.

It was only when there was a loud clatter from outside of the door that she awoke with a start. She realised that she wasn't in a field she wasn't comforted, she wasn't loved. She was there solely because she was the result of something, what that something was, she didn't know. But she knew deep down, this was not where she belonged.

Suddenly a splitting, intense pain coursed throughout her body. She was paralysed with the intense sensation of an extreme low coming and hitting her like a brick wall.

The sudden feelings of helplessness and remorse were the most and only feelings she could feel. There was no reason for this to be happening and all she could do was lay there and embrace it, ground herself and live in the moment.

Laura went to move and realised she couldn't she was strapped into her bed. She had restraints that had been placed on her arms and legs. Why? What was happening to her?

The door to her cell opened up with a loud clunk that felt like it resounded through her core. It resonated between her ears like it would if she had been on a heavy night drinking being woken too early the next day.

The Good Doctor walked into her room. He began to speak but all Laura could here were lots of echoes. "Please stop speaking doctor. I cannot hear you properly." She said confidently. Because of the searing pain, she felt she couldn't enter into any kind of conversations or even listen to what he had to say, she couldn't handle any of his games today.

The doctor moved to go and sit down next to her, he didn't just sit, he knelt next to her bed and the feeling of having someone so close to her made her feel extremely uncomfortable, especially someone that made her skin crawl. She felt a really sharp pain in her arm. She couldn't open her eyes to look over to the side to see what it was but she assumed it was some kind of injection.

However she felt didn't seem to matter, the pain had begun to ease, the thoughts began to soften and the feelings began to lose their intensity. Her entire body began to relax, it must have been whatever the pain in her arm was getting to work pretty quickly and helping her to ease. She felt a tugging at the restraints on her arms and legs. She felt the restrictions she had previously felt now being eased and a sense of freedom, only a moment later to be plunged into a new feeling of being trapped, as she realised she was still held in place.

This time it was different though, this time, it wasn't the pain or the restrictions that were paralysing her.

Again it must have been whatever was put into her arm. She came to the conclusion that she was now paralysed by medication, which was a far scarier prospect and this left her in a position to do nothing.

"Laura, I hope you are now able to hear me. I sense I may have given you a little too much medication in the cakes yesterday, which would have given you intense pain and paralysis, which may have intensified negative emotions and thought patterns. I have just given you something to counteract that, but it is a muscle relaxant so you will be unable to move for a little while. You had a conversation yesterday with a gentleman in the day room. Did he talk with you? Like you, he has been treated previously. Like you, he is in a position that he needs much more treatment. Also, like you the police may want to speak to him. Laura I am trusting that you give the police very little information when they come to speak with you, as although you have confirmed with me that you will keep your information limited, I understand the temptation there may be. Laura, do you want to spend your entire life trapped in this continuous cycle, I really don't want to have you medicated for life, or even worse"

What had he meant by worse? Despite him having given a lengthy piece of information for her to take in, Laura could only focus on those final few words, those were the ones that had counted for her. "He said nothing doctor, he dribbled and mumbled. Do I know him? Have we been here together before?" Laura felt certain in the back of her head that she knew this man, that there was a reason she felt attracted to him or that she knew him. But why? How could she feel this? She had never been allowed to have feelings for anyone other than Jerry, not even her own family. But, she had solved that problem.

It was at this point she stopped herself. She realised that she had willingly murdered her husband and children. Everything stopped. She had felt that they were a problem that needed to be solved and that she had solved them. "Doctor, I have just realised, I killed my husband and children, I saw them as a problem and although I don't remember how, or even why, I killed them, I'm glad they're dead. I don't remember any of the situation or what was the cause? I just remember getting to a point where the only escape was to poison them and then I beat him to death, choking on his own tongue wasn't a nice enough exit for him. Because of what he had put me through, he didn't deserve just to be poisoned he needed to be taught a lesson, they all did."

Awoken by the callous, coldness in Laura, The Good Doctor wasn't quite sure how to proceed. He had to answer her honestly and at this point he was relieved that she did have some heavy paralysis. "Laura, you have not only been here with him but also other places. I want to tell you everything, but I cannot until the police have gone, until they stop sniffing around you. I need to ensure that you will not give them any information that could lead them to find out about you or any of the others."

There was a discernible difference in the reaction of The Good Doctor to what there had been previously. Before, he had seemed to be dark and secretive. He had been angry and abusive, threatening and intimidating. Almost everything that Laura had been used to and had on past occasions submitted to. Maybe this was just another method of a man controlling her. Maybe this was just a technique he was trying to use to stress the importance of Laura giving as little information as possible to the police.

It didn't matter either way, she knew having had that sudden realisation that she was relieved her family were dead, had meant that she could never stand up to defend her actions. So it was either play the part and take the easy life in this place, or end up going to prison, if declared competent to do so and spending the rest of her life going through the system, whichever way she looked at it she would be held captive for the rest of her life, however long that would be.

"Laura, I am going to release your restraints, the drugs should wear off within the next 30 minutes and you should be able to get up and about, maybe when you are able to you could come and sit down to talk with me. I can give you some information, the information I think that may tide you over until this whole scenario is finished and we can let you know the full picture."

Releasing her restraints, The Good Doctor began to make a swift exit from the room with the door slamming shut behind him. Laura was still stranded on the bed, she realised that she was beginning to feel the urge to need the toilet, it hadn't been there previously but the seconds seem to prolong as time went on. She couldn't move, so she couldn't cross her legs to help her hold it in. All she could do was hope that she could hold it long enough to enable her to get some sensation back in her legs and arms to crawl across to the toilet in her cell.

Laura began to feel pain throughout her back and kidneys, emanating from the core of her body it enveloped her whole midsection. She desperately wanted the feeling to come back into her legs and arms, just to be able to try and make it over there, the few feet it would take to be able to relieve herself. The pain was becoming more intense as those prolonged seconds ticked by, it had bought a tear to her eye and it had made her begin to start stiffly wriggling her body, sometimes on purpose and sometimes involuntarily.

The tingling had begun, her fingers began to get sensation and began to twitch. She was able now to slightly move them. This was the light at the end of the tunnel for her to be able to relieve herself of what seemed like the most intense pain she had experienced since child birth.

The tears now became those of frustration instead of tears of pain. Laura couldn't quite move enough to throw herself off the bed, the last thing she wanted to do was have an accident by losing control of her bodily functions. She knew she had to be strong and hold on a little longer, to keep making those micro movements to get her blood pumping to help metabolize the sedative. Laura knew this was a battle she would have to win.

She began to count, with each second she counted she moved one of her fingers. With each minute that passed she tried to move one of her toes, forming a counting system that she was able to track. She knew he had told her around 30 minutes for her to get sensation back, could she count on this timeline or did she have to move it along and push herself to get over there. Either way at this point she knew any distraction would help.

Picking a specific spot on the ceiling in front of her, still moving her fingers and toes on count, Laura focused hard and maintained a process. I am in this moment, this moment is with me, I am being, but the being is not controlling me, I am above my physical being, I am in control. Laura repeated this mantra over and over in her head whilst staring at the spot on the wall, no matter how many movements her hands and feet were making, she knew that if she could maintain focus on something other than her needing to relieve herself, she could hopefully win the battle over her body.

Gradually the micro movements became macro movements. They became larger and more exaggerated. More joints began to free up, more limbs began to get the tingling as the drugs started to wear off.

She decided to go for it, to try moving, to start the push from the front line. Laura started to swing one leg off the bed it partially flopped but was partially was under Laura's control. She knew her next move was to slowly ease her body around and bring the other leg off the edge of the bed. As she did this, her body and lack of balance got the better of her, which lead to her banging her head on the wall. The bang resonated throughout her skull, although her sole focus at this point was getting over to the toilet giving little thought to rather heavy bump.

Her focus was maintained and with every ounce of energy that she had, she pushed herself to bring her legs level and to try and lift herself off the bed. Looking like she was well in drink, she slowly tipped her body forwards, putting the centre of balance away from the bed, she teetered on her heel half hovering over the bed half leaning forward with her direction in direct sight of the toilet. She knew she would have only one chance to make the move in fluid motion to stumble across there, remove her garments and get herself seated.

She began to tip the balance in the favour of the toilet taking those steps like a baby giraffe recently born, stumbling around unsure of how to properly stand. She knew now that she could do this and half of her wanted to feel proud, the other half just really wanted a wee.

Within moments she had made it across, de-gowned and managed to drop herself down onto the seat. The feeling of extreme relief was like no other feeling describable. The feeling of achievement was a huge accomplishment and a huge win for her. She felt proud, relieved and successful at being able to have held herself for so long when she was so desperate. Maybe I should use that mantra more often, Laura thought as she continued to sit and wait.

She finished and stepped back up to wash her hands and face. Forgetting that she was still a little uneasy on her feet, she quickly ended up sat back down on the toilet seat. At least she didn't have to move immediately for any reason. At least she could now focus on setting the next goal which was to make it to the sink. It wasn't far, a few feet at most, however it would be another thing she could start her day with in respect of it being a positive.

Slowly, she began to try again. Lifting herself by the hand rails either side of her she got to her feet, she took a moment to compose herself and took a deep breath slowly moving one foot in front of the other, keeping them shoulder width apart to ensure she had a good balance. Step by step she was making it. Step by step she was achieving her goal.

She had done it, she had made it over to the sink. It had taken all of her effort and focus, but she could again be proud of being able to put another tick on her list. What started out as being a terrible wake up, was turning around and feeling more like a positive start to the day.

Washing her hands thoroughly and splashing her face with water, Laura felt refreshed. Not only was the feeling nearly completely back all over her body, but she had now dried herself and began to calmly and confidently walk over to her dresser where she could grab some clean clothes and help herself feel even better.

Finally, she had managed it, she had got up and already had faced so many challenges and won. Laura wondered what the day might hold for her and hoped that she could push herself some more. She definitely wanted to sit and talk with The Good Doctor to find out a little more about herself not only why they had some kind of existing professional relationship but also who she was and why she had so few memories. She also had a desire to see the same man who had sat next to her dribbling the previous day, if he weren't dribbling she could easily see herself enjoying spending time in his company.

Laura picked up the tray that had been put through her hatch and sat back down on her bed. She began to eat the now cold buttered toast which had a mass produced flavour to it. She couldn't place her finger directly on it, but it tasted over sweetened and cheap. She didn't mind too much but she did have an intense hunger developing inside of her. She knew she had felt this previously but didn't really know how to control it or stop it, all she was left with was embracing it. Dealing with it, eating very slowly and waiting for the full feeling to come back to her.

It was one of the other side effects she was aware of having been medicated many times. An intense hunger that quickly wore off when eating. Before she knew it, she had reached the point at which she was now completely full. It didn't really bother her, she knew it was another thing that she was able to control. She was able at this point to stop, she had to. She looked down at the plate and smiled. She had taken three bites of the toast.

Feeling unphased by this, she got up slowly from her bed. She walked toward the cell door and banged on it to get the attention of one of the orderlies who were busy moving things up and down the corridors. "Hello..Hello, I'd like to go to the day room please can someone let me out?" she could hear a set of jingling keys moving toward her. It didn't fill her with hope knowing that all of the doors were remotely controlled but someone was responding to her, which was more important.

"Hi Laura, how are you feeling today? I will need to get the OK from AK, but please give me a few moments, I have a few other urgent things to do, but I promise I won't forget you!" She couldn't believe it, she had been acknowledged by name. It was the same kind orderly who had sat down and spoken to her in the day room yesterday, he was the one who had been the shining light in amongst a confusing midst of madness. Standing back from the door she simply responded with "Thank you"

Laura picked up in the background some music she could hear in the distance. It was classical music, but it wasn't something she was familiar with. The music seemed to penetrate her being and she could feel it through to her soul. It began to lift and turn her, Laura's body moving fluidly with it. Her arms posed like a ballerinas, her feet moving with grace and poise. She was lost in the sensation of the music for quite some time and it certainly allowed her to not sit and focus on the wait for being allowed out of her cell.

There was a clunk of the door behind her whilst she maintained the dancing within her cell. A plastered on smile of genuine happiness was on her face. It had been so long since she had felt this way, it seemed unnatural. Although to her it felt completely natural, what could have been a negative, had turned into a positive and had enabled her to feel fully relaxed ready to face the day ahead of her. No matter what that day would hold.

A banging on the door behind her snapped her back into the room, back into the moment. "Laura, I have been given the OK to let you into the day room if you would like to come out, I see your having a little dance, we do have some dance therapy going on today if you would like to join in? Let me know, I am around all day, or you can keep dancing in private, it is completely up to you."

Again Laura smiled to herself. She was enjoying herself in that moment and wanted to maintain it for a little while. So she continued to dance around her cell just being enveloped in the moment. Maybe she would go down to the day room in a little while but for now she was thoroughly feeling fulfilled by her own company which was again a rather unfamiliar feeling.

The day was moving on, the music had now gone silent and she thought to herself that it was maybe time to go and continue the puzzle she had begun yesterday. To see if she could meet or speak to anyone else.

Walking down cautiously to the day room, Laura proceeded to be vigilant of those around her. She was still wary that she may bump into the wrong person, although she wasn't sure why. Who was the wrong person? Why did she feel like this? She knew virtually no one outside of her previous family so what would she have to fear?

Having nearly tiptoed her way down there, she had made it, the sun was still shining brightly into the room and it was still penetrating the haze and creating some glorious rays of light.

Sitting right at the table where they had been the previous day was the handsome gentleman. Laura had to fight every urge she had to rush over and talk with him immediately. He sat so poised and looking deep in thought, she didn't want to disturb him but at the same time the butterflies in her stomach told her maybe that's what she really wanted and desired. She hadn't felt those butterflies in a long time and she didn't want to indulge on the feeling in that very moment, whilst also not wanting to dismiss them. Alongside that, if she rushed over to him, he would know she had an interest in him.

She aimlessly wondered around, taking in those around her. There were many very sick people in the room, there were also many highly medicated people in the room. It was slightly startling to realise that what did initially seem like a nice place to go, may actually have been some wearing off of the pills because today, even with the sunlight casting its rays into the room, it looked more like a scene from the set of a zombie film than it did a wonderful place to rest and recover.

Cutting short her tour of room, Laura made it back to the seat where the handsome gentleman was, she approached him from the rear and spoke gently. "Hello, is it possible that I could sit here with you so we could finish that jigsaw puzzle?" The man slowly turned around, with a look on his face of unease, there was a slight tension between them without there being any reason to be, an awkwardness. Without him having said a word, Laura sat down next to him and patiently waited for his response.

"Hi, I'm Sam, have we met?" Feeling a little discouraged by this, Laura previously had the premonition that there would be a grandiose relief when Sam spoke to her, that he would reveal that he couldn't talk yesterday but he wished he could do. All she could do is make a new interaction with this person that didn't remember the time they had spent together before, to her it was a meaningful experience, to him, it was nothing.

"We started a jigsaw puzzle yesterday but I think maybe you were under the effect of some medication, maybe you don't re-member, either way it is nice to meet you Sam and I am Laura." She had a confidence about her, a dominant feeling which she had not recalled in her life previously. She had never felt like she was in charge of any personal or family relationship, however in this moment she felt like the strong and dominant one. It was a good feeling to ruminate on, it was self-affirming and built her up. She felt like maybe she had slipped off into the distance as she caught her mind beginning to wonder.

"So, what are you here for?" Sam quizzed as he searched for things to communicate with her about. This sent a sudden wave of panic through her, how could she tell him that she was there because she had murdered her family following receiving a phone call? How could she be strong and confident knowing she had that potential inside of her? "I had a little situation with my family, I am here instead of prison, I should be thankful, the doctor seems to know me, I am not sure how though. I don't know or recognise him, but he seems familiar as if I do know him all too well." Sam took a moment to think. In the back of his head, he had the thought that this woman could be the one that had been all over the news that she could be "Loopy Laura" but in honesty, he didn't really care. He also twigged what she had said about the doctor, he was in a similar position and maybe they should in time figure out a way to figure this out. "What about you" followed up Laura?

He thought for a moment, not wanting to reveal that somehow, without realising he had brutally murdered a man who he thought he had a cordial conversation with. "I had a slight misunderstanding with a mugger, then when being questioned I went a bit funny, I get what you're saying about the doctor, I feel the same way, like he knows me" This had made her think, she hadn't seen anything about this in the news, maybe it was only a small situation but judging from Sam's muscular physique, any confrontation would potentially not be a good outcome for the other person.

"So you said the doctor knew you Sam, is that correct? Do you have any idea why he might know you?" Sam waited for a moment, again picking his words slowly and carefully, he was wracking his brains to try and understand how and why he may know the doctor. He still remembered being in the institution, he still remembered the doctor there looking almost identical to The Good Doctor, although the doctor at the institution was much older and seemingly more frail than this one seemed. "Well, I was at a private institution before I ended up here. There was a doctor who dealt with me directly, he knew me and he knew about me and said I had been there many times before. He looked like the main doctor here, the one that's a bit strange. But he was older. It's strange. Why do we both feel like we know him?"

Thinking that she needed to change the subject, Laura smiled a slightly sideways flirty smile at Sam "you know yesterday, when I was eating my lunch, you sat there, I was just about to take a bite of my sandwich. As I did, the largest droplet of drool came out of the corner of your mouth. It was so off-putting. Thinking about it now it has made me smile though, thank you." His face went bright red, he tugged slightly at his collar feeling a little uncomfortable at the thought of this, being unable to understand why she would thank him for it. "Well, I guess, you're welcome?" he was clearly trying to clarify in his head why she would be thanking him, it was definitely something he would be pondering over the coming days.

They both sat in silence now awkwardly taking it in turns to put pieces of the jigsaw puzzle in place. Sam reached across to the far side to slot a piece in when his hand touched Laura's. In that moment they connected, his head lifted to bring his eyes into line with hers, they tracked up from where their hands were. They both looked longingly and knowingly at each other. It was as if this moment had happened many times before, like a rediscovered love had been found. They were sat for a long time, looking deep into each other's souls.

One of the loud sirens sounded in the room, this broke their gaze, but left them both a little lost as to how to feel about the situation. Sam looked around in a panic, although he had been in the room when it had happened yesterday, he still did not make the connection that this was most likely for food being bought out to them or for medication rounds. Seeing the panic in his eyes, Laura took his hand in hers again "It's okay Sam, that'll just be for food or medication. Don't panic."

Feeling a little reassured, he drew his hand back close to himself. He had so much from this encounter to think over. They both did, how was there such a sense of familiarity? How was there such an undertone of love and understanding? It seemed both natural and unnatural at the same time. It didn't seem forced or thought out. It just felt right.

CHAPTER TWENTY ONE: BREAKING BAKELITE

Another day dawned as Terry and Herman made their way into the station. There was a sense of positivity about them as they were preparing themselves for the busy day ahead.

There had been much work going on surrounding the cases that seemed to tie up loose ends and the new information that had become available had given them what they needed to proceed with rounding up the case. The two former hapless detectives had come so far during this case and had developed both personally and professionally in that time.

"I can't believe you found your God Hermy, today is going to be the day!" Terry had an upbeat and positive aura which was contagious to the team around them. "Prep for the briefing big man, we're going to pull this guy today, he has no choice, we're going to get all three of them and get the truth about all of it!"

"I've got the files, I've got the override codes for their system. SCO19 are in the room ready to be briefed and assist with the withdrawal, it's all happening!"

Herman was like an excited school child who had eaten too much sugar. For such a large gentleman, he walked lightly on his feet and felt boundless enthusiasm for moving forwards with making the arrests. Shouting across the office, no one could avoid hearing his usually meek voice "Briefing room 5 minutes everyone on deck today please, it's going to be a big one!"

Busyness ensued throughout this usually sedate office, officers dusting off their seldom used protective gear, readying themselves to have the entirety of the plan revealed to them. Administrators preparing to take notes for the various teams that would have to come together in order for the plan to work with perfect precision.

Getting ready with his briefing feeling nervous yet confident, Herman was arranging both a whiteboard with target images along with a PowerPoint presentation of what they needed to achieve in order for the extraction to be successful. He and Terry had spent the past couple of days preparing across multiple organisations, both gaining authorisations and warrants as well as vital after thoughts which also needed to be arranged for this to be a success.

"Come on guys, get in take a desk, there's a prep pack on each desk, don't be shy, we're all here for the same job, the same reason, let's all get acquainted." The room began to fill and in the back of his mind Herman couldn't believe what he and his partner were preparing to pull off, what they were attempting to achieve, but he knew together they would be able to get through anything. If they can get through their lives outside of work with the challenges that brings, they would definitely be able to get through this operation.

Terry took to the front of the room alongside his partner. "Ok guys, Hermy's going to present you with your operation brief. Please listen as we have spent many days organising across various factions and we know there will be challenges to face and possible deviations, but, we have plans in place." Stepping aside and passing the baton, he felt so proud seeing Herman up there taking charge of the situation, his confidence was in abundance.

"Good morning ladies and gents, today we have 3 arrests to make. 2 soft arrests and one of unknown resistance. We do have the backing of SCO19, they may be required, but we don't know until we are in that situation."

"This is the plan, SCO19 - team Alpha, you will approach the guard booth, you will apprehend and cuff the guard. You will be followed once he is confirmed as secured, by the Tech team – team Zulu, who will loop the surveillance system so nothing is suspected inside of the building. Once we hear the code phrase on comms – which as stated in your mission pack is "Tango Uniform" then we will proceed to release the barrier and make our way toward the building with SCO19 team Bravo and Charlie"

Herman paused for breath, he couldn't believe he was doing all of this, he couldn't believe he was in this position of responsibility, but he certainly felt like he was rising to the occasion. He glanced over at Terry who gave him a reassuring smile and nod as if to guide him to carry on.

"Bravo and Charlie teams, you will enter the building first, this point is not secure but we will have to make the entry double time, due to the panoramic windows at the front of the building, we will need to secure the internal security before they are able to report an issue, please go in with live wires drawn, no lethal force should be used at this point unless there is a credible threat to life, remember the responsibility is on you for justification and I'm not prepared for that instance unless there isn't a trace of doubt that it was the right call to make."

"Bravo team will then secure that reception, where the remaining surveillance cameras are controlled and monitored from, again, Zulu team will lead in behind and secure the system. Bravo team will keep that area secure whilst Charlie and Delta team, will then follow up the rear. Delta team will comprise of myself and Terry, along with several tech officers, who have the emergency overrides of the security doors in the facility. We are the CO's but we are not going to be carrying side arms ourselves, so please keep that in mind."

Terry stepped up to the front of the room from sitting on a table off to the side, he being the junior commanding officer on the operation wanted to also make his mark. "Chaps, we have to move quickly and smoothly on this one. We have to ensure that no one is aware of our presence prior to us being there to apprehend the suspects. Speed and accuracy is vital to ensuring a positive outcome." He took a step back again, Herman cast him a confident and reassuring smile giving him a sense that he had his back, even though he knew he didn't really need the extra boost.

"We have four security doors that we will have to make our way through before we get to the office of Tango One – please go to page 17 of the briefing back you will see his photo, please memorise his face and ensure when we secure him, we pay particular attention, DBC's show he has previously been deceptive and injured officers on previous occasions. Aridam Kek – otherwise referred to as The Good Doctor. He is not so good, so please, ensure he is in a violent person restraint. Hands and legs cuffed. He is an older gentleman, but please don't be under any misconception, he is a dangerous individual"

The realisation had hit Terry, they were about to draw a line under what could have been decades of issues and abuses of position and power with countless unknown victims, with a truly unknown level of destruction. This only increased the desire to ensure everything went to plan and they finally got this monster to where he belonged. Clocking his colleague deep in thought Herman needed to bring him back into the moment. "Terry, can you lead the brief on the next instances please" Snapping out of his thoughts, the detective looked across and nodded his head.

"Chaps, our next targets, Tango Two and Tango Three are soft targets, patients at the facility, we believe when we have interviewed them previously they have been heavily sedated, so we need to ensure we get to them prior to anyone being able to give them any medication. So, this is where Yankee team come in, we would like to welcome you to this operation guys, we don't usually collaborate with you, but this is a bit of a special one. Here we have Doctor Yun and her team, she is a specialist in mental health and medication and will be making a primary risk assessment upon detention of both of these people. She will be assessing for any use of sedative or other medication that may have been used on them, they cannot be cuffed or taken until she has given them the all clear. If there are any signs of foul play, then we hold them there until Yankee team have cleared them and prepared them to be moved."

"We should find Tango two and three in what is known as the day room and canteen. We have to pass through another 4 security doors to allow us to get to them or maybe in their cells, numbered 85 and 88. On previous visits, most of the patients had been quite heavily medicated so we should pass without too much resistance. But we want to ensure that everyone stays safe and secure, so it is from the point of breach of door five that we will hand official control of the entire facility over to Doctor Yun. She will have full control of all staff, they will be made aware by Doctor Yun's team as we move through the building that this is the case. If you come across anyone who contravenes this, drop them, cuff them and caution them. They come in and they answer questions."

"Zulu team should have overridden the biometrics on door seven and eight by this point from the main desk, so we should be cleared to enter."

He continued "It is vital, above anything else that neither of these three communicate with each other, we cannot afford to throw any reasonable doubt on this case." Terry had put his stern voice on which was quite domineering for someone of his stature. He took a step away from the front of the briefing making way for Herman to come back in to wrap it up.

"Ok people, Pages eighteen and nineteen in your doc. pack show images of tango two and three. One male, known as Sam, tango two. He is quite muscle bound and is known for bouts of extreme violence, that and going into a state of catatonia when under extreme stress, so please, broach in a low stress position, don't ask questions and be open and honest with him. Answering his questions will help limit his stress, which should help control him, talk him through the actions you are taking and be empathetic. Tango three is known as Laura, we have never had a normal conversation with her, she has always been completely medicated, however, she is accused of brutally poisoning and bludgeoning her husband to death, please do not take her stature or poise as a guide that she is no harm, but again, use the same approach. Be calm, explain everything as you go, talk through it and explain it."

A hand appeared at the back of the room, it made Herman feel like he was a school teacher and the hand began to wave slightly, with a sight of impatience. "Yes, please go ahead"

"Officer Tyne Charlie team, what's the go code for authorisation for lethal use of force if necessary"

Like a bolt through his skull, his conscience seemed to trigger when this was asked, although it was a poignant question. Clearing his throat Herman looked over at him "the authorisation phrase is "Charlie Foxtrot", because if we are at the point of using lethal force, something has gone very wrong!" There was stifled laughter throughout the room especially from the SCO19 teams. They knew the exact definition of "Charlie Foxtrot" and what he had meant with the statement he made. Hoping that his point had hit home with the officer, he wanted to ensure that only as a very final resort would they be using lethal force. Nobody liked this resolution method, but there was always a possibility that it would be something that may have to be done, of course in the worst of cases.

"Thank you everyone, we have a very clear aim for today, we need to get these three and anyone else that shows resistance into custody, we need to keep them all separate. We need to ensure that everything does run to plan and as smoothly as possible, so please everyone do all the necessary preparation for your specific role. Prepare in your teams, make ready any necessary equipment that you require. We will meet in the car park at midday ready for the go, to the site."

The teams disbanded and went their separate ways, Terry and Herman retired to their office. Sitting down at their desks, the boys looked at each other let out small laughs of disbelief. It was not ever so long ago that they didn't really feel required in this station or in the career as a whole. It was a world away from what they were used to, requiring and running a multi-agency task force to bring in only three people. Three very questionable people, but never the less, still just three people.

"I can't believe you got to this from him working so hard to distract us from his name, Aridam Kek, unbelievable Hermy, God really is in the detail! Did you find out the definition that you were searching for?" Herman reached over his desk whilst taking a large gulp of his strong black coffee. "Erm, yeah, two names two origins, no family name. It's weird, Aridam – meaning destroyer of foes, one who wins over all of his enemies. Its origins lie in India, then Kek, meaning God of Darkness – its origins lie in Egypt. I mean it's not a normal name to call your child, I know he spent the time to disregard it as being extravagant parents who most likely had dark beliefs, but I can't help but think he has played to this a little."

Chomping on a pack of fresh pastries between them, the boys seemed full of optimism, although they knew the capture was only the initial difficulty they had to face. Once they had them, the boys would have to extract the information to try to solve the crime, which was potentially a far larger challenge than simply just asking questions and getting answers.

Herman devoured what was left of his pastry as they sat there in comfortable silence. "I forgot to tell you, I know she will take charge of the situation in the Asylum, but I have asked Doctor Yun to be present whilst we are interviewing Aridam, so that she can identify if he is trying to play any mind games on us, to see if he is trying to do anything that he had managed to do previously. Are you happy with that?"

Terry was a little frustrated that he had not been consulted about this, although he did applaud the thought that his partner hadn't wanted to be humiliated by this despicable man yet again. He could understand the thinking "Yeah, fine by me, might be good as well, maybe she will pick up on things we don't know?" Casting smiles across the room at each other, they couldn't help but feel reminded of the pride they felt in each other for how far they had come, although Herman would always be more willing to show it than his partner would. He was far more open with his thoughts, feelings and emotions and could express them far more easily.

"Come on big man, let's get prepped, not long now and sitting around isn't going to help my nerves, or your waist line if you reach for another pastry!" Feeling a little annoyed by the comment, but understanding there was no malice behind it, Herman stood and grabbed his protective vest. "I'm ready how about you!" he fired back at Terry who casually laughed, stood up and took his coat off revealing that he had been wearing his protective vest the entire time, he felt that this showed, even though he wasn't letting on, his partner was equally as anxious and excited for the operation to take place.

The boys headed out to the car park, knowing they would have a wait out there but also knowing the remainder of the team would be there waiting too. It was a big day for them and the waiting was the worst time as it was when all the creeping doubts had a chance to seep in and cause the anxiety which allowed weakness in the preparations. This was where they knew they had to be strong to be able to lead the team from the front to effect a positive outcome.

CHAPTER TWENTY TWO: CLOSING IN

The teams were assembled in the car park, it was 11:58am and everyone was ready for the departure. The boys wouldn't let the convoy leave until exactly midday, set a time frame, stick to it, get to target, execute the action plan. Nothing should deviate from the brief. The boys sat in nervous quietness along with everyone else focusing and preparing for the operation to get underway.

The vehicles engines silently ticked away as the time moved in slow motion. There was stillness in the air the sound of controlled breathing could be heard throughout the vehicle. Nervously checking his watch, Terry watched the second hand tick around counting down the seconds until he gave the command to go.

The tension built as time seemed to slow, the second hand looking like it was moving backwards once for every two moves forward it made. Round it went, tick, by tock it made its way toward the go time and both boys went to pick up the radio's to give the go, Terry yielded to Herman "Go on big man, go get them!" He lifted the radio to his mouth, taking a deep breath he paused "All teams, we are good to go!"

Pulling out of the car park of the station, these two small time detectives were hoping to break a case that may have been bigger than they ever could have thought or predicted that it would be. It could be the case that develops their careers and brings their unique skill sets into the limelight.

Trundling on, the convoy seemed to take forever to even get out of the little town, all vehicles checking in at the prescribed way points. There was still the same eerie stillness and silence in the air. There was still the same anticipation of catastrophe as there always was, these things had to be in the back of their heads. If they didn't plan for the worst case scenario and work back towards reality, how could they prepare to combat the worst. Clearly in this situation, it would be if they had advanced notice of the operation, but, everything possible had been done to foresee that this would not be the case.

The case was only revealed to the most senior officers in the division, only senior levels of health care experts had been consulted, which in turn resulted in Doctor Yun having been flown over from Russia. Only those who had demonstrated honesty and integrity throughout their distinguished careers were invited to take part in this operation.

This really was a case in the public line of sight and as such, it needed to be given the utmost time, care and attention when it came to refining the details. One wrong move, or a conversation being overheard in the pub could result in tragic circumstances for those involved or those who needed to be bought into urgent detention.

The world was passing by the vehicle in a time lapsed fashion, the moments melting away as the convoy continued on toward the Asylum. They were now beginning to draw close and the air was dense with fog that day, which gave the added element of surprise.

"We're 2 miles out, Team A take over as lead vehicle, we will wait 500 yards out until after you have secured the primary target, once ready give us the go and clear the barrier" Herman spoke clearly and concisely to ensure that there was no misinterpretation of his commands, Terry looked at him with nothing but awe, he had really come into his own throughout this investigation and his instinct to follow the details had driven him toward the resolution. He couldn't help but feel deeply for his partner in that moment seeing him as the person he really was, a confident, strong and passionate individual that saw things through even when there was no clear end in sight. Terry hoped he could, one day, be even half the man that Herman was.

The vehicles drew to a pause, the tension had built and the atmosphere was thick with anxiety as these normally docile officers were being pushed well beyond their comfort zone. The hardest part of not being on the scene at the start of the ingression was not knowing how it was progressing.

"Alpha Team for Charlie Oscar Clear lines for operational contact, we are 100 yards out and ready to begin approach. Authorisation to proceed sir?" Terry and Herman looked at each other with a nervous excitement about them "You are authorised to proceed, radio silence please from all call signs, Alpha team keep comms open." Terry had always wanted to give the go on an operation like this, he had always wanted to be a commanding officer, even if the privilege was shared, he had a smile on his face like a Cheshire cat. There was simply a double click over the airwaves for confirmation that the instruction was understood.

The following minute was filled with awkward anxiety. All that could be heard over everyone's radios was muffled movement and the silent shouting of commands. After a delayed moment, a call came over the airwaves. "Alpha team to Charlie Oscar, one in custody with limited resistance, Zulu's have dropped the barrier, you are good to go" The lead vehicle began to edge forwards waiting for the go from the boys. It was Herman who jumped to answer the call "Bravo and Charlie teams, take the lead, remember the brief, silence and speed are key - and don't forget your Zulu" Again the call was met with only a double click as both vehicles progressed beyond the rest of the convoy.

There were only three vehicles left waiting behind, but they were the ones that held the commanding officers and medical staff as well as some beat officers who would definitely come in useful with the potential for any unseen circumstances.

"Let's keep comms open, Bravo team take radio lead please" as is normal routine, a double click was heard for confirmation of the instruction being understood. "Bravo, Charlie and Zulu teams in position, authorisation to proceed sir?" Again Terry stepped up and made the call "All teams proceed as briefed, authorisation granted" More double clicks of confirmation were returned, then silence, abject silence for second after second, no open lines could be heard, no conversation, no confrontation.

After letting his mind drift from this moment, Herman was bought back into it with a start as he heard the muffles of a clear moment of confrontation. There seemed to have been more silent shouting this time, more commands for compliance from the civilian staff inside of the building, but all the team could do was trust the officers doing the jobs as briefed and hope for the positive outcome they had predicted.

There was an open line on the radio and a very heavy panting could be heard "Bravo..Team for Charlie Oscar, one in custody, some resistance shown, live wire discharged and officer caught in one of the strands, it is now all in order, Zulu dealing, no need for a big red key, one chap in Med. assess following the shock but AIO" No disturbance caused, no one aware"

When the boys heard this, they were a little shocked. The feeling of someone being tasered and having to receive primary aid treatment wasn't on the briefing, although it was a possibility having SCO19 on a job. Terry smiled at Herman "Lucky you didn't give them the clementine code" Herman wasn't sure how to react, all he could do was chuckle from his core with light relief, pick up his radio and give the go for all teams lead by themselves.

"Charlie Oscar on site, Charlie team and Delta team will proceed with Zulu's. We will hit Tango One, within 2 minutes of entry, Bravo team stand by to follow up if required, Charlie team have live wires ready and drawn" The boys cut a commanding stride moving through the lobby of the building, as they entered, they headed straight through doors one and two behind Zulu team, who were already at doors three and four working on bypassing them with the team member at the front desk.

"Doors are ISQ, you can proceed" The Zulu team member swiftly moved out of the way as the burley officers from Charlie team rushed past them. They moved forwards with their Tasers drawn, looking for the position of the office through the dimly lit corridors. Approaching the door they required, Charlie team were quickly followed by the boys. They didn't want to miss even a single moment of the arrest so that when they were writing their statements to follow up the incident, they could have complete integrity with what they told the court about the arrest of this person.

The teams took a moment, they crouched, waiting for the go, all of the required team were now present and in position, they could see Aridam sitting at his desk, only a lamp light focussing on whatever he was working on, on his desk. He appeared to pose no risk, no threat. "Sir, do we have the clementine authorisation?" Herman hesitated, he knew this was potentially too important not to have anyone to answer questions but at the same time he didn't want to have the death of a valued colleague on his conscience for the rest of his life. He was never particularly good at making the spontaneous decisions, that's why he felt such relief when Terry spoke up "Negative on clementine, live wires only." A brief thumbs up was all that was needed, the Tasers remained drawn and ready to be used if necessary although this did seem a little overkill for such a senior man who was just sitting at his desk.

"Go, Go, Go" came the shout from the rear of the team breaching the door with a swift boot, the shouts soon started "Armed police hands in the air, Armed police hands in the air" Looking up in shock, Aridam had a knowing look of what was about to happen. He raised his right hand into the air, leaving his left hand on the desk. He was holding an old fashioned fountain pen in his left hand for which he had the ink well on his desk. The officers repeated the command "Armed police, hands in the air this is the final warning, if you do not comply, we will use necessary force"

Still the doctor did not lift his left arm, opposed to lifting it, he began slowly drawing it back toward the rear side of the desk, sliding his hand slowly as if he thought they couldn't see the action he was taking. "Live wires authorised" came the shout from the leading officer, it was at this point that there were several thuds of delayed reaction. It was the Tasers being discharged in sequence all aimed at the one man. Several sets of spikes impaled the man who began to violently shake and convulse in his chair.

Knowing that these bursts were short lived, but also knowing the man could have an unknown reaction to them, the officers swiftly moved to surround the man, they couldn't yet restrain him or put him into the recovery if he required it.

His body was still residually having involuntary spasms, which sometimes happen after multiple shocks. The officers were well versed in follow up care, they had to be as a part of their job and the duty of care that comes along with carrying a firearm. A moment later, his body had calmed and the spasms had subsided. He was left in a position where there was little he could do. They decided to restrain him and bring him to his feet as he was conscious.

Herman stood in front of Aridam with a large smile on his face. "Aridam Kek, also know under the alias The Good Doctor, I am delighted to inform you that you are under arrest under suspicion of committing Murder and Murder by proxy with further potential charges yet to be established. You do not have to say anything. But, it may harm your defence if you do not mention when questioned, something which you later rely on in court. Anything you do say may be given in evidence. Do you understand?"

Aridam looked over at both Terry and Herman doing nothing but snarling and maintaining a vicious grimace on his face. This was met by the boys, who had huge grins on their faces. They knew thirty three percent of the operation was completed. They just had to continue through for the next two targets. "Detainee declined to answer, get him back to the station" Herman said in a domineering manor.

"Charlie team, let's go. Zulu team, how are doors five and six, seven and eight looking? All ISQ?" Knowing the pressure had been on them, the tech teams had proceeded with Yankee team following them. They had also been accompanied by some of the Alpha team officers, who hadn't wanted to leave the other team unassisted. This had been an oversight on the part of the boys, not thinking about them proceeding whilst the arrest was being made on Tango One.

It didn't matter, the benefit of using experienced officers was that they managed to pick up the slack or notice pinch points when they became apparent whilst operations were under way. They were able to adapt without being micro managed.

"Alpha team leader to Charlie Oscar, I am with The Zulu's and Yankee's we will proceed, we are on location and have an orderly who will take us to both cells. Bravo team, please ensure the front desk Zulu makes the doors to cell 85 and 88 ISQ, these are our soft targets, please pay caution, let a Yankee go in the cells with one officer. Once the all clear is given, restrain them and extract them."

Herman and Terry looked at each other, they didn't need to give any further instruction and their initial brief had given them all they had needed to allow the team to function without them. Again it was another benefit of working with a well experienced team that they were able to relinquish the control slightly in order to progress with being the commanding officers on the scene.

Terry grabbed his radio "Alpha leader, thank you. All call signs,

Alpha leader will take point on the soft extraction of Tango Two and Tango Three. All call signs radio silence in effect other than Alpha leader, who I ask will keep open lines." There came a double click down the radio, again this was the confirmation they needed as acknowledgment of where they were going next.

The boys began walking back to the lobby to wait and listen how the follow up arrests were going. They couldn't believe how smoothly it had gone to this point. They couldn't believe they had Aridam in custody, with only the two soft targets left to grab. Without spending too much time reflecting but feeling positive, the worry began to set in for Terry. They were not on the scene to apprehend Laura and Sam, maybe they should have been with the rest of the forward team, maybe they shouldn't have returned to the lobby to congratulate themselves on a job well done. There was after all, the greater proportion of the task outstanding.

"Alpha Leader to Charlie Oscar, Tango Two in custody, two Yankee's bringing her down, no sign of foul play. On route to Tango Three." Terry clicked his talk button twice to confirm he had received the message, he didn't know what else he could do. He knew he and Herman had most likely made the correct decision to take a step back from the front line to allow Yankee team and SCO19 to do what they needed to, but he also felt some guilt in regard to not being there and not being the arresting officer for these individuals.

"Alpha Leader to Chalie Oscar, Tango Three in custody."

Herman looked at Terry, he looked back at the doorway seeing the shadowy movements of figures coming toward them. He could do nothing more than let out an almighty "YEESSSSSSS" probably a little louder than he should have done but he had such a wave of relief that the operation had been successful and that a positive outcome had been successfully achieved. "All call signs, this is Charlie Oscar, thank you, all teams to exfil for debrief at the station and then I guess the pints are on Terry later!"

Terry smiled at him, he could tell he was proud of what they had achieved together, that he was proud of himself and of the operation they had pulled off. The hardest part, interviewing those who were most likely resistant to interview was yet to come, but a successful operation had been undertaken with all targets apprehended with minimal discharge of incapacitation weapons. Zero live rounds used, zero body bags filled. That was a positive outcome in itself.

CHAPTER TWENTY THREE: QUESTIONING OF BAKELITE

Waking with a jump, Herman had one of those dreams where he had just jumped off a cliff and opened his eyes before he hit the floor. He quickly sprung out of bed excited for the day ahead, they got to question and unravel the mystery behind the murders and the mystery behind the whole situation with the people whose lives seemed to be intrinsically linked.

He could hear Terry banging about downstairs, so decided to follow his normal morning routine. Get up, quick wash and clean then it came to getting dressed. He got into his smart suit today knowing it was going to be a big day for their careers. Who knows maybe they would even have to do a press conference once they had figured out how to charge those responsible.

Thumping down the stairs it was as if he no longer knew how walk without plodding heavily on the floor beneath him. He seemed completely incapable. Terry had just finished his second coffee of the day and was preparing all of his things to go. Strangely he was also dressed in one of his best suits, not the usual casual jeans and a t-shirt that would comprise of his "smart" dress day to day.

Herman looked over at his partner and simply nodded. They grabbed their gear and made their way out of the house. The drive to work was silent, although there was a certain positive feeling between them, both men were seemingly preparing to mentally go to battle with Aridam and the other prisoners. They had to get themselves in the correct mind-set in order to deal with it, to be professional and keep their personal feelings under wraps.

Arriving at the station a short time later, the boys still in silence, proceeded to make their way into their office. Again, sitting at their desks in silence, grabbing their coffee's in silence, the concentration on the day ahead and the mental preparation that needed to go into it was rather intense. Finally, breaking the silence, Herman looked at Terry who broke it with "are you ready for today big man, we have a big challenge to face and I don't think we are going to be straight into it, we're going to need to work him from every angle to get to the truth!" Knowing his partner was right and knowing that it would be a repetitive to even make small roads forwards, he was ready to face it.

"My good man, I'm more than ready after what that Bastard put me through. Imagine all the people he has affected over the years. Imagine all of the abominations that he has created, imagine all of the people that he has passively killed because of his experiments with those with mental disorders." This was a real thinking point for the pair of them. They knew about 3 people who may have been affected, but how many more could there have been?

Terry picked up the file from the desk "Right, shall we go for the biggest one first, I want first crack at Aridam, we just need Doctor Yun to arrive and then we can get him into interview." Herman was in agreement that his partner should have the first go at questioning him, so he picked up his phone and dialled for the doctor to see if she was at least on her way in. As he hit the call button, he realised there was no need to as he tilted his head toward the front office where he could see her sitting and waiting. "I don't want to brief her, I want her to be as appalled by it all as we are."

The partners were unsure if it was going to be easy for her to spot when he was playing games with them and when he was telling the truth about what had happened. "I really hope she is Hermy, but remember she is a specialist in her field, the same as he was, so maybe nothing will surprise her, so let's not try to anticipate anything and deal with things as they come to us, we have no clue what's going to happen."

The boys grabbed the necessary paperwork and phoned down to have him bought to an interview room. They headed through to the front office to collect the doctor. "Good morning doc, ready to go in? All we need you to do today is to keep an eye out to ensure that he isn't playing any mind games with us, we just need a straight interview to try and get to understand what has actually happened here!" The doctor looked at both of the boys nervously. She didn't know what to expect going into that interview room. She knew what to look out for when it came to people attempting to play mind games, could she spot the signs and signals in another doctor, who would know what she could be looking for as signs and identifiers?

"OK, let's get in there, let's get questioning him. Don't be worried about stopping the interview if you feel it is going wrong, or if you think he is playing games, however, if he does go into free flow and incriminates himself please don't stop him." The doctor nodded in silence gripping onto her handbag a little tighter. She was clearly anxious about what was ahead of them.

The two detectives and the doctor made their way into the interview room, Aridam and his legal consultant had already been seated to allow them to prepare. "Good morning doctor, I am now going to start the interview tape" there was a nod from the lawyer, yet complete silence from Aridam. "For the tape, this is the interview Of Aridam Kek, taken by DS Terry Picket, DC Herman Picket accompanied by Doctor Yun, for psychiatric consultation along with the Aridam's legal counsel, Roger Blower"

There was a moment of realisation which had made Aridam

look up, he looked between both of the men opposite him. He smiled his sly and knowing smile and chuckled to himself. "Well I'd have never of guessed that gentlemen, but congratulations, I hadn't realised they allowed your type to work together." The moment quickly passed, but without realising it, the doctor had been thrown off guard. This had really offended the boys and set the interview off to a very negative start.

"Now that's out of your system Aridam, we would like to ask you some questions pertaining to some people who have previously been in your care. We have two of them also in custody now, Laura and Sam, but we would like you to fill us in on Roger, the file of an unnamed man we found in your office and another girl, Adriana. Can you firstly, please explain to us about how originally they came to be in your care and the course of treatment you undertook?"

Two things happened simultaneously, initially, it was Doctor Yun, who looked at the boys and the doctor in disbelief, not only could she struggle to understand how coincidentally she could come to cover for and examine the person who was at least partially responsible for the destroyed woman she believed she had been looking after for the past year. At the same time, Aridam could not believe they had been able to find the information about these, if they had found this information what else had they had access to?

Herman looked over at The Good Doctor and smiled "Aridam, we have a little phrase we use in cases like this, that is, that God is in the details. This was certainly true for you and for this case. If we hadn't made some of the links by examining each case individually and each person individually, we wouldn't have come to find the information or to have pulled you in for questioning. What we would like you to do is take us back to the beginning where this all started we want to know what triggered these events and these people to come into your care."

The doctor sighed, it was an elongated and withdrawn movement that showed it had made him feel he was in a position where he was backed into a corner. There really was no other option than to tell the complete truth. There was no more hiding, no more covering up. It had been too much for too many years. There could be no lies by omission.

"OK chaps, the problem is, I want to be offered some protection from those who commissioned and backed my research wouldn't like to have the truth revealed. If you can guarantee my safety or at least steps toward it, I will ensure you know what you need to." This wasn't the response that the boys were expecting. Terry quickly retorted "Well, how about we get underway with talking, then we can decide if what you have is suitable to warrant the requirement for protection"

Again the doctor sighed, he knew he wasn't in a strong bargaining position but if he did talk then maybe somehow he would escape with his life.

"Well, what do you want to know?" The boys looked through their notes, unsure of where to begin. It was when Terry stopped and thought for a moment that he came to realise maybe it was a chance to let him incriminate himself. "Aridam, how about you start, take me to the beginning, but I want full disclosure on everything and everyone, how have we ended up where we are today?"

"Gents I can start at the beginning but I am not telling you everything, you will need to do some work yourselves until I have my protection, then I will tell you more. I wrote a paper on the use of Neuro-Linguistic programming in patients who suffer excessive or extreme trauma and how if you create an identifier or worsening symptoms by subliminal programming, then this should possibly be a way in which they can present themselves to a hospital or ward for onward treatment." He smiled at the men, they both knew that all he had admitted to at current was writing a medical paper. They didn't have anything on him, but they also didn't have anything they could use to offer him protection.

"Okay doctor, thank you, so what happened after you had written this paper?" The doctor was beginning to fiddle with his hands, he seemed to be getting anxious. "Well chaps, you see I was approached, the problem with my suggestion was this, there would be no way of predicting what the content of the phone call would be, you see it would be being controlled by the persons psyche, not by a prepared statement, we had to try and trick the brain into telling the person on the imaginary phone call what we wanted them to hear, that they should speak to someone or see someone for help. Not that this would be a realistic achievement, not that this would be anything they could actually undertake for real, there were too many what ifs."

"I did try and explain this to the person that contacted me regarding my paper, or should I say the organisations. You see, to have this "programming" installed in a person could save the health and emergency service lots of money, but it could also place a value marker on each persons suffering too. This as my learned colleague over here will tell you then becomes an ethical conflict. Medicine and the advancement of medical science should not be centred on being able to make a cost evaluation of care. You see you may have read the files, you may have read about my work and you may be under the impression I am a monster. I'm not, everything I have done has been the legacy of a bad decision, a bad call. If you'll pardon the pun" He smiled at his own passive joke.

Herman was feeling a connection to Aridam, a genuine sensation that he wasn't to blame, although in the back of his head he was aware that this could also be a game or portrayal of a genuine sense of regret. "DC Herman Picket and Doctor Yun taking a moment outside of the room, interview paused" he stood up and left the room, the female doctor followed swiftly behind him. They went a little way down the hall from the interview room. "Doctor Yun, I need your opinion, I am on the edge of genuinely believing him. In your professional opinion, do you think he is being genuine?" There was a moment of silence and it seemed that Doctor Yun was evaluating everything she had witnessed. "I believe he is genuine, but I also believe he is a very smart gentleman. So, only time will tell, let him take you on this journey, but I suspect he will place the blame on anyone other than himself."

They both headed back into the room, saying nothing to each other. "DC Herman Picket and Doctor Yun back in the room, interview resumed." Terry looked at them both inquisitively, he disregarded any doubts immediately and decided to continue with the interview.

"Aridam, please forgive my ignorance, but I asked you to go back to the very start. You told us about your paper and someone taking an interest in the concept, you clearly had a basis or a foundation for the study and I assume by the way you speak you had a financial backer. So, please fill me in on the blanks, show me the God." There was a pause and a prolonged silence. The sound of controlled breathing could be heard throughout the room "Once more Aridam, please fill us in on the blanks." Again the request was met with silence. It was becoming awkward as if the avenue ahead had become blocked.

"Well let me inform you of our investigation to date. We know you worked as a self-employed consultant to several large medical and pharmaceutical for the past decade. We know all of those connections started 11 years ago. We know that you were pushed to take 5 people into care to bring them onto a trial scheme, although details were sparse in the public domain. We have applied for a warrant for the stated companies to supply us with full disclosure documentation. Now, I would like to hear the information from you, as for a moment I was actually beginning to believe you that this wasn't all for protecting yourself, more-so for protecting a commercial enterprise and you were being pushed to do these things. Since you will give us no further details voluntarily, I am going to proceed with this process." Herman grinned from ear to ear as he reeled off the words, he couldn't believe he had been this coherent and confident he hadn't even meant to push The Good Doctor back into a corner.

"It would seem you have me there. Either I tell you or I let you make your own conclusions from some poorly kept and heavily edited documentation surrounding my research, study and work. OK, well if you want more, then I need more protection, I need you to ensure that I will not have my life taken whilst I sleep."

The boys looked at each other unsure they could even arrange any protection, it wasn't something either of them had been through before, but they felt they owed it to the next stage of their investigation to look at in seriousness. It was in this moment, Terry knew how he should proceed. "Aridam, DC Picket and I will go off and see what we can arrange. What I am going to ask you to do is sit here with your brief and prepare a written statement for us. We will not ask you to do anything other than this at this stage. I will ask that you then hold this until hearing what we can offer you. Then we level the playing field. Would you like to share your thoughts with me on this?"

There was a moment of uncertainty, where it seemed he was weighing up the situation. What harm could come to him by doing this, what did he have to lose? He was either all in the frame or he blew the whistle. If he did that he stood the chance of being free of it all, if he didn't whatever consequences he faced would be dire. Aridam didn't seem to be the type of person who was driven by emotion but someone who decided based on a reasoned and logical processes. He appeared to be using this method to settle on how he felt about proceeding with the suggestion Terry had made.

"OK chaps, let's do that. If you come up with a solution in which I will be protected no matter what it is, whilst I prepare a full statement then I am sure we can both benefit from this situation." "Interview paused, DS Terry Picket, DC Herman Picket and Doctor Yun leaving the room" The trio stood and exited the room.

It would seem that for that moment, the former Good Doctor had bought himself a stay of execution. Although leaving they didn't feel like they had lost out, but instead that they had just made themselves more work to do.

CHAPTER TWENTY FOUR: QUESTION THE INNOCENCE?

Sitting back at their desks accompanied by Doctor Yun, the boys couldn't help but start thinking about what they could expect in the form of a statement from Aridam. "Gentlemen, I think in honesty you need to be wary of him, I think he is playing games. I think he is leading you down a path you don't want to go down. Don't fall into his games. Let him stew in his juices. Let him prepare his statement then hold him again. Let him know you are in charge, not him."

This was a moment in which the boys had to seriously think that maybe Doctor Yun knew what she was talking about. Thinking about things from a new perspective was difficult, thinking about things alternately and unemotionally whilst changing the state of play with all of the cards already on the table.

How were they going to achieve this? "Detectives, I don't want to tell you how to do your jobs, but may I suggest you questions both Laura and Sam before you get any information about how this all came to be, then if there is any need to follow up, this can be done with them after you have seen the prepared statement."

"You know in another life, you'd have made a brilliant officer! We should do as suggested, maybe Sam and Laura can offer something up, what do you think Hermy, are you up for finding a little more of God?" Terry smiled reassuringly at them both as he seemed to be formulating a plan. Herman gave a confirming nod, he didn't quite seem so convinced of Doctor Yun, but he also couldn't be sure why, he couldn't quite put his finger on why he felt she could not be trusted.

"OK, I will go and get Sam released first, we will question him, then in one hours' time we will question Laura, Doctor Yun, I am going to ask you to retire to our canteen whilst we undertake these interviews, if we have any concerns as to their mental state, we will consult you as soon as they arise. Is that okay?" Herman enquired, she nodded and grabbed her belongings making her way out of the room. She seemed to have no insistence on being involved in other parts of the case, so there was no reason that she may be overly invested in it, maybe there was nothing to suspect.

"Let's go big man" Terry claimed cheerily as he grabbed his suit jacket and placed it over his shoulders, moving with an excitement and energy that was infectious. "Shall I meet you down there? Is the duty solicitor still here? If so, let them know, I want to go on this now!" Herman also made his way out of the room, to go and get the next one for questioning, he was excited to meet Sam, and hoped he wouldn't clam up like he had before.

Hopefully they would break some ground on the case, they were excited as Sam was an untapped resource at present. They couldn't question him about the attack on the random man, as it was not their investigation, but they could use it as a part of their case, but knew they would have to tread lightly to avoid him freezing up on them.

A short time later, they all met down at the interview room, entering altogether, everyone took their seats, Sam remained handcuffed and the boys began to prepare the tape for the interview. "This commences the interview between the detainee known as Sam, DS Terry Picket, DC Herman Picket and the duty solicitor. Good afternoon Sam, we want to ask you a few questions, we will put absolutely no pressure on you, we will guide you through the questions and we want to establish what has happened to you. Not if you're guilty of a crime." Sam had felt relieved, stepping into the room, he had wondered if he was going to be in trouble, or if he would have any side effects as he had previously. He didn't want to, he wanted to be strong and face what he had done, even if he wasn't aware of it.

"Sam, we have a history here that shows 6 years ago you were entered into the PNC system as a potential mental health risk, to yourself and others around you. You were entered in by Aridam Kek, otherwise known as The Good Doctor. Can you remember the initial treatment you received or why you ended up in his care?"

Thinking for a moment, Sam couldn't actually recall, he couldn't recall anything, his childhood, his previous career, anything up to the point a few weeks ago. "I'm sorry, try as I might and please trust me I have, I am struggling to recall anything even from recent events. I know previously I was in a place called The Institution which is, I assume, a private mental health clinic. Since then I was back at the station, I had another episode, then ended up going to the Asylum. Other than that I'm afraid my memory is blank, I couldn't tell you if I have done anything wrong or if I am blameless, I couldn't explain how I ended up this way. Do you know how it feels not to know anything about yourself other than what is happening right in that moment?" The detectives looked at each other, they knew this was most likely going to give them no path forwards and needed to think of how they could now proceed.

Herman hesitated before proceeding. "Sam, I know this is hard and I want to thank you for speaking with us so openly and honestly, If I were able to only live in the very moment I was existing, I would look favourably on it. But in the case of police work, I'm afraid it doesn't offer us much to go on. We are going to release you back into the care of Doctor Yun and the team at the Asylum. We hope to follow up with some reports about your mental state and we hope with time, maybe you will be able to recall who you are. Interview terminated, DC Picket and DS Picket leaving the room"

The detectives, left the interview room and stood outside for a moment" So, what do we do with the other 57 minutes until Laura comes?" Terry said with a smile on his face "look, I know it's a road block in this case, but did you really expect it to be anything else other than this? Don't be down hearted about it Hermy, we will get there. We will find your God, we will find the information we need. Please trust me, we will solve this case, or at least make sure Aridam is sent to prison for a long, long time!" He was begging his partner to believe him that the groundwork and investigation he had put in would be good enough to lead them forwards to a positive resolution, it was difficult for him to see in that moment, but all they could do was trudge through it bit by bit, interview by interview and see where they ended up. They could not predict the outcome until they controlled the variables.

"Look Hermy, I'll go and organise Laura to come down early. Maybe she will be able to give us something and she likes you, you built a relationship with her previously. So let's think positively about it. Go grab us a coffee, prepare a new tape in the room and I'll meet you back here in a few minutes!" Herman trudged off toward the coffee machine, he knew Terry was right and he knew that he could possibly make some forwards movement with Laura, although he didn't want to expect it.

Sitting down at the interview table, the coffee's steamed away, he sat there watching the steam dance and evaporate from the surface of the liquid, he thought how he was going to proceed with this interview, how would he instil in Laura the importance of this case and finding a resolution to it. His thoughts were interrupted as a loud buzz resounded throughout the room. The clunk of the door behind him again bought him back into the moment and away from the doubts and thoughts within his own head. In walked Laura with the duty solicitor, closely followed by Terry. Again they all seated and prepared. He took a deep breath and set the tape off recording, not knowing how he was going to open.

"Interview commencing, DC Herman Picket, DS Terry Picket, Duty solicitor and the detainee known as Laura. Laura, hello, I don't know if you will remember but we have spoken several times previously." Herman paused for confirmation, he looked over at her and couldn't help but notice the transformation she had gone through. She had a radiance about her, like something had been lifted from her soul. "Now, Laura, we know 10 years ago you were flagged on our system as being a mental health risk, since then, nothing, until the incident with your family. Do you remember the incident with your family?" She looked over at him and let out a sigh.

"Detective, yes I do remember you, you were very kind to me. You were very patient with me, unfortunately I don't think I was much help at the time, maybe I can be now. Yes, I do remember the incident with my family, regrettably I know I have killed them. I miss them every day. Even my husband." A tear came to her eye, then they came to both of her eyes. They began to tumble freely down her face "I cannot tell you why or how I came to be in that position or taking those actions, but I know in that moment, I was driven to take them, what drove me I cannot tell you. I cannot recall much apart from this. I can tell you that the doctor you arrested threatened to keep me medicated unless I refused to talk to you. He isn't a nice man."

This was a revelation for them, this was their God and gave witness that the doctor had manipulated Laura into silence. This was leverage they could use in the interview and it was on the tape so it gave them physical evidence to present to the prosecution service as to his guilt. It wasn't everything, but it was something!

"OK Laura, so he told you he would keep you medicated, do you know why? What was he trying to prevent you from revealing to us?" Shrugging her shoulders she offered nothing for them, although what she had already given them was a positive step. "OK, so, another question for you Laura. Do you remember 10 years ago how you came to be in the care of this doctor?" She put her head in her hands, she sat like this for quite some time, eventually looking up "I'm sorry, I really am, but I can only recall back to the event with my family, I see it, in my dreams and in the daytime when I zone out, I see that event happening, watching as a third person, seeing myself making those actions, but this is all I can recall. I cannot recall anything before this, try as I might."

There was a genuineness about her response, a sincere sadness within her words, she really did not have a clue how she had ended up in that position or how she could feel so badly about someone who systematically abused her physically and mentally over a long period of time.

"Thank you for your honesty Laura, we are going to release you back into the care of the Asylum, but with a new doctor. She is named Doctor Yun, she is very highly qualified in her field of study. You can trust her to aid in your recovery. Take care of yourself Laura." Again Herman had a genuine care in his voice for Laura, a soft spot, a reassurance that she would be alright. Maybe a jury would look at her actions and understand them as being enacted under diminished responsibility. Maybe she would be kept in care until she was the person she was meant to be again. Maybe she would get some answers to who she was.

"Interview terminated, DC Picket and DS Picket leaving the room" Silently and thoughtfully they made their way out of the room. The boys retired back to their office again in order to prepare for the final onslaught with Aridam. "Are you prepared for going back up against him Hermy?" Herman wasn't and he didn't think he ever would be although, he knew this was something he would have to go through in order to progress the investigation.

"Let's do this, let's get him, we need to make sure that whatever he has done, he pays for it, whatever he has put people through he goes to prison and sees out his days there." With this in mind, they called for him to be bought back to the interview room. They were now ready to proceed, with even the minor charge of threatening to drug a patient to prevent a lawful investigation, if this was their in, then they would use it.

Preparing to head back, the boys grabbed everything they needed, they knew time was of the essence. They knew acting now to detain him without the chance for release would be the only option they had, this pressure added to the anxiety of the moment. But it didn't lessen the determination. They made their way back down to the interview room and prepared them-selves. He was on his way, the moments were counting down and the tension within the room could be cut with a knife.

Aridam was bought into the room along with his lawyer, Doctor Yun followed them in shortly afterwards. He was still hand-cuffed, he proceeded toward his seat and sat himself down, slowly and cautiously. "Gentlemen, I would like to let you know I am not feeling terribly well, I will do my best to answer your questions, but please, may I see a medic as I have a slight short-ness of breath and pain within my chest." The boys had no option but to take this seriously, so it was left to Terry to go and organise some help "DS Picket leaving the room to arrange a medical consultation." Returning a moment later, he informed everyone in the room that there would be a duty doctor along shortly, this was another delay in the process, it felt like he was showing his balance of power, like he could control the momen-tum.

The boys decided to proceed with the interview despite the con-cerns of the lawyer and from Aridam. "Ok, so we have on tape confirmation that you had threatened a lady in your care, that you would keep her medicated if she attempted to speak with us, can you please either confirm or deny this allegation." Look-ing up at the boys, the doctors face had now taken on a slightly grey hue, he was grabbing at his arm "Gentlemen, I did threaten Laura that much is true. However, I am starting with what I believe to be a heart attack is the medical assistance almost here?" They knew at this point they had him, they also knew at this point there was no way they could proceed with the questioning or prosecution. But they had him.

"Interview terminated on the grounds of the suspect requiring medical assistance, all none essential personnel leaving the room." The boys stopped the interview tape and guided both Doctor Yun and the lawyer out of the room. The doctor was still on route to the station. Terry phoned through to upgrade the requirement. In that moment whilst the boys were distracted, there was a loud thud, both of them turned around to see Aridam twitching violently on the floor, froth was spewing from his mouth.

His body writhed and twitched around the floor of the room. Knowing the treatment for signs of fitting, the boys cleared everything around him, supporting his head but trying not to overly control his movement. His face had appeared to go bright red, his movements had not changed, and Terry was still on the phone with the doctor, who could offer no advice, but had just pulled into the station car park.

The twitching was beginning to tail off, the redness in his face was beginning to curtail. The breathing seemed to be a little more normal than it was previously. Although, within the next moment, it seemed to be extinct. The doctor burst into the room, throwing his bag down on the floor he began to make a rapid assessment of the symptoms. He didn't have a positive feeling about this situation. The boys had a sinking feeling about their case, what more could they now do, it didn't look like they would get to make any positive outcome with the doctor.

Grabbing some items from his bag, the doctor continued with CPR upon Aridam, this wasn't a good sign for anyone in the room. Every time he compressed his chest or attempted to put breaths in through his mouth, it appeared that his airway was obstructed. There seemed to be little that could be done. The duty doctor stopped the compressions, he looked at his watch.

"Life extinct, 16:38. I'm sorry gentlemen, I'm afraid he has passed. He's been too long without oxygen"

"Doctors dead" claimed Terry "OK, please everyone leave everything exactly as it was and exit the room. We need to bag up our clothes, I will call the boss down to come and take charge."

Herman stood unable to speak and clearly the situation had a major effect on him. Terry guided him out of the room. Not only was the future of this case now in question, but also the future for the boys. A death in custody was something no officer ever wished to face.

CHAPTER TWENTY FIVE: CONCLUDING BAKELITE

A few weeks had passed since the incident with Aridam, Terry and Herman had been suspended and dragged through interviews and a coroner's investigation along with internal police investigations to try and determine what had happened. It had concluded that the doctor had died from a very severe heart attack. What bought it on had been inconclusive. They could not determine the cause medically.

The investigation into the doctor's activities had been postponed whilst the boys were suspended and whilst the investigation into his death had taken place. Although it was important to the boys to continue with the case, there was no one of interest or to their knowledge, in immediate danger. There was definitely no-one who could help advance the case.

They didn't know what they should now do, the prosecution service wouldn't push to prosecute someone posthumously and the police service wouldn't want to waste funds on spending more time investigating the case if there was no one to be held accountable. What more could be done? Did the case now just go cold? No matter what they approached it with, it could never be fully resolved.

It appeared that the only way forward was to put the case in the filing system and wait for it to show its ugly face again in the future. Cases like this had a habit of coming back up, they had a nasty way of showing themselves again. But until it happened, there was nothing they could do with it. They were at a loss.

"Well Hermy, what do we do now, all we have on the table is a couple of low rent burglaries, we can easily deal with those, hammer the usual suspects out. Get them closed off. Nothing will compare to the size of the case we've been on recently, can you imagine dealing with something like that again. I hope for it not to happen too soon"

Herman looked at his partner, he knew that this had been quite a lot for Terry to go through and to experience, neither of them had been through anything like this previously, or expected ever to have anything like this land on their desks again.

"It was quite exciting though wasn't it, the thrill of the chase, the twists and turns, being in the national papers, just not being a nobody. I'm going to miss it, I'm going to feel a bit useless now looking into burglaries and day to day bread and butter jobs. They all seem a bit mundane. I don't know if this will be enough for me anymore."

On that negative thought, it was time for the day to draw to a close, for the boys to head home and spend some quality time together again. They hadn't spent much time with each other since the wedding. They had to put themselves on the back burner due to this career making case. Which all now seemed to be for nothing.

The boys made it home earlier than usual, they sat down and cuddled up on the sofa. They turned on the television the news seemed to be being shown on every channel, there had been an outbreak of some serious illness in India and it had travelled across land to several other neighbouring countries. The worry was that it would spread globally.

"B'ah we don't need to worry about stuff like that Hermy, it'll never make it over here and it'll never have any effect on us will it!" Terry claimed dismissing it. It was something that worried Herman like any immediate thought of danger or threat would always be likely to.

Whilst they were cuddled up his mind was never really in the room. He still wanted to solve the case, although they had been told to leave it behind.

The boys had also begun to revert back to their previous habits. Turning into work later in the day, going to the pub for lunch, not showing enthusiasm for what they had to do. Herman had begun to pile the weight on again as he had returned to eating to cure the boredom and lack of challenge he was feeling.

Having been milling it over in his head for quite some time, Herman asked "What if we missed something with the case, what if we could find it?" as they sat trying to avoid showing any interest to the television. Terry looked over at him and smiled "you have to let it go Hermy, leave the what-ifs and live in the moment, we've been told to drop the case. We've been told to re-visit it, if it ever comes up again. But until that point, we've been told to leave it."

Disappointed in his partner's lack of interest in being pulled back into it, Herman could find no motivation to move onto anything else. When something sits unresolved and he knew there was more to it, he couldn't just leave it. He didn't want to. He felt incomplete.

Terry gave Herman an extra-long cuddle, he knew this was something that he needed. He needed to be there for him, to hold him when he was feeling low and useless, to be his safety net. To care for him and tell him it was all going to be OK.

"OK buddy, I will leave it." he smiled reassuringly and gave him a warming embrace. This was all Herman needed in that moment. Although it wasn't a long term solution.

He couldn't switch off from the case, they had nothing terribly interesting coming up and there was a global threat from some radical illness. But he knew he had nothing to worry about as long as his partner was by his side. The what-if's and what-have-been events would have to disappear for the evening whilst they spent the time together and had only each other on their minds.

Herman was struggling having no closure on the case, there were too many unanswered questions, but he knew he couldn't show that. He knew he couldn't say it, because Terry simply wouldn't understand.

They knew in that moment, they had each other and nothing else mattered.

AFTERWORD

Thank you for taking the time to read my debut novel.

Whilst for some this ending may have been frustrating, there is more to come, there is more information to be had.

Terry & Herman do have many more investigations and we would love for you to join us along the way.

Postmodern fragmentation is, for me, the epitome of mental health crisis. Sometimes we can break down into tiny pieces and only when we have the full picture or can see more clearly can we begin to rebuild ourselves. But, only once we have worked through those initial periods

What started as a therapy and difficulty in communicating has turned into many pages of glorious release.
Being able to speak without speaking, being able to express without directly expressing.